WAR-CRY!

There pealed out a singularly penetrating yell, most startling in its suddenness and nerve-racking with its terrible long-drawn and sustained wildness.

"Comanche war-cry!" hissed Pilchuck. "Some buck has glimpsed our men below. Wait! We want the shootin' to begin below and above. Then mebbe the Indians will run this way."

Scarcely had the scout ceased his rapid whisper when a Sharps rifle awoke the sleeping echoes. It came from Starwell's detachment below.

Despite Pilchuck's orders, some of his men began to fire.

"All right, if you can't wait. But shoot high," he shouted.

Twenty Creedmoors thundered in unison from that rocky slope. It seemed to Tom then that hell had broken loose. He had aimed and shot at a running brave. His hands shook to spoil his aim and his face streamed with cold sweat. All the men were loading and firing, and he was in the midst of a cracking din.

The Buffalo Hunter

Zane Grey

Edited by

Loren Grey

BELMONT TOWER BOOKS • NEW YORK CITY

A BELMONT TOWER BOOK

Published by

Tower Publications, Inc.
Two Park Avenue
New York, N.Y. 10016

INTRODUCTION

Zane Grey is considered by many to be one of the greatest Western story-tellers who ever lived. Here in this volume are thrilling examples of his gift, which ranged in scope from the early West to a more modern era as well.

None of these stories has appeared in paperback in the United States and Canada before; in fact, "On Location" and "John Silver's Revenge" have never been previously published before in any form.

They are as vivid and alive to the reader's imagination as the best Western stories ever written.

Loren Grey

CONTENTS

The Buffalo Hunters

Preface

After the searing experiences that had divided and
alienated his family during the Civil War, Tom Doan
had drifted West because he could no longer stand the
bitterness that living in his boyhood neighborhood had
created in him. The West was a new land and virtually
free from scars of the conflict. Tom had wanted to be a
rancher, but he had no money and the odd jobs he held
paid too poorly to accumulate any savings. Finally,
albeit reluctantly, because killing buffalo offered none
of the challenge he had found in hunting wild
game—but there was money to be had—Tom joined up
with a buffalo-hunting expedition, headed by Clark
Hudnall and Jude Pilchuck. They were two rugged
westerners with whom Tom soon developed a friend-
ship. Also along on the expedition was Milly Fayre,
step-daughter of a hide hunter named Randall Jett.
Tom's and Milly's growing fondness for each other soon
incurred the bitter enmity of Jett, whom Tom
suspected had designs on Milly himself.

Tom found buffalo hunting to be unromantic,
grueling work. Shooting buffalo was ridiculously easy
because there were endless herds on the plains and most

of them seemed to have little fear of the hunters, but a most bloody and arduous task was skinning the animals and curing the hides. Tom soon sickened of the slaughter, but kept on because he felt he needed the money, and because Milly was part of the band.

Then, after returning from a hunting expedition one day, Tom found that Jett had split with Hudnall, virtually kidnapped Milly, and taken her off with his own party. Some days later, Tom learned to his horror that Jett's expedition had been set upon by Indians, and that most of them had been killed, and Milly was missing. Not long after that, the Indians also attacked part of Hudnall's expedition, and Hudnall himself was killed. The Indian raids had now developed into a full-fledged war and it was necessary for all the remaining hunting expeditions to ban together for protection.

Tom could not bring himself to speculate on what Milly's fate might be if she survived the raid and was captured by the Indians. She would be better off dead. There was little left for him now, with his sweetheart dead or captured and the best of his friends murdered by the Indians. But he stayed on grimly with Pilchuck and his men, because survival seemed to be the only motive he could muster.

CHAPTER 1

Pilchuck's band contained fifty-two men, most of whom owned, or had borrowed, Creedmor Sharps .45 calibre rifles for this expedition. These guns were more reliable and of longer range than the fig fifties. Each man took at least two hundred loaded cartridges. Besides that, reloading tools and loads of extra ammunition were included in the supplies. Four wagonloads of food and camp equipment, grain for the horses, and medical necessities were taken in charge of the best drivers.

This force was divided into three companies—one of twenty men under Pilchuck, and two, of sixteen men each, under old buffalo-hunters. This was to facilitate camping operations and to be in readiness to split into three fighting groups.

Tom Doan was in Pilchuck's company, along with Stronghurl, Burn Hudnall, Ory Tacks, Starwell, Spades Harkaway, the Indian called Bear Claws, Roberts, and others whom Tom knew. There were at least eight or ten hunters, long used to the range, and grim, laconic men who would have made any fighting force formidable.

Pilchuck, Bear Claws, Starwell, and Tom formed an advance guard, riding two miles ahead of the caval-cade. Both the scout and Starwell had powerful field-glasses. The rear guard consisted of three picked men under Harkaway. The route lay straight for the Staked Plain and was covered at the rate of fifteen miles a day. At night a strong guard was maintained.

On the fourth day the expedition reached the eastern wall of the Staked Plain, a stark, ragged, looming escarpment, notched at long distances by canyons, and extending north and south out of sight. This bold upheaval of rock and earth now gave at close hand an inkling of the wild and inhospitable nature of the Staked Plain.

The tracks of Hudnall's wagon led into a deep-mouthed canyon down whose rugged bottom poured a clear stream of water. Grass was abundant. Groves of cottonwood trees filled the level benches. Game of all kinds abounded in these fastnesses and fled before the approach of the hunters. Before noon of that day a small herd of buffalo, surprised in an open grassy park, stampeded up the canyon, completely obliterating the wagon tracks Pilchuck was following, and all other signs of the Comanches.

This flight of the buffalo, on the other hand, helped to make a way where it was possible to get the four wagons of supplies up on the Staked Plain. Many horses and strong hands made short work of this labor.

The Mexican scout led straight to the spot where there had recently been a large encampment of Comanches. They had been gone for days, no doubt having got wind of the campaign against them. The tracks of Hudnall's wagon were found again.

As it was now late in the day, camp was pitched here with the three forces of hunters close together. By dark, supper was finished, the horses were picketed and herded, guards were on duty, and Pilchuck was in council with his two scouts and the more experienced of his men. It was decided to hold that camp for the next day, and send out detachments with the scouts to try to locate the Comanches.

Round the camp fire that night Tom made the further acquaintance of Spades Harkaway, and found him a unique character, reticent as to himself, but not unwilling to talk about Texas, the buffalo, and the Indians. He had twice crossed the Staked Plain from its western boundary, the Pecos River, to the headwaters of the Brazos on the east.

Late next day the Mexican scout returned with the information that he had found the main encampment of the Comanches. He had been on a reconnoitre alone. Bear Claws and Pilchuck, who had essayed to follow the tracks of Hudnall's wagon, had actually lost all sign of them. For miles they had trailed the marks of the iron shod wheels over an area of hard packed gravel, only to lose them farther on in tough, short, springy grass that after the recent rain left no trace.

"The Indian says he can find the wagon tracks by making a wide circle to get off the grass," Pilchuck informed Starwell, "but that might take days. Besides, the Indians sent the wagon off their main trail. Reckon they expected pursuit. Anyway, we'll not risk it."

When Pilchuck made this decision he did not yet know that the Mexican had located the Comanches. Upon consulting with him the information came out that a large band of Indians had been encamped in a canyon, and undoubtedly their look outs had seen him.

This was verified next day, after a hard ride. An Indian band, large enough to have hundreds of horses, had hastily abandoned the encampment in the canyon and had climbed up on the plain, there to scatter in all directions. Plain trails were left in several cases, but these Bear Claws would not pay any attention to them. The Mexican sided with him. They concentrated on dinner trails over harder ground to follow.

It was after dark when Pilchuck and his men got back to camp, hungry and weary from a long day in the saddle. Next morning camp was moved ten miles to the west, to a secluded spot within easy striking distance of the place where Bear Claws left off trailing the night before.

That day the Osage Indian lost track of the Comanches for the reason that the trail, always dim, finally vanished altogether. Three days more of searching the fastness within riding distance of this camp availed nothing. Camp had to be moved again, this time at the Indian's suggestion, across the baffling stretch of plain to a wild and forbidding chaos of ruined cliffs, from which center many shallow canyons wandered for some leagues.

13

"Reckon we've got to rely on our field glasses to see them before they see us," said Pilchuck.

When the sun rose high enough next morning to burn out the shadows, Pilchuck stood with his scouts and some of his men on the crest of the rocky wilderness.

"Shore that's a hole!" he ejaculated.

Far and wide heaved the broken billows of grey rock, like an immense ragged sea, barren, monotonous, from which the heat veils rose in curtains. Here and there a tufted cedar raised its dwarf head, but for the most part there was no green to break the stark nudity. Naked eyes of white men could only see the appalling beauty of the place and enable the mind to grasp the deceiving nature of its distance, size, and colour. Pilchuck took a long survey with his field glass.

"Reckon all them meanderin' gorges head in one big canyon way down there," he said, handing the glass to Starwell.

"I agree with you, an' I'm gamblin' the Comanches are there," replied Starwell, in turn handling the glass to the man nearest him.

Tom had a good look at that magnified jumble of rocks and clefts, and the wonder of its wildness awed and thrilled him.

Standing next to Tom was Bear Claws, the Osage Indian, and so motionless, so striking was he as he gazed with dark, piercing eyes across the void, that Tom marvelled at him and felt imminence of some startling fact. Pilchuck observed this also, for as he stood behind the Indian he watched him steadily.

Bear Claws was over six feet tall, lithe, lean, erect, with something of the look of an eagle about him. His bronze, impassive face bore traces of vermilion paint. Around his neck was the bear claw necklace from which the hunters had nicknamed him. In the back of his scalp lock, a twisted knot of hair, he had stuck the tail feathers of a prairie bird. Bright bracelets of steel shone on his wrists. He was naked to his beaded and quilled breech clout.

"Me," he grunted, reaching for Pilchuck's field glass,

without taking his fixed gaze from what held him. With both hands then he put the glass to his eyes.

"Ugh!" he exclaimed instantly.

It was a moment of excitement and suspense for the watching men. Pilchuck restrained Starwell's impatience. Tom felt a cold ripple run over his body, and then as the Indian said, "Comanches" the ripple seemed suddenly to be strung with fire. He thought of Milly Fayre.

Bear Claws held the glass immovable, with stiff hand, while he stepped from behind it, and drew Pilchuck to the exact spot where he had stood. His long reaching arm seemed grotesque while his body moved guardedly. He was endeavouring to keep the glass levelled at the exact spot that had held him.

Pilchuck fastened hard down on the glass, that wavered slightly and then gradually became still. To the watching men he evidently was an eternity. But at last he spoke: "By thunder! he's right. I can just make out...Indians on trail—goin' down—head of that canyon all these rocks draws run into...Starwell, take a look...Hold there, over that first splinter of cliff, in a line with the high red bluff—an' search at its base."

Other glasses were now in use, and more than one of the hunters caught a glimpse of the Comanches before they disappeared.

The hunters retraced their steps from that high point and returned to camp. Pilchuck took the scouts to search for a well-hidden pocket or head of a box canyon where wagons and horses not needed could be concealed to advantage and protected by a small number of men. This was found, very fortunately, in the direction of the Indian encampment, and several miles closer. The move was made expeditiously before dark.

"Reckon this is pretty good," said Pilchuck with satisfaction. "We are far enough away to be missed by any scout they send out to circle their camp. That's an old Indian trick— to ride a circle round a hidin' place, thus crossin' any trail of men sneakin' close. It hardly seems possible we can surprise a bunch of Staked Plain Comanches, but the chance shore looks good."

In the darkest hour before dawn forty grim men rode out of camp behind the Mexican and Pilchuck.

Tom Doan rode next to Bear Claws, the fifth of that cavalcade, and following him came Spades Harkaway. No one spoke. The hoofs of the horses gave forth only dull, sodden sounds, inaudible at little distance. There was an opaque misshapen moon, orange in color, hanging low over the uneven plain. The morning star, white, luminous, like a marvelous beacon, stood high above the blanching velvet of the eastern sky.

They travelled at walk or trot, according to the nature of the ground, until the moon went down and all the stars had paled, except the great one in the east. This, too, soon grew wan. The grey of dawn was at hand. Dismounting in the lee of a low ledge, where brush grew thick and the horses could be tied, Pilchuck left two men on guard and led the others on foot behind the noiseless Mexican.

In less than a quarter of a mile the Mexican whispered something and slipped to his hands and knees. Pilchuck and his followers, two and three abreast, kept close to his heels. The fact that the Mexican crept on very slowly and made absolutely no sound had the effect of constraining those behind him to proceed as stealthily. This wrought upon the nerves of the men.

Tom Doan had never experienced such suspense. Just ahead of him lay the unknown ground never seen by him or any of his white comrades, and it held, no one knew how close, a peril soon to be encountered.

The dawn was growing lighter and rows of rocks ahead could be distinguished. The ground began to slope. Beyond what seemed a grey space, probably a canyon, rose a dim vague bulk, uneven and woolly. Soon it showed to be canyon slope with brush on the rim.

Tom, finding that he often rustled the weeds or scraped on the hard ground, devoted himself to using his eyes as well as muscles to help him crawl silently. Thus it was that he did not look up until Pilchuck's low "Hist!" halted everybody.

Then Tom saw with starting eyes a deep bend in a wonderful gully, where on a green level of some acres in extent were a large number of Indian tepees. A stream wound through the middle of this oval, and its low rush and gurgle were the only sounds to break the stillness of the morning. Hundreds of Indian ponies were grazing, standing, or lying down all over this meadow like level. Not an Indian appeared in sight, but as the light was still grey and dim, there could not be any certainty as to that.

Pilchuck raised himself to peer over a rock, and he studied the lay of the encampment, the narrow gateways above and below, and the approaches from the slope on his side. Then he slipped back to face the line of crouching men.

"By holdin' high we're in range right here," he whispered tensely. "Starwell, take ten men an' crawl back a little, then round an' down to a point even with where this canyon narrows below. Harkaway, you take ten man an' go above, an' slip down same way. Go slow. Don't make noise. Don't stand up. We can then see each other's positions an' command all but the far side of this canyon. That's a big camp—there's two hundred Indians, more if they have their families. An' I reckon they have. Now, Indians always fight harder under such conditions. We're in for a hell of a fight. But don't intentionally shoot squaws an' kids. That's all." With only the slightest rustle and scrape, and deep intake of breath, the two detachments under Starwell and Harkaway crept back among the stones out of sight. Then absolute silence once more reigned.

Pilchuck's men lay flat, some of them more favorably located than others, peering from behind stones. No one spoke. They all waited. Meanwhile the grey dawn broadened to daylight.

"Ugh!" grunted Bear Claws, deep in his throat. His sinewy hand gripped Tom's shoulder.

Tom raised his head a couple of inches, and he spied a tall Indian standing before a tepee, facing the east, where faint streaks of pink and rose heralded the sunrise.

Presently another Indian brave appeared, and another, then several squaws, and in a comparatively short time the camp became active. Columns of blue smoke arose lazily on the still air. The ponies began to move about.

"Ugh!" exclaimed Bear Claws, and this time he touched Pilchuck, directing him towards a certain point in the encampment.

At that juncture there pealed out a singularly penetrating yell, most startling in its suddenness and nerve-racking with its terrible long-drawn and sustained wildness.

"Commanche war-cry!" hissed Pilchuck. "Some buck has glimpsed our men below. Wait! We want the shootin' to begin below an' above. Then mebbe the Indians will run this way."

Scarcely had the scout ceased his rapid whisper when a Sharps rifle awoke the sleeping echoes. It came from Starwell's detachment below.

In an instant the Indian camp became a scene of wild rush and shrill cry, above which pealed sharp, quick shouts—the voice of authority. A heavy volley from Starwell's men was signal for Harkaway's to open up. The puffs of white smoke over the stone betrayed the whereabouts of both detachments. A rattle of Winchesters from the camp below told how speedily many of the Indians had got into action.

Despite Pilchuck's orders, some of his men began to fire.

"All right, if you can't wait. But shoot high," he shouted.

Twenty Creedmoors thundered in unison from that rocky slope. It seemed to Tom then that hell had broken loose. He had aimed and shot at a running brave. His hands shook to spoil his aim and his face streamed with cold sweat. All the men were loading and firing, and he was in the midst of a cracking din.

In a few moments the first blending roar of guns and yells broke, and there intervened a less consistent din. Pandemonium reigned down in that encampment, yet there must have been many crafty Indians. Already the front line of tepees was in flames, sending up streaks of smoke, behind which the women and children were dimly seen running for the opposite slope. A number of frightened mustangs were racing with flying manes and tails up and down the canyon, but the majority appeared to be under control of the Indians, and corralled at the widest point. Soon many braves, women, and children dragging packs and horses were seen through or round the smoke on the opposite slope.

The Comanche braves below then lived up to their reputation as the most daring and wonderful horsemen of the plains. To draw the fire of the hunters, numbers of them, half naked demons, yelling, with rifles in hand, rode their mustangs bareback, with magnificent affront and tremendous speed, straight at the gateway of the canyon. They ran a gauntlet of leaden hail.

Tom saw braves pitch headlong to the earth. He saw mustangs plunge and throw their riders far. And he also saw Indians ride fleet as the storm winds under the volleys from the slope, to escape down the canyon.

No sooner had one bunch of rider braves attempted this than another drove their mustangs pell-mell at the openings. They favored the lower gate beneath Starwell's detachment, being quick to catch some little advantage there. The foremost of four Indians, a lean wild brave, magnificently mounted, made such a wonderful target with his defiance and horsemanship that he drew practically all the fire. He rode to his death, but his three companions flashed through the gateway in safety.

"Hold men! Hold!" yelled Pilchuck suddenly at this juncture. "Load up an' wait. We're in for a charge or a trick."

Following with sharp gaze where the scout pointed, Tom saw through smoke and heat the little puffs of white, all along behind the burning front line of tepees. There were many braves lying flat behind stones, trees, camp duffle, everything that would hide a man. Bullets whistled over Tom's head and spanged from the rocks on each side of him.

"Watch that bunch of horses!" called Pilchuck warningly. "There's fifty if there's one. Reckon we've bit off more'n we can chew."

Dimly through the now thinning smoke Tom could see the bunch of riders designated by Pilchuck. They were planning some audacious break, like that of the braves who had sacrificed themselves to help their families to escape. This would be different, manifestly, for all the women and children, and the young braves with them, had disappeared over the far slope. It was war now.

"Jude, they're too smart to charge us," said a grizzled old hunter. "I'll swear thet bunch is aimin' to make a break to git by an' above us."

"Wal, if they do, we'll be in a hell of a pickle," replied the scout. "I'll ask Bear Claws what he makes of it."

The Osage readily replied, "No weyno," which Tom interpreted as being anything but good for the hunters.

The Mexican urged Pilchuck to work back to higher ground, but the scout grimly shook his head.

Suddenly, with remarkable swiftness, the compact bunch of Indian horsemen disintegrated and seemed to spill both to right and left.

"What the hell!" muttered Pilchuck.

One line of Comanche riders swerved below the camp, the other above, and they rode strung out in single file, going in opposite directions. Starwell and Harkaway reserved their fire, expecting some trick. When half way to each gate, the leader of each string wheeled at right angles to head straight for the slope.

"By God! They're goin' between us!" exclaimed Pilchuck. "Men, we've shore got to stick now an' fight for our lives."

At two hundred yards these incomparable riders were as hard to hit with bullets as birds on the wing. Starwell's detachment began to shoot and Harkaway's followed suit. Their guns were drowned in the dreadful war-cry of the Comanches. It seemed wilder, more piercing now, closer, a united sound, filling the ears, horrid yet not discordant, full of death, but for all that a magnificent blending of human voices. It was the cry of a wild tribe for life.

It lifted Tom's hair stiff on his head. He watched with staring eyes. How those mustangs leaped! They crossed the open level below, the danger zone of leaden hail, without a break in their speeding line. When they reached the base of the slope, they were perked to their haunches, and in a flash each one was riderless. The Comanches had taken to the rocks.

"Ahuh! I reckoned so," growled Pilchuck. "Pretty slick, if I do say it. Men, we've got crawlin' snakes to deal with now. You shore have to look sharp."

This sudden manoeuver had the same effect upon the Starwell and Harkaway detachments as it had on Pilchuck's. It almost turned the tables on the white men. How grave it was perhaps only the experienced plainsmen realized. They all reserved their fire, manifestly directing attention to this new and hidden peril. The Comanches left in camp, a considerable number, redoubled their shots.

"Men, reckon it ain't time yet to say everyone for himself," declared Pilchuck. "But we've shore got to crawl up to the level. Spread out, an' crawl flat on your bellies, an' keep rocks behind you."

Thus began a retreat fraught with great risk. Bullets from the Winchesters spanged off the rocks, puffing white powder dust into the air. And these bullets came from the rear. The Comanches on each side had vanished like lizards into the maze of boulders. But every hunter realized these Indians were worming their way to places of advantage.

Tom essayed to keep up with Bear Claws, but this was impossible by crawling. The Osage wriggled like a snake. Pilchuck, too, covered ground remarkable for a large man. Others crawled fast or slowly, according to their abilities. Thus the detachment, which had heretofore kept together, gradually disintegrated.

It had been a short two hundred yards from the top of this slope to the position the hunters had abandoned. Crawling back seemed interminable and insurmountable to Tom. Yet he saw how imperative it was to get there.

Some one was close behind Tom, crawling laboriously, panting heavily. It was Ory Tacks. As he was fat and round, the exertion was almost beyond his endurance and the risks were great. Tom had himself to think of, yet he wondered if he should not help Ory. Roberts crawled a little to Tom's left. He, too, was slow. An old white haired buffalo hunter named Calkins had taken Pilchunk's place on Tom's right. The others were above, fast wriggling out of sight.

A bullet zipped off a stone close to Tom and sang into the air. It had come from another direction. Another bullet, striking in front of him, scattered dust and gravel in his face. Then bullets hissed low down, just over the rocks. The Comanches were not yet above the hunters. Calkins called low for those back of him to hurry, that the word has been passed back from Pilchuck.

Tom was crawling as flat as a flounder, dragging a heavy gun. He could not make faster time. He was burning with sweat, yet cold as ice, and the crack of Winchesters had the discordance of a nightmare.

"Doan," called Roberts sharply, "the fellow behind you's been hit."

Tom peered round. Ory Tacks lay with face down. His fat body was quivering.

"Ory! Ory! Are you hit?" flashed Tom.

"I should smile," he groaned, lifting a pale face. His old slouch hat was still in place and a tuft of tow-colored hair stuck out through a hole. "Never mind—me."

"Roberts, come help me," called Tom, and began to back down towards Ory. Roberts did likewise, and they both reached the young man about the same time.

"Much obliged to see you," said Ory gratefully, as they took hold of his arms, one on each side.

Up to that moment Tom had been mostly stultified

22

by emotion utterly new to him. It had been close to panic, for he had found himself hard put to it to keep from leaping up to run. But something in connection with Ory's misfortune strung Tom suddenly and acutely to another mood. Grim realization and anger drove away his fear.

"Drag him; he cain't help himself," panted Roberts.

Then began what Tom felt to be the most heartbreaking labor imaginable. They had to crawl and drag the wounded Ory uphill. Tom locked his left arm under Ory's and, dragging his rifle in his right hand, he jerked and hunched himself along. Bullets now began to whistle and patter from the other side, signifying that the Commanches to the right had located the crawling hunters. Suddenly above Tom boomed a heavy Creedmoor—then two booms followed in succession.

"Good! It was about time," panted Roberts.

Tom felt the coldness leave his marrow for good. It was flight now. Pilchuck, Bear Claws, the Mexican, and some of the old plainsmen had reached the top of the slope and had opened on the Comanches. This spurred him, if not to greater effort, which was impossible, at least to dogged and unquenchable endurance. Roberts whistled through his nose; his lean face was bathed with sweat. Ory Tacks struggled bravely to help himself along, though it was plain his agony was tremendous.

The slope grew less steep and more thickly strewn with large rocks. Tom heard no more bullets whiz up from direction of the encampment. They came from both sides, and the reports of Winchesters, sharp and rattling above the Creedmoors, covered a wide half-circle. Farther away the guns of the Starwell and Harkaway forces rang out steadily, if not often. It had become a hot battle, and the men were no longer shooting at puffs of white smoke.

Not a moment too soon did Tom and Roberts drag Tacks over the top of the slope into a zone of large boulders, behind which Pilchuck and his men were fighting. For almost at the last instant Tom heard a dull spat of lead striking flesh. Roberts' left arm, on which he was hunching himself along, crumpled under him, and he dropped flat.

"They busted me," he declared huskily, then let go of Tacks, and floundered behind a rock.

Tom, by superhuman exertion, dragged Ory farther on, behind a long, low ledge, from which a hunter was shooting. Then Tom collapsed. But as he sank flat he heard the boy's grateful "Much obliged, Tom." For a few moments then, Tom was deaf and blind to the battle. There was a bursting riot within his breast, and an overtaxed heart fluttering to recover. It seemed long that he lay prostrate, utterly unable to lift face or hand. But gradually that passed. Pilchuck crawled close, smelling of sweat, dust, and powder.

"Tom, are you hurt?" he queried, shaking him.

"No—only—all in," whispered Tom huskily between pants. "We had to drag Ory up here. He's hit; so's Roberts."

"I'll take a look at them," said the scout. "We're shore in better position here. Reckon we can hold the red devils off. Lucky Starwell an' Harkaway are behind them, on both sides. We're in for a siege. . . . Bullets flyin' from east an' west. Peep out mighty careful an' look for an Indian. Don't shoot at smoke."

Tom crawled a little to the left and cautiously took up a position where he could peer from behind the long, flat rock. He could see nothing move. An uneven field of boulders, large and small, stretched away, with narrow aisles of grey grass and ground between. The firing had diminished greatly. Both sides were conserving ammunition. Not for several moments did Tom espy a puff of white smoke, and that came from a heavy Creedmoor four hundred yards or more away, from a point above where Starwell's men had guarded the gateway of the canyon.

Meanwhile, as he watched for something to shoot at, he could hear Pilchuck working over the wounded men, and ascertained that Roberts had been shot through the arm, not, however, to break the bones, and

24

Ory Tacks had a broken hip. Tom realized the gravity of such a wound out there in the wilderness.

"I'd be much obliged for a drink of water," was all Tom heard Ory say.

Pilchuck crawled away and did not return. Ory Tacks and Roberts lay at the base of the low edge, out of range of bullets for the present. But they lay in the sun and already the sun was hot. The scout had chosen a small oval space irregularly surrounded by boulders and outcroppings of rough ledges. By twisting his head Tom could spy eight or ten of Pilchuck's force, some facing east behind their fortifications, others west. Tom heard both profanity and loquacious humour. The Mexican and the Osage were not in sight.

Then Tom peeped out from behind his own covert. This time his quick eye caught a glimpse of something moving, like a rabbit slipping into brush. Above that place then slid out a red streak and a thin blue-white cloud of smoke. Sputt! A bullet hit the corner of his rock and whined away. Tom dodged back, suddenly aghast, and hot with anger. A sharp-eyed Indian had seen him. Tom wormed his way back of the long rock to the other end. Behind the next rock lay the old white haired hunter, bare headed, with sweat and tobacco stains upon his grizzled face.

"Take it easy an' slow," he advised Tom complacently. "Comanches can't stand a long fight. They're riders, an' all we need is patience. On the ground we can lick hell out of them."

The old plainsman's nonchalance was incredible, yet vastly helpful to Tom. He put a hard curb on his impetuosity, and forced himself to wait and think carefully of every action before he undertook it. Therefore he found a position where he could command a certain limited field of rocks without risk to himself. It was like peeping through a knot hole too small for any enemy to see at a distance. From this vantage point Tom caught fleeting glimpses and flashes of color—grey and bronze, once a speck of red. But

25

these vanished before he could bring his rifle into play.

"If you see suthin' move, shoot quick as lightin'," said the old plainsman. "It might be a gopher or cottontail, but take no chances. It's likely to be a two-legged varmint."

The hours passed swiftly for the fighters. Another wounded man joined Roberts and Ory Tacks, and the ordeal must have been frightful for them. Tom forgot them; so did all the defenders of that position. The glaring sun poured down its heat. Stones and guns were so hot they burned. No breeze stirred. And the fight went on, favorable for the buffalo hunters because of their fortifications, unfavorable in regard to time. They were all parching with thrist. By chance or blunder the canteens had been left on the saddles and water had come to be almost as precious as powder. The old plainsman cursed the Staked Plain. Tom's mouth appeared full of cotton waste. He had kept pebbles in his mouth till he was sick of them.

Noon went by. Afternoon came. The sun, hotter than ever, began to slope to the west. And the fight went on, narrowing down as to distance, intensifying as to spirit, magnifying peril to both sides. The Creedmoors from the Starwell and Harkaway forces kept up the bulk of the shooting. They were directing most of their fire down into the encampment, no doubt to keep the Comanches there from joining their comrades on the slope. Mustangs showed on the farther points, and evidently had strayed.

Presently Pilchuck came crawling on hands and knees, without his rifle or coat. A bloody patch showed on his shoulder.

"Tom, reckon I got punctured a little," he said. "It ain't bad, but it's bleedin' like hell. Tear my shirt sleeve off an' tie it round under my arm over my shoulder tight."

An ugly bullet hole showed angrily in the upper part of the scout's shoulder, apparently just through the flesh.

"Notice that bullet come from behind," said

Pilchuck. "There shore was a mean redskin on your side. He hit two of us before I plugged him. There, good. . . . Now how's the rest of your hospital?"

"I don't know. Afraid I forgot," replied Tom, aghast.

"Wal, I'll see."

He crawled over to the wounded man and spoke. Tom heard Roberts answer, but Ory Tacks was silent. That disturbed Tom. Then the scout came back to him.

"Roberts is sufferin' some, but he's O.K. The young feller, though, is dyin', I'm afraid. Shot in the groin. Mebbe—"

"Pilchuck! Ory didn't seem bad hurt."

"Wal, he is, an' if we don't get some water he'll go," declared the scout emphatically. "Fact is, we're all bad off for water. It's shore hot. What a dumbhead I was to forget the canteens!"

"I'll go after them," returned Tom, like a flash.

"It's not a bad idee," said Pilchuck after a moment's reflection. "Reckon it'd be no riskier than stayin' here."

"Direct me. Where'd you leave the horses?"

The scout faced south, at right angles with the crossfire from the Comanches, and presently extended his long arm.

"See that low bluff, not far, the last one reachin' down into this basin. It's behind there. You can't miss it. Lucky the rocks from here on are thick as cabbages."

"I can make it," declared Tom doggedly. "But to get back. That stumps me."

"Easy. You've got to go slow, pickin' the best cover. Just lay a line of little stones as you crawl along. Reckon the Comanches are all on these two sides of us. But there *might* be some tryin' to surround us."

"Anything more?" queried Tom briefly.

The scout apparently had no thought of the tremendousness of this enterprize to Tom. It was as if he had naturally expected of Tom what he would do himself if he had not been partially incapacitated. Tom realized he had never in his life received such a compliment. It swelled his heart. He felt light, hard, tense, vibrating to a strange excitation.

27

"Wal, I can't think of anythin'," replied the scout. "Comin' back be slower'n molasses, an' get the drift of the fight. We're holdin' these Redskins off. But I reckon Starwell an' Harkaway have been doin' more. If I don't miss my guess, they've spilled blood down in the canyon. Comanches are great on horseback, but they can't stick out a fight like this. If they rush us, we're goners. If they don't they'll quit before sunset."

CHAPTER 2

Milly Fayre rode out of Sprague's Post on the front of a freighter's wagon, sitting between Jett and his wife. The rest of Jett's outfit followed close behind, Follonsbee and Pruitt in the second wagon, and Catlee driving the last.

For as long as Milly could see the Hudnalls, she waved her red scarf in farewell. Then when her friends passed out of sight Milly turned slowly to face the boundless prairie, barren of life, suddenly fearful in its meaning, and she sank down, stricken in heart. What she had dreaded was now an actuality. The courage that had inspired her when she wrote the letter to Tom Doan, leaving it with Mrs. Hudnall, was a courage inspired by love, not by hope. So it seemed now.

"Milly, you ain't actin' much like a boy, spite them boy's clothes" said Jett, with an attempt at levity. "Pile over in the back of the wagon an' lay down."

Kindness from Jett was astounding, and was gratefully received by Milly. Doing as she was bidden, she found a comfortable place on the unrolled packs of bedding, with her head in a shade of the wagon seat. It developed then that Jett's apparent kindness had been only a ruse to get her away so he could converse with his wife in low, earnest tones. Milly might have heard all or part of that conversation, but she was not interested and did not listen.

The hours passed, and Jett's deep, low voice appeared never to rest or cease. He did not make a noon stop, as was customary among the buffalo hunters. And he drove until sunset.

'Forty miles, bedam!' he said with satisfaction as he threw the reins.

29

Whether Milly would have it so or not, she dropped at once back into the old camp life and its tasks. How well she remembered! The smoke of the camp fire made her eyes smart and brought tingling as well as hatefull memories.

The other wagons drove up rather late, and once more Milly found herself under the hawk eyes of Follonsbee and the half-veiled hidden look of the crooked-faced Pruitt. Her masculine garb, emphasizing her shapely slenderness, manifestly drew the gaze of these men. They seemed fascinated by it, as if they both had discovered something. Neither of them spoke to her. Catlee, however, gave her a kindly nod. He seemed more plodding in mind than she remembered him.

One by one the old associations returned to her, and presently her fleeting happiness with the Hudnalls had the remoteness and unreality of a dream. She was again Jett's step-daughter, quick to start at his harsh voice. Was that harshness the same? She seemed to have a vague impression of a difference in his voice, in him, in all of his outfit, in the atmosphere around them.

A stopping-place had been chosen at one of the stream crossings where hundreds of buffalo-hunters had camped that year, a fact Jett growled about, complaining of lack of grass and wood. Water was plentiful, and it was cold, a welcome circumstance to the travellers. Jett had an inordinate thirst, probably owing to his addition to rum at Sprague's.

"Fetch some more drinkin' water," he ordered Milly.

She took the pail and went down the bank under the big, rustling, green cottonwoods. Catlee was at the stream, watering the horses.

"I seen you comin', an' I says, Who's that boy?" he said with a grin. "I forgot."

"I forgot, too," she replied dubiously. "I don't like these—these pants. But I've made a discovery, Catlee. I'm more comfortable round camp."

"Don't wonder. You used to drag your skirts round....Gimme your bucket. I'll fill it where the water's clear."

He waded in beyond where the horses were drinking and dipped the pail. "Nothin' like good cold water after a day's hot ride."

"Jett drank nearly all I got before and sent me for more."

"He's burnin' up inside with red liquor," returned Catlee bluntly.

Milly did not have any reply to make to that, but she thanked Catlee and, taking the pail, she poured out a little water so she would not spill it as she walked.

"Milly, I'm sorry you had to come back with Jett," said Catlee.

She paused, turning to look at him, surprised at his tone. His bronzed face lacked the heat, the dissolute shades common to Jett and the other men. Milly remembered then that Catlee, in her opinion, had not seemed like the rest of Jett's outfit.

"Sorry? Why?" she asked.

"I know Sprague. He's from Missouri. He told me about you an' your friend Tom Doan."

"Sprague told you—about—about Tom!" faltered Milly, suddenly blushing. "Why, who told him?"

"Mrs. Hudnall," he said. "Sprague took interest in you, it 'pears. An' his wife is thick with the Hudnall women. Anyway, he was sorry Jett took you away, an' so am I."

Milly's confusion and pain at the mention of Tom did not quite render her blind to this man's sympathy. She forced away the wave of emotion. Her mind quickened to the actuality of her being once more in Jett's power and that she had only her wits and courage to rely upon. This hard-faced, apparently dull and sombre man might befriend her. Milly suddenly conceived the inspiration to win him to her cause.

"So am I sorry, Catlee," she said sadly, and her quick tears were genuine. Indeed, they had started to flow at mention of Tom's name. "I—I'm engaged to Tom Doan.... I was—so—so happy. And I'd never had any happy times before.... Now I've been dragged away. Jett's my stepfather. I'm not of age. I had to come.... And I'm terribly afraid of him."

"I reckon," rejoined Catlee darkly, "you've reason to be. He an' the woman quarrelled at Sprague's. He wanted to leave her behind. For that matter, the four of them drank a good deal, an' fought over the hide money."

"For pity's sake, be my friend!" appealed Milly.

The man stared at her, as if uncomprehending, yet somehow stirred.

"Catlee," she said, seeing her advantage and stepping back to lay a hand softly on his arm, "did you ever have a sister or a sweetheart?"

"Reckon not, or I'd be another kind of man," he returned, with something of pathos.

"But you're not bad," she went on swiftly.

"Me not bad! Child, you're crazy! I never was anythin' else. An' now I'm a hide thief."

"Oh, it's true then? Jett is a hide thief. I knew something was terribly wrong."

"Grid, don't you tell Jett I said that," replied Catlee almost harshly.

"No, I won't. I promise. You can trust me," she returned hurriedly. "And I could trust you. I don't think you're really bad. Jett has led you into this. He's bad. I hate him."

"Yes, Jett's bad all right, an' he means bad by you. I reckon I thought you knowed an' didn't care."

"Care! If he harms me, I'll kill him and myself," she whispered passionately.

The man seemed to be confronted with something new in his experience.

"So that's how a good girl feels!" he muttered.

"Yes. And I ask you—beg of you to be a man, a friend."

"There comes Pruitt," interrupted Catlee, turning to his horses. "Don't let him or any of them see you talkin' to me."

Supper was cooked and eaten. The men, except Catlee, were not hungry as usual, and appeared to be wearing off the effects of hard drinking. They spoke but seldom, and then only to ask for something out of

32

reach on the spread canvas. Darkness settled down while Milly dried the pans and cups. Catlee came up with a huge armload of wood, which he dropped with a crash, a little too near Pruitt to suit his irascible mood.

"Say, you Missouri hay-seed, can't you see my feet?" he demanded.

"I could if I looked. They're big enough," retorted Catlee. I ain't wonderin' you have such care of them."

"Ain't you? Shore I'd like to know why?" queried Pruitt.

"I reckon what little brains you've got are in them."

"You damn Yank." ejaculated the little rebel, as amazed as enranged. "I've shot men for less'n thet."

"Reckon you have," rejoined Catlee with slow, cool sarcasm. "But in the back! An' I'm lookin' at you."

Milly heard and saw this by-play from the shadow beyond the campfire circle. If that were Catlee's answer to her appeal, it was a change, sudden and bewildering. The thrill she sustained was more like a shudder. In that moment·she sensed a far reaching influence, a something which had to do with future events. Catlee stalked off into the gloom of the cottonwood, where he had made his bed.

"Rand, are you sure thet feller is what you said he was—a Missouri farm-hand, tired of workin' for nothin'? demanded Follonsbee.

"Hank, I ain't sure of anythin' an' I don't give a whoop," replied the leader.

"Thet's natural, for you,' said the other with sarcasm. "You don't know the West as I know it. Catlee struck me queer.... When he called Pruitt, so cool-like, I had come to mind men of the Cole Younger stripe. If so ..."

"Aw, it's nothin'," cut in Pruitt. "Jett spoke my sentiments about our Yankee pard. It riles me to think of him gettin' a share of our hide money."

Jett coughed, an unusual thing for him to do. "Who said Catlee got a share?" he queried.

Follonsbee lifted his lean head to peer at the leader. Pruitt, who was sitting back to a stump, his distorted face gleaming red in the camp fire light, moved slowly forward to gaze in turn. Both men were silent; both of them questioned with their whole bodies. But Jett had no answer. He calmly lit his pipe and flipped the match into the fire.

"Shore, now that I tax myself, I cain't remember thet anybody said Catlee got a share," replied Pruitt, with deliberation. "But I thought he did. An' I know Hank thought so."

"I'd have gambled on it," said Follonsbee.

"Catlee gets wages, that's all," asserted the leader.

"Ahuuh! An' who gets his share of the hide money?" demanded Pruitt.

"I do," rejoined Jett shortly.

"Jett, I'm tellin' you that's in line with your holdin' out money for supplies at Sprague's," said Follonsbee earnestly. "You furnish the outfit, grub, everythin', an share even with all of us, includin' your woman. You got your share, an' her share, an' now Catlee's share."

"I'm willin' to argue it out with you, but not on an equal divvy basis."

There followed a long silence. The men smoked. The fire burned down, so that their faces were but pale gleams. Milly sought her bed, which she had made in the wagon. Jett had sacrificed tents to make room for equal weight of buffalo hides. He had unrolled his blankets under the wagon, where the sullen woman had repaired soon after dark. Milly took off her boy's shoes and folded the coat for a pillow; then, slipping under the blankets, she stretched out, glad for the relief.

Jett, Follonsbee, and Pruitt remained around the camp fire, quarrelling in low voices; and that sound was the last Milly heard as slumber claimed her.

Milly's eyes opened to the bright light of day, and pale blue sky seemed canopied over her. Not the canvas roof of her tent! Where was she? The smell of cottonwood smoke brought her to a surging shock of realization. Then Jett's harsh voice, which had always made her shrink with fear, sent a creeping fire along her veins.

She lay a moment longer, calling to the spirit that had

34

awakened last night; and it augmented while she seemed to grow strangely older. She would endure; she would fight; she would think. So that when she presented herself at the camp fire she was outwardly a quiet, obedient, impassive girl, but inwardly a cunning, daring woman.

Not half a dozen words were spoken around the breakfast canvas. Jett rushed the tasks. Sunrise shone on the three wagons moving south at a brisk pase.

Milly had asked Catlee to fix her a comfortable place in the back of Jett's wagon. He had done so, adding of his own accord an improvised sunshade of canvas. She had watched him from the wagon seat, hoping he would speak to her or look at her in a way that would confirm her hopes. But the teamster was silent and kept his head lowered. Nevertheless, Milly did not regard his taciturnity as unfavorable to her. There had been about Catlee, last night when he had muttered "So that's how a good girl feels," a something which spoke to Milly's intuition. She could not prove anything. But she felt. This man would befriend her. A subtle unconscious influence was working on his mind. It was her presence, her plight, her appeal.

Milly thought of a thousand plans to escape, to get word to Doan, to acquaint buffalo hunters with the fact of her being practically a prisoner, to betray that Jett was a hide thief. Nothing definitely clear and satisfactory occurred to her. But the fact of her new knowledge of Jett stood out tremendously. It was an infallible weapon to employ if the right opportunity presented. But a futile attempt at that would result fatally for her. Jett would most surely kill her.

It seemed to Milly as she evolved in her mind plan after plan that the wisest thing to do would be to play submissive slave to Jett until he reached the end of the drive south; and there to persuade Catlee to take her at once to Hudnall's camp, where she would betray Jett. If Catlee would not help her, then she must go alone or, failing that, wait for Tom Doan to find her.

Before the morning was far advanced Jett gave wide

berth to an oncoming outfit. Milly was not aware of this until the unusual jolting caused her to rise to her knees and look out. Jett had driven off the main road, taking a low place, where other drivers had made short cuts. Four freight wagons heavily laden with hides were passing at some distance to the right. The foremost team of horses was white—Milly thought she recognized it as Hudnall's. Her heart rushed to her lips. But she had seen many white teams, and all of them had affected her that way. If she leaped out and ran to find she was mistaken, she would lose every chance she had. Besides, as she gazed, she imagined she was wrong. So with a deep sigh she dropped back to her seat.

The hours passed quickly. Milly pondered until she was weary, then fell asleep, and did not awaken until another camp was reached. And the first words she heard were Jett's speaking to Follonsbee as he drove up abreast of the leader, "Wasn't that Hudnall's outfit we passed?"

"First two teams was," replied Follonsbee. "That young skinner of Hudnall's was leadin' an' that ugly feller was drivin' the second team. I didn't know the other outfits."

Soon the men were back from attending to the horses, and this evening they were hungry. Meeting outcoming freighters with buffalo hides had for the moment turned the minds of Jett and his two lieutenants from their differences.

"How many hides in them outfits? queried Jett.

"It weren't a big haul," replied Follonsbee.

"Shore was big enough to make us turn off the road," said Pruitt meaningly.

Jett glared at him. Then Catlee drawled: "Funny they didn't see us. But we went down on our side some. That first driver was Hudnall's man, Tom Doan."

"Ahuh. Well, suppose it was?" returned Jett, nonplussed at this remark from the habitually unobserving Catlee.

"Nothing. I just recognized him," replied Catlee casually as he lowered his eyes.

36

When he raised them a moment later, to look across the canvas supper cloth at Milly, she saw them as never before, sharp as a dagger, with a single bright gleam. He wanted her to know that he had seen Tom Doan. Milly dropped her own gaze and she spilled a little of her coffee. She dared not trust her flashing interpretation of this man's glance. It seemed like a gleam of lightning from what had hitherto been dead ashes. Thereafter he paid no attention to her, nor to any of the others; and upon finishing the meal and finishing his chore of cutting firewood he vanished.

Jett had his two disgruntled men take up their quarrel and spent a long, noisy, angry hour round the camp fire.

The next day came and passed, with no difference for Milly except that Catlee now avoided her, never seemed to notice her; and that she hung out her red scarf with a hopeful thrill in its significance. Then one by one the days rolled by, and under the wheels of the wagons.

Seven days, and then the straggling lost bands of buffalo! The hot, summer air was drowsy; the gently waving prairie bore heaps of bones; skulking coyotes sneaked back from the road. A thousand times Milly Fayre looked back down the endless road she had travelled. No wagon came in sight!

Noon on the ninth day brought Jett within sight of the prairie-wide herd of buffalo. He halted to point it out to his sullen, unseeing men; and later he reined in again, this time to turn his ear to the hot stinking wind.

"Aha! Listen!" he called back to Follonsbee.

Milly heard the "Boom! Boom! Boom!" of guns, near and far, incessant and potent. Strangely, for once she was glad to hear them!

All that hot midday she reclined on the improvised seat in her wagon, holding her scarf to her nostrils and looking out her wagon occasionally at the sordid ugliness of abandoned camp sites. The buffalo hunters had moved on up the river that now showed its wandering line of green timber.

Milly took a last backward gaze down the prairie

37

road just as Jett turned off to go into the woods. Far away Milly saw a dot on the horizon—a white and black dot. Maybe it was Tom Doan's horses and wagon! He could not be far behind. It was as well now, perhaps, that he had not caught up with Jett. The buffalo range had been reached; and it could not be long before her situation would be changed.

Jett drove off the prairie, into the timber, along a well-defined shady road where many camps had been pitched and then down into the brakes. Brutal and fearless driver that he was, he urged his horses right through the tangled undergrowth that bent with the onslaught of the wagon, to spring back erect after it had passed. Follonsbee came crashing next. Jett drove down into the bottom lands clear to a deep shining river.

Milly would not allow herself to be distressed because Jett meant to hide his camp, for she knew that any one hunting wagon tracks and camps would surely not miss him. In a way Milly was glad of the shade, the murmur of the river, the songs of the birds, and the absence of the stench. A camp on the edge of the prairie, with the rotten carcasses of buffalo close at hand, the dust and heat, the flies and bugs, would be well-nigh unendurable.

Jett halted his team in a shady glade of cottonwoods just back from the river, and Milly then discovered that this was the scene of Jett's previous encampment. His tents and fireplace, boxes and bales, evidently had not been molested during his absence.

"Turn horses loose an' unload the wagons," he ordered his men. "I'll take a look for my saddle horses."

"No fear of hosses leavin' grass an' water," rejoined Follonsbee. "But there might be hoss thieves on the range."

"Haw! haw! laughed Pruitt in his mean way. "Shore you know these heah buff-hunters are all honest men."

Jett strode off into the green brakes. The men unloaded the wagons and set the boxes and bags of supplies under a cottonwood. Mrs. Jett opened a tent near the fire place.

"Miss," said Catlee, "the canvas wagon cover you had before got ripped to pieces. There ain't any tent for you till that one's mended."

"Can't I stay in the wagon?" she asked.

"Don't see why not. We'll hardly be movin' or haulin' very soon."

It was late in the afternoon when the rays of the sun began to lose heat. Milly was sorely in need of a little freedom of limbs. She had been cramped and inactive so long. So she walked to and fro under the trees. This camp was the most secluded Jett had ever chosen far from the prairie, down in the brakes at the edge of the river, hidden by trees from the opposite densely foliaged bank. If it had not hinted of a sinister meaning and was not indeed a prison for Milly, she could have revelled in it. If she had to spend much time there, she would be grateful for its quiet, cleanliness, and beauty. She strolled along the green bank until Mrs. Jett curtly called her to help get supper.

About the time it was ready Jett returned with muddy boots and clothes covered with burrs and bits of brush.

"Found all the horses except the bay mare," he announced. "An' tomorrow we can go back to work. I'm aimin' at hard work, men."

"Huh! I'd like to know what you call all we've done," replied Follonsbee.

"Wal, Jett, there shore won't be *any* work aboot heah till you settle up," added Pruitt, crisply.

Jett's huge frame jerked with a shock of surprise and fury he must have felt.

"So that's et?" he queried thickly. "Waited till you got way down here!"

"We shore did, boss," returned Pruitt.

In sullen silence, then, Jett began and finished his supper. Plain it was he had received a hard, unexpected blow, one he seemed scarcely prepared to cope with. He had no further words with his men, but he drew his wife aside; and they were in earnest conversation when Milly fell asleep.

Next day brought forward a situation Milly had not

39

calculated on. Jett had no discussion whatever with his men and, saddling his horse he rode off alone. The woman sulked. Follonsbee and Pruitt, manifestly satisfied with their stand, played cards interminably, now and then halting to talk in low tones over something vital to them. Catlee rigged himself a crude fishing tackle and repaired to the river bank, where he had found a shady seat within sight of the camp.

Milly was left to herself. Her first act, after the tasks of the morning were ended, was to hang up her red scarf in a conspicuous place. Then she had nothing to do but kill time. With the men in camp, this was not easy. Apparently she had liberty. No orders had been given her, but perhaps this was owing to the timid meekness she had pretended. She might have wandered away into the brakes or have trailed the wagon tracks up to the prairie. But she could not decide that this was best. For the present she could only wait.

Already the boom of guns floated in on the summer air from all sides, increasing for a while, until along the up-river prairie there was almost continuous detonation. Every boom, perhaps, meant the heart or lungs of a noble animal torn to shreds for the sake of his hide. As Milly settled down again to the actual presence of this slaughter she accepted the fact with melancholy resignation.

In the course of her strolling round the camp Milly gravitated towards Catlee, where he sat contentedly smoking his pipe and fishing. She watched him, trying to make up her mind to approach him on the subject nearest her heart. But she knew that the men and Mrs. Jett could see her and that any such action might arouse suspicion. Therefore she desited. Once Catlee turned, apparently casually, and his grey gaze took her in and the camp. Then he winked at her.

CHAPTER 3

Jett's outfit fell into idleness for more days than Milly could remember. She waited for time to pass, and no one would have suspected her longing. When Jett returned to camp from one of his lonely rides, Milly would hear his horse breaking the brush along the trail, and she could never repress a wild throb of hope. It might be Tom! But it was always Jett.

One day Jett returned in great perturbation, apparently exhausted. His horse was jaded. Follonsbee and Pruitt were curious to no end, for Jett did not vouchsafe any explanation. Whatever had happened, however, brought about a change in him and his habits. He stayed in camp.

The business of hide hunting had been abandoned, not improbably in Jett's mind for a temporary period, until his men weakened. But they did not weaken; they grew stronger. More days of this enforced idleness crystallised a growing influence—they would never again follow the extraordinary labours of hunting and skinning buffalo. Whatever had been Jett's unity of outfit was destroyed.

Milly heard the woman tell Jett this, and the ensuing

scene had been violent. It marked, further, the revelation of Mrs. Jett's long hidden hand in the game. She was the mainspring of Jett's calculated thinking, and when the other men realized this it precipitated something darkly sombre into the situation. Follonsbee and Pruitt had manifestly been playing a hand they felt sure would win. Jett could no longer hunt hides, or steal them either, without his men. All of these lonely rides of his had been taken to find other accomplices, whom Follonsbee and Pruitt knew could not be obtained there on the buffalo range.

Milly heard the bitter quarrel which ensued between Jett and his wife and the two lieutenants. Catlee was always there listening and watching, but he took no part in any of their talks or quarrels. He was outside. They did not count him at all. Yet he should have been counted immeasurably, Milly concluded. Like herself, Catlee was an intense though silent participator in this drama.

The content of that quarrel was simple. Jett had weakened to the extent of wanting to settle in part with his men. Follonsbee and Pruitt were not willing to take what he offered, and the woman, most tenacious and calculating of all of them, refused to allow Jett to relinquish any share of their profits.

There was a deadlock, and the argument put aside for the present. Follonsbee and Pruitt walked away from camp; Jett and his wife repaired to their tent, where they conversed heatedly; Catlee and Milly cooked the supper. Milly did not know when the absent men returned.

Next day the atmosphere of Jett's outfit had undergone further change. The leader was a worried and tormented man, beset by a woman with will of steel and heart of hate; and he saw opposed to him Westerners whose reaction now seemed formidable and deadly. That had roused an immovable stubborness in him.

Milly saw the disintegration of this group, and what she could not divine herself she gathered from study of Catlee. Indeed, he was the most remarkable of the outfit—he whom the others never considered at all. Not that Milly could understand her impressions. If she tried to analyse Catlee's effect upon her, it only led to doubt. As for Jett and his men, they were a divided outfit, wearing towards dissolution, answering to the wildness of the time and place. The evil that they had done hovered over them, about to enact retribution.

Milly began to dread the issue, though the breaking up of this outfit augured well for her. Then any day Tom Doan, with Hudnall and his men, might ride into Jett's camp. That meant deliverance for her, in one way or another. If Jett refused to let her go, she had but to betray him. Milly held her courage all through this long ordeal, yet she felt more and more the looming of a shadow.

Towards the close of the afternoon the tension relaxed. Follonsbee and Pruitt sauntered off with their heads together; Jett fell asleep under a cottonwood, and his sullen wife slouched into her tent; Catlee sat on a log by the river bank, not fishing or smoking, but deep in thought.

Milly, answering the long-resisted impulse, slipped to his side.

"Catlee, I must tell you," she whispered. "This—all this I've gone through has got on my nerves. I've waited and hoped and prayed for Tom Doan.... He doesn't come. He has missed this road. I might have stood it longer, but this fight between the Jetts and his men wears on me. I'm scared. Something awful will happen. I can't stand it.... I know you're my friend, oh, I know it!.... But you must help me. Catlee, you're no—no—you're not like these people. But whatever you were, or are, remember your mother and save me before—before."

Milly's voice failed her. Liberating her fears and hopes had spent her force in expression.

"Lass, have you said all you want to?" queried Catlee, in tense undertone.

"Yes—yes—I could only repeat," faltered Milly, but she held out trembling hands to him.

The man's face underweant a change, but not on the

surface. It seemed light agitation transpiring beneath a mask.

"Don't go out of my sight," he said.

But Milly had seen or heard something terrible. She backed away from Catlee, sensing this was what he wanted her to do. Yet not out of his sight. What had he meant by that? It signified a crisis. All the time he had known what was to happen, and all this time he had been her friend. This was what had been on his mind as he watched and listened.

Returning to the wagon that was her abode, she climbed to the seat and sank there, with wide eyes and beating heart. She could see Catlee sitting like a statue staring into the river. Mrs. Jett came out of her tent with slow, dragging step, and a face drawn, pale, and malignant. Her eyes were beady, the corners of her hard mouth curved down. Heavy, slovenly, she moved to awaken Jett with a kick of foot no less gentle than her mien.

"Come out of it, you loafer," she said. "My mind's made up. We'll break camp at daylight tomorrow....As you ain't got nerve to kill these men, you can have it out with them tonight. But I'm keepin' the money and we're goin' tomorrow."

"Ahuh! ejaculated Jett with a husky finality.

The habit of camp tasks was strong in her, as in all of her companions. Methodically she bestirred herself round the boxes of supplies. Catlee fetched firewood as if he had been ordered to do so. Follonsbee and Pruitt returned to squat under a cottonwood, with faces like ghouls. Jett went into his tent, and when he came out he was wiping his yellow beard. He coughed huskily, as always when drinking.

For once, Milly made no move to help. No one called her. It was as if she had not been there. Each member of that outfit was clamped by his or her own thoughts. Supper was prepared and eaten in a silence of unnatural calm. Lull before the storm!

Catlee brought Milly something to eat, which he tendered without speaking. Milly looked down into his

44

eyes, and it seemed to her that she had been mistaken in the kindly nature of the man. As he turned away she noticed a gun in his belt. It was unusual for buffalo hunters to go armed in such manner.

After supper Mrs. Jett left her husband to do her chores, and slouched towards her tent with a significant, "I'm packin' an' I want to get done before dark."

Milly saw Follonsbee motion for Pruitt and Catlee to draw aside. When they had gone in separate directions, Follonsbee approached Jett.

"Rand, it's the last deal an' the cards are runnin' bad," he said.

"Ahuh," ejaculated the giant, without looking up.

"Your woman has stacked the deck on us," went on Follonsbee, without rancor. "We ain't blamin' you altogether for this mess."

"Hank, I'm talked out," replied Jett heavily.

"You've been drinking too much," went on the other in conciliatory tones, "but you're sober now an' I'm goin' to try once more. Will you listen?"

"I ain't deaf."

"You'd be better off if you was ... Now, Rand, here's the straight of it, right off the shoulder. You've done us dirt. But square up an' all will be as before. We've got another chance here for a big haul—four thousand hides if there's one, an' easy. Use your sense. It's only this greedy woman who's changed you. Beat some sense into her or chuck her in the river. It's man to man now. An' I'm tellin' you, Pruitt is a dirty little rebel rattlesnake. He'll sting. I'm puttin' it to you honest an' level-headed. If this goes on another day, it'll be too late. We're riskin' a lot here. The hunters will find out we're not killin' buffalo. We ought to load up an' *move*."

"We're going tomorrow," replied Jett gloomily.

"Who?"

"It's my outfit an' I'm movin'. If you an' Pruitt want to stay here, I'll divide supplies."

"You're most obligin'," returned Follonsbee sarcastically. "But I reckon if you divide anythin' it'll be money, outfit, an' all."

45

"That's where the hitch comes in," snarled Jett.

"Are you plumb off your head, man?" queried the other in weary amazement. "You can't just do anythin' else."

"Haw Haw," guffawed Jett.

Follonsbee dropped his lean, vulture face and paced to and fro, his hands locked behind his back. Suddenly he shouted for Pruitt. The little rebel came on the run.

"Andy, I've talked fair to Jett, an' it ain't no use," said Follonsbee. "He an' the woman are breakin' camp tomorrow."

"Early mornin, hey?" queried Pruitt.

"Yes, an' he's offered to let us stay here with half the supplies. I told him if he divided anythin', it'd be money, outfit, an' all."

"Wal, what'd he say?"

"That here was just where the hitch come in. I told him he couldn't do anythin' else but divide, an' then he hawed hawed in my face."

"You don't say. Wal, he ain't very polite, is he?.... Hank, I'm through talkin' nice to Jett. If I talk any more I'll shore have somethin' hard to say. Give him till mawnin' to think it over."

Pruitt's sulky temper was not in evidence during this short interview. Milly could not see his face, but his tone and the poise of his head were unlike him.

"Will you fellers have a drink with me?" asked Jett in grim disdain.

They walked off without replying. Milly peered round. Catlee leaned against a tree close by, within earshot, and the look he cast Jett was illuminating. Jett was new to the frontier, though he had answered quickly to its evil influence. But otherwise he had not developed. The man's quick decline from honest living had been the easiest way to satisfay a naturally greedy soul. Drink, the rough life of the open, had paved the way. His taking to this frontier woman was perhaps the worst step. And now the sordid nature of him lowered him beneath these thieves, who had probably put the evil chances in his way. But Jett did not understand

Western men, much less desperadoes such as Follonsbee and Pruitt.

Darkness settled down over the camp and the river.
The crickets and frogs were less in evidence with their
chirping and trilling. The camp fire had died out, and
soon the dim light in Jett's tent was extinguished. The
lonely night seemed to envelop Milly and strike terror
to her soul. What was the portent of the wild mourn of
the wolves? Yet there came an intuitive, irresistible
hope—tomorrow she might be free. Somewhere
within a few miles Tom Doan lay asleep, perhaps
dreaming of her, as she was thinking of him.

Milly heard Catlee's stealthy tread. He had moved
his bed near her wagon, and his presence there was
significant of his unobtrusive guardianship. It relieved
her distraught nerves, and soon after that her eyelids
wearily closed.

Milly awoke with a start. The stars above were wan
in a pale sky; a camp fire crackled with newly burning
sticks; the odor of wood smoke permeated the air. The
wagon in which she lay was shaking. Then she heard the
pound of hoofs, the clink and rattle of harness, and a
low, husky voice she recognized. Jett was hitching up.

With a catch in her breath and a gush of blood along
her veins Milly raised herself out of her bed and peered
over the side of the wagon. The dark, heavy form of
Mrs. Jett could be discerned in the flickering light of the
fire; contrary to her usual phlegmatic action, she was
moving with a celerity that spoke eloquently of the
nature of that departure. Apparently none of the others
were stirring. Milly moved to the other side of the
wagon and peered down, just making out Catlee's bed
under the cottonwood. A dark form appeared against
the dim background. Milly saw it move, and presently
satisfied herself that Catlee was sitting on his bed,
pulling on his boots.

Jett's huge figure loomed up, passing the wagon.
Milly dropped down so she would not be seen. He
spoke in a low, husky voice to the woman. She did not
reply. Presently Milly heard again the soft thud of hoofs

47

coming closer, to cease just back of her wagon. Next she heard the creak and flop of leather. Jett was saddling the fast horses he used in hunting. Again Milly cautiously raised her head. She saw Jett in quick, sharp, decisive, yet nervous action. He haltered both horses to the back of the wagon and slipped nose bags over their heads. The horses began to munch the oats in the bags.

In a moment more Jett approached the wagon and lifted something over the footboard, just as Milly sank back into her bed. His quick heavy breathing denoted a laboring under excitement. She smelled rum on him. He disappeared and soon returned to deposit another pack in the back of the wagon. This action he repeated several times. Next Milly heard him fumbling with the wire that held the water keg to the wagon. He tipped the keg, and the slap and gurgle of water told of the quantity.

"Half full," he muttered to himself. "That'll do for today." His heavy footsteps moved away, and then came sound of his hoarse whisper to the woman. She replied:

"Reckon they'll show up. We'll not get away so easy, if I know men in this country. You'd better keep a rifle in your hand."

"Eat an' drink now, pronto," she said. "We won't stop to wash an' take these things. I packed some."

The boil of the coffee pot could be heard, and then a hot sizzle as the water boiled over into the fire. Some one removed it. Again Milly peeped out of the wagon side. Dawn was at hand. All was grey, shadowy, obscure beyond the trees, but near at hand it was light enough to see. Jett and the woman were eating. His rifle leaned against the mess box. They ate hurriedly, in silence.

Just then a low rumble like thunder broke the stillness of the morning. Deep, distant, weird, it denoted a thunderstorm to Milly. Yet how long and strangely it held on!

Jett lifted his big head like a listening deer.

"Stampede, by gosh! First one this summer. Lucky it's across the river."

"Stampede!" echoed the woman slowly. "Hum! Are there lots of buffalo across here?"

"They'd make a tolerable herd if they got bunched. I ain't in love with the idee. They might start the big herd on this side. We're aimin' to cross the prairie to Red River. An' even if we had two days' start, a runnin' herd would catch us."

"I don't agree with you, Jett," remarked the woman. "Anyway, we're goin', buffalo or no buffalo."

Milly listened to the low, distant rumble. What a strange sound. Did it not come from far away? Did she imagine it almost imperceptibly swelled in volume? She strained to hear. It lessened, died away, began again, and though ever so faint, filled her ears.

Imperceptibly the grey dawn had yielded to daylight. The Jetts had about finished their meal. Whatever was going to happen must befall soon. Milly strove to control her fearful curiosity. Her heart beat high. This issue mattered mightily to her. Peeping over the far side of her wagon, she saw Catlee sitting on his bed, watching the Jetts from his angle. He saw Milly. Under the brim of his sombrero his eyes appeared to be black holes. He motioned Milly to keep down out of sight. Instinctively she obeyed, sinking back to her bed; and then, irresistibly impelled, she moved to the other side, farther up under the low wagon seat, and peeped out from under it.

At that juncture Pruitt and Follonsbee strode from somewhere to confront the Jett's. The little rebel struck terror to her heart. Follonsbee resembled, as always, a bird of prey, but now about to strike.

"Jett, you ain't bravin' it out?" asked Pruitt, cool and laconic. "Shore you ain't aimin' to leave heah without a divvy."

"I'm leavin' two wagons, six horses, an' most of the outfit," replied Jett gruffly. He stared at Pruitt. Something was seeking an entrance into his mind.

"You're lucky to get that," snapped the woman.

"Listen to her, Hank," said Pruitt, turning to Follonsbee.

"I'm listenin', an' I don't have to hear no more. She

stacked this deal," replied Pruitt's comrade stridently. Only the timbre of his voice showed his passion; he was as slow and easy as Pruitt.

"Talk to me," shouted Jett, beginning to give way to the stress of a situation beyond him. "Let my wife . . ."

"Wife? Aw, hell!" interposed Pruitt contemptuously. "This Hardin' woman ain't your wife any more than she's mine. . . . Jett, you're yellow, an' you're shore talkin' to men who ain't yellow, whatever else they are."

Jett cursed low and deep, and fumed in his effort to confront these men as an equal. But it was not in him. Fiercely he questioned the woman. "Did you tell them we wasn't married yet?"

"Reckon I did. It was when you was silly over this black-eyed stepdaughter of yours," she replied suddenly.

Assuredly Jett would have struck her down but for the unforgettable proximity of Pruitt and Follonsbee. The latter laughed coarsely. Pruitt took a stride forward. His manner was careless, casual, but the set of muscles, the action of him, indicated something different.

"Jett, did *you* tell your woman you wanted to get rid of her—so's you could have your black-eyed wench?" demanded the little rebel, with all his insolent meanness. "You shore told us—an' you wasn't so orful drunk."

The woman seemed to tower and her face grew black.

"I didn't," yelled Jett.

Wordlessly the woman turned to question these accusers.

"Jett's a lyin' yellow skunk," declared Pruitt. "He shore meant to give the girl your place. 'Cause he wouldn't give her to me or Hank heah!"

"It's true," corroborated Follonsbee. "It's Jett an' not us who's lyin'. Why, I wouldn't lie to save both your dirty lives."

That convinced the woman, and she turned on Jett with incoherent fury. He tried to yell a break into her tirade; and not till he had seized her in brutal hands, to shake her as if she had been a rat, did she stop. Then, after a pause, in which she glared at him with the hate of a jade, she panted: "I'll put that little hussy's eyes out.... An' Rand Jett, you'll never get a dollar of this hide money."

"Shut up or I'll mash your jaw!" he shouted hoarsely.

"Haw! Haw!" laughed Follonsbee in glee that seemed only in his tones. He did not move hand or foot.

"Jett, I'm shore hopin' we can leave you to this sweet lady," cut in Pruitt, "for you deserve it. But I'm feared your bull-headedness will aboot force our deal.... Once more an' last time, damn you, will you divvy hide money, outfit, an' supplies, as you agreed?"

"Naw, I won't, declared Jett fiercely. He looked a driven man; and strangely his gaze of hate was for the woman and not the man who menaced him.

"Then we'll take it all!" flashed Pruitt ringingly.

In violent shock, Jett wheeled to face Pruitt, at last with comprehension. What he saw turned his skin white back of his yellow beard. His large, hard, bright blue eyes suddenly fixed in wild stare on Pruitt. And he began to shake. Suddenly, he dived for his rifle.

Milly's gaze had been riveted on Jett. Dimly she had seen Pruitt, but not to note look or action. Her fascinated spell broke to a horror of what was coming. Swiftly she dropped down to cover and wrapped her head in the blankets of her bed. Tightly she pulled them over ears and eyes, and twisted and rolled. And deep concussions seemed to beat at her brain. The wagon lurched. The blackness that enveloped her was not all from the blankets. Her senses seemed whirling dizzily. Then hearing and thought returned to a degree of discrimination.

She listened. There was no sound she could discern while under the folds of blankets. She was suffocating. She threw them off. Then she lay there. All was still. No sound! A low thunder of stampeding buffalo floated across the river. Milly listened for voices. The camp appeared deserted. Had these men run off into the

51

brakes? Something was ended. She could only wail, lying there in a tremble.

Suddenly she heard a soft step close to the wagon. Then Catlee's hat and face appeared over the side. He looked down at her with eyes the like of which Milly had never seen in a human.

"Lass, it's half over, but the worst's to come," he whispered, and with dark, grey gleaming gaze on her, bright, almost smiling, he dropped down out of her sight. He had not seen her desperation. He had not appealed to her to bear up under this tragedy. His look, his whisper, had made of her a comrade, brave to stand the outcome. Likewise they were a warning for herself to interpret, a suggestion of his imminent part in this terrible affair. They strung Milly's nerves to high tension. What might her part be? Compared with this experience, the West had dealt to women fatality and catastrophe which dwarfed hers. Life was sweet, never more so than at that moment, when memory of Tom Doan flashed back to her. She felt the grim and sombre presence of death; she felt the imminence of further developments, sinister, harrowing, revolving more around her. Must she surrender to her emotions? Milly bit and choked them back. She needed all the strength, will, and nerve possible to a woman; and in her extremity, with a racked heart, and unseeing eyes on the cottonwoods above, she propelled her spirit with the thought of Tom Doan, to endure or achieve anything.

Low voices diverted the current of her mind. Some persons, at least two, were returning from the river bank. Milly sat up, to took over the wagon side. Follonsbee and Pruit were entering the camp clearing. Neither Jett nor the woman was to be seen. Milly suffered no shock; she had not expected to see them. Pruitt was wet and muddy to his hips.

"Shore may as well stay heah an' hunt hides, same as the other outfits," he was saying.

"I'm agin' stayin'," replied Follonsbee.

"Wal, we won't argue aboot it. Shore, I ain't carin' much one way or other," responded Pruitt.

52

They reached the camp fire, the burned out sticks of which Pruitt kicked with a wet boot. Follonsbee held his hands over the heat, though they could not have been chilled. The morning was warm. Milly saw his hand quivering very slightly.

"Shore we ought to have got that job off our hands long ago," said Pruitt. "Wal, Hank, heah's my idee. Let's pull out, ford the river below, an' strike for the Brazos. There's buffalo, an' this main herd won't be long comin'."

"Suits me good," responded the other in relief. "Now, let's have everythin' clear. We've shared the hide money Jett's woman had. How about the rest of the outfit?"

"Same way, share an' share alike."

"Ahuh! The deals' made. Shake on it," said Follonsbee, extending his hand.

Pruitt met it half-way with his own.

"Hank, we stuck together for aboot two years, an' I reckon we're a good team."

"How about the girl?" suddenly demanded Follonsbee.

Their backs were turned to Milly, who heard this query with the sharp ears of expectation. She was fortified by her own resolve and the still hidden presence of Catlee.

"Wal, if I didn't forgit aboot our black-eyed wench!" ejaculated Pruitt, slapping his leg.

"Toss you for her, or cut the cards?" asked Follonsbee, with his sleek, narrow, beak-like head lowered.

"No, you don't. Yo're shore too lucky.... We'll share the girl same as the rest of the outfit."

"All right. It'll be a two-man outfit, half of everythin; for each, even the girl. Then we can't squabble.... But, say, we forget Catlee. Where the hell's he been?"

"Reckon he was scared. Mebbe he's runnin' yet."

"Nope. I tell you, Andy, your hate of Yanks has got you figgerin' this Catlee wrong," protested Follonsbee.

"That farm hand," replied the other bluntly. "I don't

53

know *what* he is, but he's got me figgerin' we'd better give him a hoss an' pack an' turn him loose."

Pruitt pondered this suggestion for a moment and then somberly shook his head. That idea did not appeal to him, while at the same time it manifestly introduced another and uncertain element into the situation.

Milly heard quick rustling footsteps behind her. Catlee appeared round the wagon, with a gun levelled low in his hand. Follonsbee saw him first and let out a startled exclamation. Pruitt jerked up. Then he froze.

"Howdy, men?" was Catlee's greeting, in a voice these companions evidently had never heard him use before.

Follonsbee uttered a gasp of amazed conviction.

"Andy, I told you!"

Pruitt scarcely moved a muscle, unless in the flicker of an eyelash. He did not change expression. He hissed out, "Who'n hell are you *now*?" That was his swift acceptance of Follonsbee's reiterated hints.

"Small matter," replied Catlee, as with weapon quiveringly extended he sheered round squarely in front of Pruitt, "but if it'd please you to be acquainted with me at this late day, you can bow to Sam Davis."

"Ahuh! Late pard of the Youngers," retorted Follonsbee, going white in the face.

"Reckon I'm used to hard company," whipped out Catlee stingingly, "but never yet took to sharin' innocent little girls!"

Pruitt suffered no suggestion of Follonsbee's weakening to the power of a name, whatever it was. The levelled weapon, covering him and his comrade, was the great factor in his reaction. Not for the slightest fraction of a second did he take his dancing, furious gaze from Catlee. The uselessness of more words seemed marked in his almost imperceptible gathering of muscular force. All the power of sight and mind was transfixed on Catlee's eyes, to read there the intent that preceded action. He chose an instant, probably the one which Catlee decided, and like a flash threw his gun.

As it left his hip and snapped, Catlee's gun crashed. The force of the bullet knocked Pruitt flat.

"Hurry, Hank! he yelled, his fierce, wild tone of terrible realization. Flinging the empty weapon he had forgotten to load, he lurched like a crippled panther to get his hands on Jett's rifle.

Milly saw only the intrepid Pruitt, but she heard Catlee's second shot and the sodden thud of Follonsbee falling. He made no outcry. Pruitt's actions were almost too swift to follow, so swift that Catlee missed him as he grasped and carried Jett's rifle over the mess box. Up he sprang, grotesque, misshapen, yet wonderfully agile, to discharge the heavy rifle even as he received Catlee's fire square in his chest. Staggering backward, he dropped the weapon, his arms spread, and he seemed to fall step by step. An awful blankness blotted out the ferocity of his crooked face. Step by step he fell backward over the bank into the river. A sounding splash followed his disappearance.

Milly's gaze wavered. A silence intervened. Her lungs seemed to expand. The appalling fixity of her attention broke with a shock, and she looked at Catlee. He lay on the ground beside the camp fire. His hand twitched, releasing the smoking gun. Milly leaped out of the wagon and ran to him.

She knelt. His hat was off; his face was vague, changing. The grey storm of his eyes seemed fading.

"Oh—oh, Catlee!" cried Milly poignantly.

"Good luck!" he whispered. His lips set, his eyelids fluttered, all his body quivered to a relaxation. He had been shot through the breast.

"My God! How awful! He's dead! They're all dead. I'm left alone. It's over. . . . Brave Catlee! Oh, he saved me! But what can I do?"

Milly's outburst was silenced by the shrill neigh of one of the horses hitched to the wagon. It was a neigh that heralded the sight or scent of another horse. Wild and sharp it then pealed out in a whistling answer from across the river.

Milly joyfully bounded erect to peer out under the cottonwoods. But her joy sustained a bewildering check, and it died when a steadier glance revealed mounted Indians riding down into the river. For one moment Milly stared, trying her fingers in her horror; then the spirit born of these hours ran through her like a white flame and, climbing to the seat of the wagon, she whipped up the reins.

Her instinct was to escape. She had no time to think of a better way. And the horses, restive, not wholly recovered from fright, needed no urging. They broke into trot, dragging the saddled animals behind the wagon. Out of the clearing, into the brakes they crashed, and were hard to hold. Road there was none, but a wide lane of crushed weeds and brush marked where Jett had driven the wagon in, and later had ridden to and fro on horseback. The team followed it, and they tore through the bending clumps of brush that hung over it and bumped over logs. Branches of trees struck Milly as she passed, blinding her for a moment. When she could see clearly again, the horses were no longer in the lane through the brush. They had swerved to one side or the other, she did not know which. But she kept her sense of direction: to the right was down-river, and to the left was the prairie, the main herd of buffalo, and the camps of the hunters.

She must get out into the open quickly. If the Indians had not heard her drive away, there would be a little time before they would strike out on her tail through the brakes.

"Oh, I forgot," she cried. "They heard the horse neigh." And with a sinking of her daring spirit let the horses have free rein. They quickened their gait, but showed no sign of bolting. They wanted to get out of that jungle, and they broke a path through thickets, over rotten logs, and under matted hanging vines. Milly had all she could do to keep from being torn from her seat.

They got by the worst of the brakes and Milly saw light ahead low down through the trees, but it seemed to be in the wrong direction. She should turn more to the left. Her efforts to head the iron-jawed team in that direction were unavailing. They kept to a straight course out into the light. But this open had deceived Milly, and probably the horses, too. It was a wide, bare

56

strip of sand where a tributary of the Pease flowed in wet season. Here the horses slowed to a dragging walk, yet soon crossed the sand to enter the brakes again.

Here in the shade and dust, and the melee of the threshing branches round her face, Milly lost all sense of the right direction. She realized her peril, yet did not despair. Something had always happened; it would happen to save her again.

Suddenly a crashing of brush in front of her stopped her heart. She almost fell back into the wagon. A huge brown buffalo-bull tore ahead of her, passing to the left. Milly recovered. Then again she heard crashing ahead of her to one side, and more at a distance. There were buffalo in the brakes.

Above the swish of brush and rattle of wagon and pound of hoofs she began to hear a low, rumbling thunder, apparently to the fore and her right.

"They said stampede!" she said fearfully.

The horses heard it and were excited, or else the scent and proximity of stray buffalo had been the cause of their faster, less regular gait. Milly assayed again to swerve them to the left, but in vain. And, indeed, that left side grew more and more impractical, owing to obstructions which shunted the horses in an opposite direction. Quite unexpectedly, then, they burst out of the brakes into open prairie.

Milly was as amazed as frightened. The plain was so dusty, she could not see a mile, and strings of buffalo were disappearing into a yellow, broken pall. They appeared to be loping in their easy, lumbering way. The thunder was louder now, though still a strange low roar, and it came out of the dust curtain which obscured the prairie. The horses, snorting, not liking dust or buffalo, loped for a mile, then slowed to a walk and halted. Milly tried to get her bearings. The whole horizon to fore and right was streaky with dust and moving buffalo. From behind her the line of river timber extended on her right to fade in the obscurity of dust. This established her position. She had crossed the brakes of the tributary and was now headed east. The buffalo were then coming out of the south and they were crossing the Pease. Milly realized that she was far out of her proper course, and must make a wide turn to the left, across the dry stream-bed, and then go up the river to the camps of the hide-hunters.

Suddenly, she missed something. The two saddle-horses! They had broken off in the rough ride. Milly looked back at the dark, ragged line of timber from where she had come. The air was clearer that way. Movement and flash attracted her gaze. She saw animals run out into the open. Wild, lean, colored ponies with riders! They stretched out in swift motion, graceful, wild, incomparably a constrast to the horses of white hunters.

Milly realized she was being pursued by Indians.

CHAPTER 4

Milly screamed at the horses and swung the lash, beating them into a gallop. The lightly loaded wagon lurched and bounced over the hummocky prairie, throwing her off the seat and from side to side. A heavy strain on the reins threatened to tear her arms from their sockets.

It was this physical action that averted a panic-stricken flight. The horses broke from gallop into run, and they caught flight with scattered groups and lines of buffalo. Milly was in the throes of the keenest terror that had yet beset her, but she did not quite lose her reason. There were a few moments fraught with heart numbing, blood-curdling sensations which, on the other hand, were counteracted by the violence of the race over the prairie, straight for the straggling strings of the buffalo herd. The horses plunged, hurtling the wagon along; the wind, now tainted with dust and scent of buffalo, rushed into Milly's face and waved her hair; the tremendous drag on the reins, at first scarcely perceptible, in her great excitement began to hurt hands, wrists, arms, shoulders in a degree that compelled attention. But the race itself, the flight, the breakneck pace across the prairie, with stampeding buffalo before and Commanche Indians behind—it was too great, too magnificent, too terrible to prostrate this girl. Opposed to all the fears possible to a girl was the thing roused in her by love, by example of a thief who had died to save her, by the marvel of the moment.

Milly gazed back over her shoulder. The Commanches had gained. They were not half a mile away, riding now in wide formation, naked, gaudy, lean, feathered, swift, and wild as a gale of wind in the tall prairie grass.

"Better death among the buffalo!" cried Milly, and she turned to wrap both reins round her left wrist, to lash out with the whip, and to scream: *Run! Run! Run!*

Buffalo loped ahead of her to each side and behind in straggling groups and lines, all headed in the same direction as the vague denser bunches to the right. Here the dust pall moved like broken clouds, showing light and dark.

She became aware of increasing fullness in her ears. The low rumble had changed to a clattering trample, yet there seemed more. The sound grew; it came closer; it swelled to a roar; and presently she located it in the rear.

She turned with startled gaze and saw a long, bobbing, black, ragged mass pouring like a wooly flood out over the prairie. A sea of buffalo! They were moving at a lope, ponderously, regularly, and the scalloped head of that immense herd crossed the line between Milly and the Commanches. It swept on. It dammed and blocked the way. Milly saw the vermillion paint on the naked bodies and faces of these savages as they wheeled their lean horses to race along with the buffalo.

Then thin whorls of rising dust obscured them from Milly's sight. A half-mile of black, bobbing humps moved between her and the Comanches. She uttered a wild cry that was joy, wonder, reverence, and acceptance of the thing she had trusted. Thicker grew the dust mantle; wider the herd; a greater volume of sound! The Comanches might now have been a thousand miles away, for all the harm they could do her.

As they vanished in the obscurity of dust, so also did they fade from Milly's mind!

Milly drove a plunging, maddened team of horses in the midst of buffalo as far as the eye could see. Her intelligence told her that she was now in greater peril of death than at any time heretofore, yet, though her hair rose stiff and her tongue clove to the roof of her mouth, she could not feel the same as when Pruitt had parcelled her, share-and-share with Follonsbee, or when those lean, wild-riding Comanches had been swooping down on her. Strangely, though there was natural terror in the moment, she did not seem afraid of the buffalo.

The thick massed herd was on her left, and appeared to have but few open patches; to the fore and all on the other side there were as many grey spaces of prairie showing as black, loping blotches of buffalo. Her horses were running while the buffalo were loping, thus she kept gaining on groups near her and passing them. Always they sheered away, some of the bulls kicking out with wonderful quickness. But in the main they gave space to the swifter horses and the lumbering wagon.

The dust rose in sheets, now thin, now thick, and obscured everything beyond a quarter of a mile distant. Milly was surrounded, hemmed in, carried onward by a pondering moving pendulum. The trampling roar of hoofs was deafening, but it was not now like thunder. It was too close. It did not swell or rumble or roll. It roared.

A thousand tufted tails switched out of that mass, and ten times that many shaggy humps bobbed in sight. What queer sensation this action gave Milly—queer above all the other sensations! It struck her as ludicrous.

The larger, denser mass on the left had loped up at somewhat faster gait than those groups Milly had first encountered. It forged ahead for a time, then gradually absorbed all the buffalo, until they were moving in unison. Slowly they appeared to pack together, to obliterate the open spaces, and to close in on the horses. That was what Milly feared most.

The horses took their bits between their teeth and ran

headlong. Milly had to slack the reins or be pulled out of the seat. They plunged into the rear of the moving buffalo to make no impression other than to split the phalanx for a few rods and be kicked from all sides. Here the horses reared, plunged, and sent out above the steady roar a piercing scream of terror. Milly had never before heard the scream of a horse. She could do nothing but cling to the loose reins and the wagon seat and gaze with distended eyes. One of the white horses, Jett's favourite, plunged to his knees. The instant was one when Milly seemed to be clamped by paralysis. The other white horse plunged on, dragging his mate to his feet and into the race again.

Then the space around horses and wagons closed in, narrowed to an oval with only a few yeards clear to the fore and on each side. Behind, the huge, lowered, shaggy heads almost bobbed against the wagon.

The time of supreme suspense had come to Milly. She had heard that buffalo would run over and crush any obstruction in their path. She seemed about to become the victim of such a blind juggernaut. Her horses had been compelled to slacken their gait to accomodate that of the buffalo. They could neither forge ahead, nor swerve to one side or other, nor stop. They were blocked, hemmed in, and pushed. And their terror was extreme. They plunged in unison and singly; they screamed and bit at the kicking buffalo. It was a miracle that leg or harness or wheel was not broken.

A violent jolt nearly unseated Milly. The wagon had been struck from behind. Fearfully she looked back. A stupid-faced old bull with shaggy head as large as a barrel was wagging along almost under the end of the wagon-bed. He had bumped into it. Then the space on the left closed in until buffalo were right alongside the wheels. Milly wrung her hands. A big black bull rubbed his rump against the hind wheel. The iron tyre revolving fast scraped hard on his side. Quick as a flash the bull lowered head and elevated rear, kicking out viciously. One of his legs went between the spokes. A crack rang out above the trample of hoofs. The bull went down.

Milly could not cry out. She clung to the seat with all her strength. Then began a terrific commotion. The horses plunged as the drag on the wagon held them back. Buffalo began to pile high over the one that had fallen, and a wave of action seemed to permeate all of them.

Those rushing forward pounded against the hind wheels, and split round them until the pressure became so great that they seemed to lift the wagon and carry it along, forcing the horses ahead.

Milly could not shut her eyes. They were fascinated by this heaving mass. The continuous roar, the endless motion towards certain catastrophe, were driving her mad. Then this bump and scrape and lurch, this frightful proximity of the encroaching buffalo, this pell-mell pandemonium behind, was too much for her. The strength of hands and will left her. The wagon tilted, turned sidewise, and stopped with a shock. An appalling sound seemed to take the place of motion. The buffalo behind began to lift their great heads, to pile high over those in front, to crowd in a terrific straining wave of black, hideous and irresistible, like an incoming tide. Heads and horns and hair, tufted tails, a dense, rounded, moving tussling sea of buffalo bore down on the wagon. The sound now was a thundering roar. Dust hung low. The air was suffocating. Milly's nose and lungs seemed to close. She fell backward over the seat and fainted.

When she opened her eyes it was as if she had come out of a nightmare. She lay on her back. She gazed upward to a sky thinly filmed over by dust clouds. Had she slept?

Suddenly she understood the meaning of motion and the sensation of filled ears. The wagon was moving steadily, she could not tell how fast, and from all sides rose a low, clattering roar of hoofs.

"Oh, it must be—something happened—the horses went on—the wagon did not turn over!" she cried.

But she feared to rise and look out. She listened and felt. There was a vast difference. The wagon moved on steadily, smoothly, without lurch or lump; the sound of hoofs filled the air, yet not loudly or with such a cutting trample. She reasoned that the pace had slowed much. Where was she? How long had she lain unconscious? What would be the end of this awful race?

Nothing happened. She found her breathing easier and her nostrils less stopped by dust and odor of buffalo. Her mouth was parched with thirst. There was a slow, torrid beat of her pulse. Her skin appeared moist and hot. Then she saw the sun, quite high, a strange magenta hue, seen through the dust clouds. It had been just after daylight when she escaped from Jett's camp. Ah! She remembered Catlee! Sam Davis, one of the Youngers' clan! Hours had passed and she was still surrounded by buffalo. The end had not come then; it had been averted, but it was inevitable. What she had passed through! Life was cruel. Hers had been an unhappy fate. Suddenly, she thought of Tom Doan, and life, courage, and hope surged with the magic of love. Something had happened to save her.

Milly sat up. She saw grey prairie—and then, some fifty yards distant, the brown shaggy bodies of buffalo in lazy lope. The wagon was keeping the same slow speed. Milly staggered up to lean against the seat and peer ahead. Wonderful to see, Jett's white team was contentedly trotting along, some rods in the rear of straggling buffalo. She could scarcely believe what she saw. The horses were no longer frightened.

On the other side wider space intervened before buffalo covered the grey prairie. She could see a long way—miles, it seemed—and there were as many black streaks of buffalo as grey strips of grass. To the fore Milly beheld the same scene, only greater in extent. Buffalo showed as far as sight could penetrate, but they were no longer massed or moving fast.

"It's not a stampede," Milly told herself in sudden realization. "It never was. . . . They're just traveling. They don't mind the wagon—the horses—not any more. Oh, I shall get out!"

The knotted reins hung over the brake where she had left them. Milly climbed to the driver's seat and took them up.

The horses responded to her control, not in accelerated trot, but by a lifting of ears and a throwing of heads. They were glad to be under guidance again. They trotted on as if no buffalo were near. It amazed Milly, this change. But she could tell by the sweat and froth and cakes of dust on them that they had travelled far and long before coming to this indifference.

Milly did not drive the horses, though she held the reins taut enough for them to feel she was there; she sat stiff in the seat, calling to them, watching and thrilling, nervously and fearfully suspicious of the moving enclosure which carried her onward a prisoner. Time passed swiftly. The sun burned down on her. And the hour came when the buffalo lumbered to a walk.

They were no different from cattle now, Milly thought. Then the dust clouds floated away, and she could see over the backs of buffalo on all sides, out to the boundless prairie. The blue sky overhead seemed to have a welcome for her. The horses slowed down. Gradually the form of the open space surrounding the wagon widened, changed its shape as buffalo in groups wandered out from the herd. Little light, tawny calves appeared to run playfully into the open. They did not play as if they were tired.

Milly watched them with a birth of love in her heart for them, and a gratitude to the whole herd for its service to her. No doubt now that she was saved. Nearly a whole day had passed since the Indians had seen her disappear, and leagues of prairie had been covered. The direction she was being taken was north, and that she knew to be favorable to her. Sooner or later these buffalo would split or pass her; then she would have another problem to consider.

But how interminably they travelled on. No doubt the annual instinct to migrate northward had been the cause of this movement. If they stampeded across the Pease, which had not seemed to her the case, they had at once calmed to a gait the hunters called their regular ranging mode of travel. Her peril at one time had been great, but if this herd had caught her in a stampede, she would have been lost.

The stragglers that from time to time came near her paid no attention to horses or wagon. They were as tame as cows. They puffed along, wagging their big heads, apparently asleep as they travelled. The open lanes and aisles and patches changed shape, closed to reopen, yet on the whole there was a gradual widening. The herd was spreading. Milly could see the ragged rear a couple of miles back, where it marked its dark line against the grey prairie. Westward the mass was thick and wide; it was thin and straggly on the east. Northward the black, creeping tide of backs extended to the horizon.

Milly rode on, escorted by a million beasts of the plain, and they came to mean more to her than she could understand. They were alien, vigorous, self-sufficient; and they were doomed by the hide-hunters. She could not think of anything save the great, shaggy, stolid old bulls, the sleeker, smaller cows, and the tawny, romping calves. So wonderful an adventure, so vast a number of hoofed creatures, so strangely trooping up out of the dusty river brakes to envelop her, so different when she and they and the horses had become accustomed to one another—these ideas were the gist of her thoughts. It was a strange, unreal concentration on buffalo.

The afternoon waned. The sun sank low in the west and turned gold. A time came when Milly saw with amazement that the front leagues of buffalo had disappeared over the horizon, now close at hand. They had come to the edge of slope on river brake. What would this mean to her?

When the wagon reached the line where the wooly backs had gone down out of sight, Milly saw a slope covered with spreading buffalo that ended in a winding green belt of trees. In places shone the glancing brightness of water. Beyond, on a level immense plain, miles and miles of buffalo were moving like armies of ants. They were spreading on all sides, and those in the lead had stopped to graze. The immensity of the scene, its beauty and life and tragedy, would remain in Milly's memory all her days. She saw the whole herd, and it

66

was a spectacle to uplift her heart. While the horses walked on with the buffalo streaming down that slope, Milly gazed in rapt attention. How endless the grey, level prairie below! She understood why the buffalo loved it, how it had nourished them, what a wild, lonely home it was. Faint threads of other rivers crossed the grey; and the green hue was welcome contrast to the monotony. Duskily red the sun was setting, and it cast its glow over the plain and buffalo. In the distance purple mantled the horizon. Far to the northwest a faint, dark ruggedness of land or cloud seemed limned against the sunset-flushed sky. Was that land? If so, it was the Llano Estacado.

Milly's horses reached the belt of trees and entered a grove through and round which the buffalo were travelling. She felt the breaking of the enclosure of beasts that had so long encompassed her. It brought a change of thoughts. She was free to let the remainder of the herd pass. Driving down behind a thick clump of cottonwoods, she turned into a green pocket and halted. Wearily the horses stood, heaving, untempted by the grass. On each side of Milly streams and strings and groups of buffalo passed to go down into the river, from which a loud, continuous splashing rose. She waited, watching on one side, then the other. The solid masses had gone by; the ranks behind thinned as they came on; and at last straggling groups with many calves brought up the rear. These hurried on, rustling the bush, on to splash into the shallow ford. Then the violence of agitated water ceased; the low trample of hoofs ceased.

Silence! It was not real. For a whole day Milly's ears had been filled and harassed by a continuous trample, at first a roar, then a clatter, then a slow beat, beat, beat of hoofs, but always a trample. She could not get used to silence. She felt lost. A rush of sensations seemed impending. But only a dreamy stillness pervaded the river's edge, a hot, drowsy, thick air, empty of life. The unnaturally silent moment flung at her the loneliness and wildness of the place. Alone! She was lost on the prairie.

"Oh, what shall I do now?" she cried.

There was everything to do—to care for the horses and for herself, so to preserve strength; to choose a direction, and to travel on and on, until she found a road that would lead her to some camp or post. Suddenly she sank down into a heap. The thought of the enormous problem crushed her for a moment. She was in the throes of a reaction.

"But I mustn't *think*," she whispered fiercely. "I must *do*!"

And she clambered out of the wagon. The grove sloped down to the green bench where she had waited for the buffalo to pass. Grass was abundant. The horses would not stray. She moved to unhitch them, and had begun when it occurred to her that she would have to hitch them up again. To this end she studied every buckle and strap. Many a time she had helped round horses on the farm; the intricacies of harness were not an entire mystery to her. Then she had watched Jett and Catlee hitch up this team. Still, she studied everything carefully. Then she unbuttoned the traces and removed the harness. The horses rolled in a dusty place which the buffalo had trampled barren, and they rose dirty and yellow to shake a cloud from their backs. Then with snorts they trotted down to the water.

Milly was reminded of her own burning thirst, and she ran down to the water's edge where, unmindful of its muddy colour, she threw herself flat and drank until she could hold no more. "Never know—water—could taste so good," she panted. Returning to the wagon, she climbed up in it to examine its contents. She found a bag of oats for the horses, a box containing utensils for cooking, another full of food supplies, a bale of blankets, and lastly an axe and a shovel.

"Robinson Crusoe had no more," said Milly to herself, and then stood aghast at her levity. Was she not lost on the prairie? Might not Indians ride down upon her? Milly considered the probabilities. "God has answered my prayer," she concluded gravely, and dismissed fears for the time being.

In the box of utensils she found matches, which were

next to food for importance, and thus encouraged she lifted out what she needed. Among the articles of food were a loaf of bread and a bag of biscuits. Suddenly her mouth became flooded with saliva and she had to bite into a biscuit. There were also cooked meat and both jerked venison and buffalo. Salt and pepper, sugar, coffee, dried apples she found, and then did not explore the box to the uttermost.

"I'll not starve, anyway," murmured Milly.

Next she gathered dry bits of bark and wood, of which there was abundance, and assayed to start a fire. Success crowned her efforts, though she burned her fingers. Then, taking up the pail, she descended the bank to the river and filled it with water, which was not clarifying in the slow current. Returning, she poured some into the coffee-pot and put that in the edge of the fire. Next, while waiting for the water to boil, she cut strips of the cooked buffalo meat and heated them in a pan. She had misgivings about what her cooking might be. Nevertheless, she sat down presently and ate as heartily as ever before in her life.

Twilight had fallen when she looked up from the last task. The west was rose with an afterglow of sunset. All at once, now that action had to be suspended, she was confronted with reality. The emotion of reality!

"Oh, I'm lost—alone—helpless!" she exclaimed. "It's growing dark. I was always afraid of the dark."

And she shivered there through a long moment of feeling. She would be compelled to think now. She could not force sleep. How impossible to fall asleep! Panthers, bears, wildcats, and wolves lived in these river brakes. She felt in her coat for the little Derringer. It was gone. She had no weapons save the axe, and she could not wield that effectively.

Yet she did not at once seek the apparent security of her bed in the wagon. She walked about, though close by. She peered into the gathering shadows. She listened. The silence had been relieved by crickets and frogs. Slowly the black night mantled the river bottom, and the trains of stars twinkled in the blue dome.

The presence of the horses, as they grazed near, brought something of comfort, if not relief. She remembered a dog she had loved. Rover—if she only had him now! Then she climbed into the wagon, and without removing even her boots, she crawled into the blankets. They had been disarranged in the rought ride. She needed them more to hide under than for warmth. The soft night seemed drowsily lulling.

Her body cried out with its aches and pains and weariness, with the deep internal riot round her heart. Not all at once could she lie still. But gradually began a slow sinking, as if she were settling down, down, and all at once she lay like a log. It was too warm under the blanket, yet when she threw it back and saw the white stars, so strange, so watchful, she grew more aware of her plight and covered her face again. At length her body relaxed. Then her mind grew active, reverting to the terrible tragedy of Jett's outfit. Catlee! All the time he had watched over her. He had killed for her—had died for her. A man who confessed he had never been anything else than bad! Something great loomed in Milly's simple mind. Could Jett have had any good in him! She prayed for their souls.

They had left her alone, and she must find her way. And into that dark gulf of mind flashed the thought and the vision of Tom Doan. Milly began to weep. It was too terrible, the remembrance of him, and his love and kisses, of his offer of marriage and of his plan for their home. It was terrible to dwell upon when she was lost in the prairie. She might never see him again! But she must try with all her power to find her way out.

"I—will try—for him!" she sobbed, and remembered her prayers. Then grief and worry succumbed to exhaustion; she drifted into slumber.

The singing of birds awakened Milly. The sun had risen; the green leaves were fluttering with a silken rustle. It took a moment for realization of her situation to rush into thought. Yet the darkness of mind, the old reluctance to return to consciousness, was absent this morning.

When she got to her knees and knelt there, stretching her bruised and cramped muscles, she looked over the wagon to see the white horses grazing near under the cottonwoods. Sleek grey deer were grazing with them, as tame as cattle. A rabbit crossed the aisle of green. The morning held a strange bright beauty and peace.

Milly brushed out her tangled short curls. Her face was burned from the wind and sun of yesterday's ride. Then she climbed out of the wagon, ready for the day. She did not have to dress, and she thought bathing her face might make the sunburn worse.

First she put a quart of oats in each nose-bag and carried them out to the horses. She did not need to go far. Both horses saw her and came to meet her; slipping the nose-bags in place, she led them to the wagon and haltered them. Breakfast did not take long to prepare and eat. Then she cleaned the utensils, packed them away in the box, shook out her blankets, and rolled them. This left the task which worried her—that of hitching up.

But when she came to undertake it she found that she remembered where every part of the harness belonged. To lift the heavy wagon tongue and hold it while she snapped the hooks into rings required all her strength.

The moment of decision had come. Milly turned to mount the wagon.

Not reluctant, indeed, were the horses. They had grazed and drank their fill and they knew their noses were pointed homeward, away from the buffalo fields. Milly had all she could do to hold them. She drove out of the grove, to the right where the buffalo had worn a wide-trodden belt down to the stream. The last fifty yards were quite downhill. Milly reined in to scrutinize her first obstacle of the day.

Thousands of buffalo had forded the stream here. Far as she could see, the banks on both sides were trodden fresh and dark with tracks. At this point the stream was perhaps three feet deep and forty wide; nothing for strong and nimble buffalo to ford. But these buffalo had not been hampered with a wagon. Still, the

71

crossing was not especially bad. Jett would not have given it a second glance. He would have plunged across. They sandy bottom would assuredly be hard-packed. Milly had only to start right, not too carefully, and to keep the horses going.

She threw on the brake and called to the horses. "Get up! Whitey! Specks! Easy now!"

They trotted down the slope—faster—faster. Milly leaned back on the reins. Her face blanched. Her teeth clenched. It was fearful, yet it roused defiance. She could drive them. They were eager, unafraid. The wagon propelled them. Plunge! The water crashed and splashed high. And the wagon bounced after them, to souse into the stream, over the front wheels. Milly was deluged. But she called to the horses. They took the stream at a trot. It was no deeper than their knees, and they sent sheets of muddy water ahead of them. The opposite bank was low, easy for them; and Milly, before she realised it, pulled up on the level, open prairie.

"Easy, and I got a bath!" she cried exultantly. "Oh, Whitey and Specks, I love you!"

She searched for her scarf to wipe her wet face and hair. But it, too, like her little gun, was gone. She had lost it. No! She recalled that she had left it tied on the hoop of the wagon cover in Jett's camp. The memory startled her. Suppose Tom Doan should at last find Jett's camp and see her red scarf. But that misery for him could never be. The Indians would have made blackened embers of that camp.

Milly took her direction from the sun and drove out upon the prairie. It was a grey, beautiful plain, luxuriant with ripened grass, sloping very gently to the north. Far to the eastward she espied the black horizon—a wide line of buffalo. They had grazed down the stream. In the bright sunlight the whole panorama was splendid and stirring to her.

The horses started at a trot, and in the thick grass slowed to a steady walk. The wagon was light, the ground level; and this powerful team had no serious

72

task ahead of them if they were only guided aright. Milly was excited, thrilled, and yet troubled. The adventure was tremendous, but the responsiblity too great except for moments of defiance or exaltation. She could not all the time remain keyed-up with a spirit that was unquenchable.

Several miles of travel brought her to the summit of the gradual slope of valley, and here, as on the side from which she had come, she obtained a commanding view of the surrounding country. It was grand, but she had eyes only for the northwest. Across the leagues of billowy prairie, so grey and monotonous and lonely, there stood a purple escarpment, remote and calling. It was the Llano Estacado. Milly recognised it, and seemed for an instant to forget the sense of being lost. But it was far away, and the northern end disappeared in purple haze. On the other hand, it was a landmark ever-present from high points, and somewhere between it and her present position ran the road of the buffalo hunters.

To her left meandered the green line of trees, like a fringed ribbon on the soft grey of prairie, and it headed towards the Staked Plain, where she knew all these Texas streams had their source.

"I could reach the road today or tomorrow if I drove straight west," thought Milly.

It was a sore temptation, but her good sense forbade her to take such added risk. The Comanches were between her and the buffalo camps. She must aim diagonally across the prairie, towards the extreme northwest corner of the escarpment, and perhaps in four or five days she would strike the road. Then she would know the camping grounds, and would surely fall in with oncoming hunters or outgoing freighters. To find water at night, and to cross such streams as she met—these were her present problems.

Meanwhile, as she drove on, thinking only of this incredible journey, she could not help seeing and being momentarily thrilled by the wild creatures of the prairie.

Sleek, grey, white-rumped antelope scarcely bothered to trot out of her path, and with long ears erect they watched her pass. Wild? These beautiful prairie deer were not wild. Milly believed she could in time have had them eating out of her hand, like she had the squirrels and birds at the Pease River camp. It was men who made animals wild.

She ranged the wide grey expanse for sight of buffalo. There were none. She saw a band of coyotes sneaking round the antelope. Farther on she espied a gaunt wolf, almost white, watching her from a ridge-top.

Milly drove from early morning until an hour before sunset, when she reached the only water of the day. It was a pond in a sandy streambed. There were fringes of hackberry brush along the banks, but no sheltering trees. Farther west some six or eight miles she thought she espied the green of timber, but that was far away and off her line of direction. She must take what afforded; and to this end she unhitched, turned the horses loose, and made the simple preparations for her own wants.

Next morning Milly was up early, and on the way before sunrise. She started well. But at the end of the first hour she ran into rough prairie, hindering travel. The luxuriant prairie grass failed, and the grey earth carried only a scanty covering. The horses ploughed up dust that rose and blew back upon her; the sun grew hot and glaring; and there was a wide area of shallow washes, ditches, and gullies, like the depressions of a wash-board. Having plodded miles into this zone, she could not turn back, unless absolutely baulked, so she applied herself to careful driving, and kept on, true as possible, to the distant purple landmark.

The strong horses, used to a heavy hand, could not altogether be controlled by Milly, and they plunged into many places without her sanction. What with holding the reins as best she could, constant heed to brake and distance, and worry lest she would damage a wheel, she was in grievous straits most of that day. It passed swiftly, swallowed up in miles on hard going, and left no time for scanning the prairie or fearful imaginings. It was work.

Towards evening she drew out of this zone and came presently to good grass once more, and just at dusk hauled up to a timber belt that bordered water. The thirsty horses stamped to get down to it. Milly laboured to unhitch them, and when the task was done she sank to the ground to rest. But she was driven to secure firewood while there was light enough. She felt too tired to eat, yet she knew she must eat or else fail altogether of strength. The long hanging to the reins was what had exhausted Milly. Her hands hurt, her arms ached, her shoulders sagged. Driving that iron-mouthed team was a man's job. Milly was no weakling, but her weight and muscular force were inadequate to the demand of such driving.

Supper, bed, night, sleep—they all passed swiftly, and again the sun rose. Milly could not find a place to ford the stream. It was not depth of water that prevented it, but high banks unsafe to attempt. For miles she drove along it, glad of the green foliage and singing birds and wild creatures, and especially glad that its course for most of the morning ran a little west of north. When, however, it made an abrupt turn to the west, she knew she must cross. She assayed the best ford she could find, and made it safely, wet, shaken, frightened, and nearly pulled apart. On that far side she rested in the shade, and wept while she ate.

When about to start again she remembered that the men had never passed a stream or pond without watering the horses. Whereupon she took the bucket and went down to fill it. Four trips were necessary to satisfy the thirst of Whitey and Specks. She had done well.

"We had two dry camps between Sprague's and the Pease," she said, and thought she must not forget that.

The afternoon drive began favourably. The sun was somewhat hazed over, reducing the heat; a level prairie afforded smooth travel; the horses had settled down into steady solid work. The miles came slowly, but surely.

Milly's courage had not failed, but she was beset by physical ills, and the attendant moods, fancies, and thoughts that could not everlastingly be overcome. She grew to hate the boundless prairie-land, so barren of life, of any colour but grey, of things that might mitigate the deceit of distance. Nothing save grey level and purple haze! It wore on her, ever flinging at her the attributes of the prairie openness, a wind, empty of sound, movement, the above of solitude, the abode of loneliness. Lonely, lonely land! She was as much lost as ever. There was no road, no river, no camp, no mountain, only the dim upflung false Llano Estacado, unattainable as ever.

But while Milly succumbed to her ills and her woes, the horses plodded on. They knew what they had to accomplish, and were equal to it. They crowded the hours and miles behind them, and bore Milly to another watercourse, a wide glade-bordered enlargement of a stream, where ducks and cranes and kingfishers gave life to the melancholy scene.

While she performed her tasks the lake changed from blue to gold, and at last mirrored the rose of sunset sky. Then dusk fell sadly and night came, dark, lonely, pierced by the penetrating trill of frogs and the dismal cry of a water-fowl. They kept Milly awake and she could not shake the encroachment of morbid thoughts. Where was she? What had become of her? The vast gloomy prairie encompassed her, held her a prisoner, threatened her with madness. She had feared Indians, rivers, accidents, but now only the insupportable loneliness. Would she not die of it and be eaten by buzzards? The stars that had been so beautiful, watching, and helpful, now seemed pitiless, remote, and aloof, with their pale eyes on her, a girl lost on the endless prairie. What was beyond those stars? Not a soul, no kindly great spirit to guide her out of this wilderness? Milly prayed once more.

She dragged herself from bed next day, long after sunrise, and had spirit to begin the ordeal.

Whitey and Specks waited in camp for their oats. Milly scorned herself for dreading they would run away, leaving her utterly alone. She fed them and caressed them, and talked as if they were human. "You belong to me," she said. "I was Jett's stepdaughter. He's gone. And you're mine...If you ever get me out of this—"

But she did not think she would ever get out now, unless Providence remembered her again. She had no hunger. A fever consumed her and she drank copiously of water. Hitching up was a dragging job. The heavy wagon tongue nearly broke her back. At last she was in the driver's seat. Whitey and Specks started of their own accord, splashed across the shallow lake, and pulled up on the grey, flat expanse.

Milly was either ill or almost spent, she did not know which. She had power to sit up, hold the reins, and guide the horses towards that futile illusive landmark days away on the horizon, but she could not control her mind.

The wandering roll of prairie-land mocked her with its shining grey distances, its illusive endlessness, and its veils of heat. The hot sun rose, glared down, slanted to the west, and waned. She found no water that sunset. The horses had no drink. Milly mixed their oats with water from the keg. Hunger exceeded all her sensations, even the pains; and tenaciously she clung to her one idea of effort, to keep trying, to follow judgment she had made at the outset. She ate, and crawled into her wagon-bed, no longer afraid of night and loneliness. So tired—so tired she wanted to die!

But the sun awakened her and the will to go on survived. The faithful horses waited, whinnying at her approach. Mechanically she worked, yet was aware of clumsiness and pain; that she must water them that day. The prairie smoked with heat. It beckoned, flaunted, slanted to the hot, steely sky. She closed her eyes and slept with the reins in her hands; she awakened to jolt of wagon and crunching of stone. Thunder rumbled out of the sky and clouds obscured the sun. She drove into a storm, black and windy, with driving sheets of cool rain and white zigzag ropes of lightning, crashing thunder, and a long roll across the heavens. She was drenched to the skin and strangely refreshed. That fiery band round her head had snapped and gone. The horses splashed into a buffalo-wallow and drank of the fresh rainwater.

Away the storm rolled, purple clouds and pall of drifting grey and sheets of flame. The north showed blue again, and presently the sun shone. The horses steamed; the prairie smoked. Milly's clothes dried as the grey miles passed behind the tireless team.

The day's journey ended at a river, and as if her troubles need be multiplied, it was unfordable at that point. Milly camped. And the morning found her slower, stiffer, yet stern to go on. This river, too—could it have been the Louisiana Red?—had a northwest trend. All day she followed it, often in the shade of trees. No tracks, no trails, no old camps—the region was like a barren land.

Next morning she found a unused buffalo ford. The tracks were old. They stirred her sluggish blood, her submerged hopes. If only she could drop the reins and rest her hands, her arms! But the faithful horses had to be guided. Would she ever come to a road? Was this whole world devoid of the manifestations of travel? Miles and miles, as grey and as monotonous as a dead sea!

Then she drove into a zone of buffalo carcasses, and was startled into wonder, hope, and wild thought. Where was she? Fifty—maybe a hundred miles east of the Staked Plain, and still lost! These carcasses were black and dried; they had no odour; they were ghastly heaps of bones and hides. She drove ten miles across this belt of death and decay; and no sign of horses or wagon cheered her aching heart.

Milly lost track of hours, days, time. Sunset, a camp by water, black night with hateful stars, the false dawn, day with its grey leagues and blistering sun, the white

78

horses forever moving on and on and on, night, blackness, light once more, and horrible weary pangs.

"*What's this?*" cried Milly, and wide flew her eyes. She was lying back in the wagon, where she had fallen from faintness. She remembered. It had been early morning. But now the sun was high. The wagon creaked, swayed, moved on to strange accompaniment—clip-clop, clip-clop, clip-clop. The horses were trotting on hard road. Was she dreaming? She closed her eyes the better to listen. Clip-clop, clip-clop, clip-clop! This was no lying trick of her jaded ears, worn out from silence.

"Oh—thank heaven!" panted Milly. "It's a road—a road!" And she struggled to rise. Grey endless prairie, as always, but split to the horizon by a white hard road! She staggered to the seat. But driving was not necessary. The reins were looped round the brake. Whitey and Specks needed no guidance now, no urging, no help. They were on the homeward stretch. With steady clip-clop they trotted on, clicking off the miles. Whitey was lame and Specks had a clanging shoe, but these were small matters.

Milly sank down overwhelmed with joy. On the Fort Elliott road! The Llano Estacado showed no longer the deceiving purple of distance. It showed grey and drab, shadowy clefts, rock walls, and canyons. She forced herself to eat and drink, though the dried meat and bread were hard to swallow. She must brace up. Many were the buffalo hunters who travelled this road. Surely before the hour was gone she would see a white wagon on the horizon. Milly lifted her head to gaze backward towards the South, and then forward towards the north. The prairie was still a lonely land. Yet how different!

She rested, she thought, she gazed the hours away; and something came back to her.

Afternoon waned and sunset came; and with the fading of rosy and golden light the horses snorted their scent of water. Milly was stronger. Hope had wonderfully revived her, and she called to the horses.

Another horizon line reached! It was the crest of one

of the prairie slopes. Long had it been unattainable, hiding while it beckoned onward. A green-mantled stream crossed just below. Milly's aching and exhausted heart throbbed to sudden recognition. She had camped here. She knew those cotton woods. And strong sweet wine of renewed life fired her veins.

Whitey and Specks remembered. This was the cold, sweet water from the uplands, well-loved by the buffalo. They snorted and lifted dusty, shaggy hoofs to plod on and stop. Milly looked down on the green bank where Catlee had voiced his sympathy.

Another sunset, one of gold and red out of purple clouds, burned over the prairie-land. The sloping shadows crept along the distant valleys; the grassy undulating expanse shone with dusky fire. And a winding river, like a bright thread, lost itself in the far dim reaches.

Milly Fayre drove Whitey and Specks across the cattle-dotted pasture which flanked the river banks outside of Sprague's Post.

Horses mingled with the cattle. Between the road and the cottonwoods camps sent up their curling columns of blue smoke. Tents gleamed rosily in the sunset glow. Dogs ran out to herald the coming of another team. Curious buffalo hunters on the way south dropped out to halt Milly. Natives of the Post strolled across from the store to question the traveller from the buffalo fields.

"Howdy, sonny!" greeted a white-haired old Westerner, with keen blue eyes flashing over weary horses, and a wagon with its single occupant. "All by yourself?"

"Yes," replied Milly, amazed to hear her husky voice.

Men crowded closer, kindly, interested, beginning to wonder.

"Whar you from?" queried the old man.

"Pease River," replied Milly.

"Aw, say now, sonny, you're—" Then he checked his query and came closer to lay a hand on the smoking horse nearest to him. The rugged faces, some bronzed, some with the paleness that was not long of the prairie, were lifted to Milly. They seemed beautiful, so full of life, kindness. The dimmed in Milly's sight because of her tears.

"Yes, Pease River," she replied, hurriedly and low. "My outfit fought—killed one another. . . . Comanches swam the river. . . . I drove Whitey and Specks through the brakes. . . . The Indians chased us. . . . We ran into stampeded buffalo. . . . Driven all day—surrounded—dust and roar. . . . Oh, it was terrible! But they slowed up—they carried us all day—forty miles. . . . Since then I've camped and driven, camped and driven—days, days, days, I don't know how many!

A silence ensued after Milly's long, poignant speech. Then the old Westerner scratched his beard in perplexity.

"Sonny, air you jest foolin' us or jest out of your haid? You shore look fagged out."

"It's gospel truth," panted Milly.

"My boy," began the kindly interrogator with graver voice, and again his keen gaze swept over grimy horses and travel-work wagon.

"Boy!" exclaimed Milly, as spiritedly as her huskiness would permit. "I'm no boy! I'm a girl—Milly Fayre."

CHAPTER 5

Tom raised himself as high as he dared and studied what he could see of the field in the direction of the bluff. A man might trust himself boldly to that jumble of rocks. Accordingly, he crawled on hands and knees to the end of this stone-like corral, and there, stretching on his left side, with left hand extended and right dragging his rifle, he crawled as swiftly and noiselessly as possible. He peered only ahead of him. There was no use to look at the aisles between the rocks at the right and left, because he had to pass these openings, and looking was not going to help him. Trusting to luck and daring, he went on. Fear had left him. All he asked was luck and strength enough to get back with the water.

After the first ten or a dozen rods were behind him, there came an easing of a terrible strain. His comrades behind him were shooting now something like a volley, which action he knew was Pilchuck's way of diverting possible discovery of him. The Indians were shooting more, too; and he began to draw considerably away from the crossfire. He heard no more bullets whiz over his head. As it was impossible to rawl in a straight line, owing to rocks impeding his progress, he deviated from the course set by Pilchuck. This entailed the necessity of lifting himself every few moments so that he could peep over the rocks to keep the direction of the bluff. These brief actions were fraught with suspense. They exposed him perilously, but they were absolutely imperative.

Again Tom lost his direction. He was coming to a zone more open, and surely not far from the bluff that was his objective point. Usually he had chosen a high and large stone from which to peep. At this juncture not one of such size was available. Low down along the side of a flat stone he peered out. All he could see was a rather wide space, not thickly studded with rocks. But from that angle the bluff was not in sight.

Something like a sharp puff of wind whipped by. He heard a hiss. Then he felt a shock, solid, terrific, followed by a tearing, burning pain across his back. Almost the same instant came the bursting crack of a rifle. A half-naked Indian; red-skinned, snake-like, stood with smoking rifle, savage expectation on his dark face.

Tom fell flat behind the rock. In one second he gripped his rifle hard and cocked it, while his muscles gathered and strung for a mighty effort.

Tom leaped up and shot in the same action. It seemed he did not see the Indian clearly until after the discharge of the rifle. The Indian's gun was levelled. But it flew aside, strangely, as if propelled. And on the same instant there was a metallic crack. Tom's bullet had struck the breech of the Indian's gun and had glanced.

The Indian gasped and staggered. He seemed to push his gun away from him. It fell to the ground. Blood gushed from his mouth. He was swaying, yet he pulled out a knife and made at Tom.

For a second Tom stood transfixed. The Indian came lurching with the knife. Then Tom jumped just in time to avoid its sweep. Horror gave place to fury. He had no time to reload, so he whirled his rifle, making a club of it. But he missed the Indian, and such was the force of the blow he had aimed that he nearly lost his balance. As it was he righted himself to find the Indian lunging down with the knife.

Like a flash Tom's left hand caught the descending wrist and gripped it. Then he tried to swing the rifle with his right. But the Indian intercepted the blow and held the rifle.

Thus on the moment both were rendered helpless to force the issue. They held each other grimly.

It was a deadlock. Tom exerted himself to the utmost to hold that quivering blade from his body. He saw the advantage was on his side. Blood poured from a wound in the Indian's throat. The nearness of it, the terrible nature of the moment, the unabatable ferocity and courage of his red adversary were almost too much for Tom. He all but sank under the strain.

Then came a sudden shuddering convulsion on the part of the Indian, a last supreme effort. It was so great that it broke Tom's hold. But even as the Indian wrenched free, his strength failed. The corded strung muscles suddenly relaxed. He dropped the knife. He swayed and fell.

Tom bent over him. The Indian gazed upward, conscious. Then the hate in his eyes gave way to a blankness. He was dead, Tom slowly realized.

In a moment more Tom was alive to the situation. He had conquered here. But he was not yet out of danger. If any Indians had seen this encounter, they would have shot him before this.

Crouching down, Tom peered round until he had again located his objective point. Then he ran as fast as his spent strength permitted and soon reached the red bluff. But he did not locate the hiding place of the horse until Jake Devine saw him and called. Tom staggered round the bluff and into the pocket where the horses were concealed.

Devine came rattling down from a ledge, where evidently he had been watching. Then Al Thorndyke, the other guard, appeared from the opposite quarter. They ran to Tom.

"Say, you're all bloody!" declared Jake, aghast.

"Tom, I see thet fight," added Thorndyke sharply. "But I couldn't shoot for fear of hittin' you."

"I'm hit—I don't know how bad," panted Tom. "But it can't be very bad.... Hurry up, boys. I came after water. Tie me up. I've got to rustle back."

"We'll shore go with you," said Devine.

They tore Tom's shirt off. It was wringing wet and as red as a flag.

"Reckon you sweat a heap," put in Thorndyke encouragingly.

Tom winced as one of them ran a finger in the wound on his back.

"Nothin' bad. Long, deep cut," said Devine. "Fetch water, Al."

The two men washed Tom's wound and bandaged it tightly with a scarf.

"I've got to take some canteens back," declared Tom.

"I'll go. You stay with Al," replied Devine.

"Wal, I ain't a-goin' to stay. I've got to git in thet fight," asserted Thorndyke.

Tom heard a rattling volley of Creedmoors, punctuated by the sharper, lighter cracking of Winchester.

Devine's logic was unanswerable. So Tom made no further objection. The three men took two canteens each and their rifles, and harried forth.

Tom led the way. It was easy walking, but when he reached the point where he thought it needful to stoop, the hard work commenced. The heavy canteens swung round and hung from his neck.

He reached the spot where he had fought the Comanche, and here he crouched down. Devine and Thorndyke came up with him. The Indian lay stark, his eyes wide open, his hands spread.

"Fellers, I'll fetch thet Indian's gun an' belt," said Devine practically.

Soon Tom lay flat to crawl like a snake. It was well that he had laid a trail. Tom kept the lead, ten feet in front of Thorndyke, who was a like distance ahead of

85

Devine. Tom had to stop every little while to rest. His lungs appeared to stand the test, but his muscles were weak. Still he knew he could make the distance. The long drink of water he had taken had revived him.

They had crawled close to where Pilchuck and his men were shooting, and therefore within the zone of the Indians' fire, when a bullet kicked up the dust in front of Tom. He hesitated. Then a bullet clipped the crown of his hat. This spurred him to a spasmodic scrambling forward to cover behind a boulder. From there Tom squirmed round to look back. Jake Devine was kneeling with levelled rifle, which on the instant belched fire and smoke. Jake dropped down and crawled forward. His face was black and his eyes blazed.

"Thet Redskin is feed fer lizards," he said grimly. "Go on, Tom."

At last Tom and his comrades reached the smoky place that marked Pilchuck's position.

"I ain't hankerin' fer this part of the job," said Devine. "Suppose they take us for Redskins."

But Pilchuck was too wise a leader to allow blunders of that nature. He was on the look-out, and his grimy, sweaty, stern face relaxed at sight of Tom.

"Shore was good work, Tom," he said. "It's next door to hell here. Hurry to Ory an' Roberts."

Tom hurried to where the young man lay, under a sunshade Roberts had rigged up with his shirt and stick. Roberts gave Tom a husky greeting. Manifestly his voice was almost gone. Ory's face was pale and clammy. When Tom lifted his head he opened his eyes and tried to speak. But he could not.

"Ory, here's water," said Tom and held a canteen to the boy's pale lips.

Never until that moment had Tom appreciated the preciousness of water. He watched Ory drink, and had his reward in the wan smile of gratitude. "Much obliged, Tom," whispered Ory, and lay back with a strange look. Then he shut his eyes and appeared to relax. Tom did not like the uneasy impression he received on the moment, but in the excitement he did not think any more about it.

Roberts handed the canteen to the other wounded fellow and watched him drink. Then he slaked his own thirst.

"Say! he ejaculated, with a deep breath, "thet shore was all I needed."

The white-headed ol plainsman crawled over for his share.

"Son, them canteens will lick Nigger Horse," he said.

"What! Are we fightin' that chief?" queried Tom in amazement.

"Accordin' to Pilchuck we're doin' jest that," responded the plainsman cheerfully. "Old Nigger an' a thousand of his Redskins, more or less."

Then Tom crawled to the vantage point behind the rock he had used before, and gave himself up to this phase of the fight. It did not take longer than a moment to realise what Pilchuck had meant. There was scarcely a second without its boom of Creedmoor or crack of Winchester. A little cloud of white smoke hung above every boulder. Tom exercised the utmost vigilance in the matter of exposing himself to the Indians' fire. He was almost spent, and suffering excruciating pain from his wound. How infernally hot the sun burned down! His rifle and the stones were as fire to his hands. But as he began to peer out for an Indian to shoot at, and worked back into the fight, he forgot his pangs, and then what had seemed the intolerable conditions.

Slowly the pitch of the fight augmented, until it was raging with a reckless fury on the part of the Comanches, and a desperate resistance on that of the besieged. Sooner or later Tom was forced to realise in his own reactions the fact that the fighting and the peril had increased to an alarming extent. A stinging bullet-crease in his shoulder was the first awakening shock he sustained. He had answered to the Indians' growing recklessness. He had been exposing himself more and redoubling his fire. He had missed Indians slipping stealthily from boulder to boulder—

opportunities that only intense excitement and haste had made him fail to grasp. Then, when he crouched back, forced to cover, aghast at this second wound, he became fully aware of the attack.

The Comanches had pressed closer and closer, not better concealed by the pall of smoke that overhung the scene.

"Hold your fire! Look out for a charge!" yelled Pilchuck in a stentorian voice.

The booming of Creedmoors ceased, and that permitted a clearer distinguishing of the Indians' fire. Their Winchesters were rattling in a continuous volley, and a hail of lead whistled over and into the boulder corral. Manifestly the Indians had massed on the west side, between Starwell's position and Pilchuck's. This occasioned the leader to draw up his men in line with Tom's fortification. Closer and hotter grew the Indian's fire. Through the blue haze of smoke and heat Tom saw dim, swiftly-moving shapes, like phantoms. They were Comanches, gliding from covert to covert, and leaping from boulder to boulder. Tom's heart seemed to choke him. If the Indians were in strong enough force they would effect a massacre of Pilchuck's men. Suddenly, as Tom dwelt fearfully on such a contingency, the firing abruptly ceased. A silence fraught with suspense ensued, strange after the heavy shooting.

"It's a trick. Look sharp!" Pilchuck warned his men.

"Wal, seein' this fight's ag'in the extermination of the buffalo, I reckon old Nigger Horse will do or die," said Jake Devine.

"If you'd ask me I'd say these hoss-ridin' Redskins was up to their last dodge on foot," averred the old white-headed plainsman.

"Look out, it's not our last dodge," replied Pilchuck.

Scarcely had he spoken when the Indians opened up with a heavy volley at alarmingly close range. Pilchuck shouted an order that was not intelligible in the cracking of firearms. But only its contents were needed. The big buffalo guns answered with a roar. In another moment firing became so fast and furious that it blended as a continuous thundering in Tom's ears. He saw the rush of the Indians, incredibly swift and vague through the smoke, and he worked his rifle so hard that it grew hot. Above the roar of guns he heard the strange ear-splitting yell of the Comanches. Almost at the same instant smoke veiled the scene, more to the advantage of the white men than the red. The Creedmoors thundered as continuously as before, and the volume of sound must have been damning to the desperate courage of the Comanches. Perhaps they had not counted on so strong a force and resistance. Their war-cry pealed to a shrill pitch and ceased; and following that the rattling volleys fell off. Then Pilchuck ordered his men to stop shooting.

Tom saw the old white-haired plainsman stand up and survey the smoke-hazed slope. Then he dropped down.

"Fellars, they're draggin' off their dead an' crippled," he said. "They're licked, an' we ought to chase them clear to their hosses."

"Right," replied Pilchuck grimly. "But wait till we're sure."

Tom could not see anything of the retreat, if such it was. The smoke mantle was lifting above the boulders. With the sudden release of strain the men reated according to their individual natures. Those new to such fighting were silent, as was Tom, and lay flat. Jake Devine was loquacious in his complaints that he had not downed any Comanches. The old plainsman urged Pilchuck to chase the Indians. Then when the receding fire of the enemy ceased altogether Tom heard yells close at hand.

"That's Harkaway," said the scout eagerly, and he called out a reply.

Soon Harkaway and his men came stooping and crawling to join Pilchuck. They were panting from exertion.

"Boss, they're workin' down," he said breathlessly.

"Mebbe it's a trick," replied the wary scout. "I'll sneak out an' take a look."

Tom drew back from his position and eased his cramped limbs. His shirt was wet with blood. Examination showed his second bullet wound to be a slight one, but exceedingly annoying. He got Devine to tie it up, running a scarf under his arm and over his shoulder.

"Wal, a couple more scratches will make an old residenter out of you, Tom," he said dryly.

Tom was about to make some fitting reply when Pilchuck returned in haste.

"Men, it's goin' to be our day," he said, his grey eyes alight with piercing intensity. "If we rout old Nigger Horse it'll be the first victory for the whites in this buffalo war. Us hunters will have done what the soldiers couldn't do. Harkaway, you stay here with two of your men to guard these cripples. All the rest of you grab extra cartridges an' follow me."

Tom was not the last to get his hands into that cartridge bag, nor to fall in line after the scout. Once out of the zone of smoke, he was thrilled to see Indians disappearing over the edge of the slope. There was a good deal of shooting below, and the unmistakable booming reports told of Creedmoors in action. From the sound, Tom judged Starwell had changed his position. But this could not be ascertained for sure until the brow of the slope was reached. Pilchuck advanced cautiously, gradually growing bolder, as ambush appeared less probably, and the time came when he broke into a run.

"String out, an' come fast," he called back.

Tom fell in behind Jake Devine, and keeping some paces back, he attended to the difficulty of running over the rough ground. Thus it was he did not look up until he reached the edge of the slope. Here he found Pilchuck and some of the men in a group, gazing, talking, and gesticulating all at once. Tom's breast was heaving from the hard run. He was hot and wet. But it was certain that a reviving thrill ran over him. The Comanches were in retreat. There was no doubt of that. It was still an orderly retreat, with a line of warriors guarding the rear. Tom saw Indians dragging and carrying their wounded and dead; others were gathering in the horses; and the mass was centered in the middle of the encampment, where there were signs of great haste.

One by one Pilchuck's arriving men added to the group on the slope.

"Starwell has the idea," declared Pilchuck. "See. He's moved this way an' down. He can still cover that gate an' also reach the camp."

"Jude, we shore hev our chance now," spoke up the old white-haired plainsman.

"I reckon," replied the scout. "Now listen, men. When I give the word we'll charge down this hill. Each an' every one of you yell like the devil, run a dozen jumps, drop down on your knee an' shoot. Then load, get up, an' do the same over again. Head for that pile of rocks this side of Starwell's position."

Silence followed the scout's trenchant speech. Then ensued a tightening of belts, a clinking of cartridges, a rasping of the mechanism of the Creedmoors. Tom was all ready, quivering for the word, yet glad of a few moments' rest. Pilchuck and the old plainsman stood close together, keen eyes on the Indian encampment. The sun was low over the escarpment to the west and it was losing its heat. The canyon seemed full of golden lights and blue haze, through which flashed and gleamed moving objects, horses, Indians, and collapsing tepees—a colourful and exciting scene. The rear guard of Indians backed slowly to the centre of the encampment. Their horses were being brought in readiness. Tom could not help but see the execution of a shrewd Indian brain. Still, there were signs of a possible panic. Already the Comanches had suffered in this fight, as was shown by the number of those incapacitated. Already the far slope of the canyon was covered by ponies dragging travois.

The sudden breaking up of the rearguard, as these Indians leaped for their horses, was a signal for Pilchuck.

"Charge, men!" he yelled harshly, and plunged down the slope.

"Hi, fellers," shouted Jake Devine, "old Nigger Horse is my meat."

In a moment Pilchuck's men were spread out on the jump, yelling like fiends and brandishing their weapons. Tom was well to the fore, close behind Devine and Pilchuck. Their heavy boots sent the loose stones flying and rattling down the hill. White puffs of smoke showed suddenly down in the encampment and were followed by the rattle of Winchesters. Presnetly Pilchuck plunged to a halt and, kneeling, levelled his Creedmoor. His action was swiftly followed by his men. His Creedmoor boomed; those of Devine and the plainsman next, and then the others thundered in unison. It was a long-range shot and Tom aimed generally at the commotion in the encampment. Pandemonium broke loose down there. All order seemed to vanish in a rushing melee. Pilchuck leaped up with a hoarse command, which his men answered in wild, exulting whoops. And they plunged again down the slope faster, rendered reckless by the success of their boldness.

Tom felt himself a part of that charging line of furious buffalo-hunters, and had imbibed the courage of the mass. Like the others, he had calculated on the Indians charging back to meet them thus precipitating a pitched battle. But this was not the case. The Indians began returning the fire from all parts of the canyon. It was a hasty action, however, and did not appear formidable. They were not bent on escape. That give irresistible momentum to the charge of Pilchuck's force. Starwell and his men, seeing the Indians routed, left their covert and likewise plunged down, firing and yelling.

Tom, following the example of the men before him, ran and knelt and fired four times in rapid succession on the way down to the level floor of the canyon. By this time all the Indians were mounted and the mass of them abandoned the idea of a slow climb up the opposite slope. They broke for the canyon gate. This meant they had to lessen the long range between them and Pilchuck's force, a fact that did not daunt them. Their lean, racy mustangs were quickly in a running stride, and each rider was presenting a rifle towards the enemy.

"HOLD HERE, MEN!" bawled Pilchuck stridently. "If they charge us take to the rocks!"

Tom no longer heard the bang of any individual gun, not even his own. And he was loading and firing as fast as possible. A roar filled his ears, and the ground seemed to shake with the furious trample of the mustangs racing by. How long and low they stretched out, how lean and wild their riders! What matchless horsemen these Comanches. Even in the hot grip of that fighting moment Tom thrilled at the magnificent defiance of these Indians, courting death by that ride, to save their burdened comrades climbing the slope. Some of them met that death. Tom saw riders throw up their arms and pitch headlong to the ground. Mustangs leaped high in convulsive action, and plunged down to roll over and over.

Tom seemed aware of the thinning of Pilchuck's ranks. And when the order came to run down the canyon to prevent a possible massacre of Starwell and his men, who had impetuously advanced too far, some were left behind. From that moment Tom lost clear perception of the progress of the fight. The blood rage that obsessed the frontiersman was communicated to him. He plunged with the others; he felt their nearness; he heard their hoarse yells and the boom of their guns; but he seemed to be fighting alone for the sake of the fight itself. The last of that mounted band of Comanches swooped across towards Starwell's men, driving them to the rocks. Pilchuck's force, charging down the level, came abreast of them, and there in the open a terrible, brief, and decisive battle ensued.

If the Comanches had not halted in the face of the booming Creedmoors there would have been an end to Pilchuck's buffalo hunters. They would have been run down. But the Indians were not equal to victory at such cost. They shot as they had ridden, furiously, without direct attention. As for the white men, fury made them only the more efficient. They advanced, yelling, curshing, shooting, and loading like men possessed of devils. The smoke and din seemed to envelop Tom. His gun scorched his hands and powder burned his face. When he reloaded he seemed to reel and fumble over his breech lock. The compact mass of Indians disintegrated to strings and streams, vague, lean, wild, and savage figures hard to aim at. Then something struck Tom and the vagueness became obscurity.

CHAPTER 6

In 1876 more than two hundred thousand buffalo-hides were shipped east over the Santa Fe Railroad, and hundreds of thousands in addition went north from Fort Worth, Texas.

For this great number of hides that reached Eastern and foreign markets there were at least twice the number of hides sacrificed on the range. Old Buffalo hunters generally agreed on the causes for this lamentable fact. Inexperienced hunters did not learn to poison the hides, which were soon destroyed by hide-bugs. Then as many buffalo were crippled as killed outright and skinned, and these wounded ones stole away to die in coulees or the brakes of the rivers. Lastly a large percentage of buffalo was chased by hunters into the quagmires and quicksands along the numerous streams, there to perish.

The year 1877 saw the last of the raids by Comanches and Kiowas, a condition brought about solely by the long campaign of united bands of buffalo hunters, who chased and fought these Indians all over the Staked Plain. But this campaign was really a part of the destruction of the buffalo, and that destruction broke forever the strength of these hard-riding Indians.

In the winter and spring of that year the number of hide-hunting outfits doubled and trebled and quadrupled; and from the Red River to the Brazos, over the immense tract of Texas prairie, every river, stream, pond, waterhole and spring, everywhere buffalo could drink, was ambushed by hunters with heavy guns. The poor animals that were not shot down had to keep on travelling until the time came when a terrible parching thrist made them mad. Then, when in their wanderings to find some place to drink they scented water, they would stampede, and in their madness to assuage an insupportable thirst would plunge over one another in great waves, crushing to death those underneath.

Tom Doan, during the year and a half of the Indian raids, fought through three campaigns against Comanches, Kiowas, and Llano Estacado Apaches.

Pilchuck's first organizing of buffalo-hunters into a unit to fight Comanches drove the wedge that split the Indians; and likewise it inspired and roused the hide-hunters from the Territory line to the Rio Grande. Thus there was a war on the several tribes, as well as continued slaughter of the buffalo.

In the spring of 1877, when, according to the scouts, the backbone of the southwest raiding tribes had been broken, Tom Doan bade good-bye to Burn Hudnall, his friend and comrade for so long. Dave Stronghurl had months before gone back to Sprague's Post to join his wife and people.

"I reckon I'm even with the Comanches," he said grimly. That was his only reference to his father's murder.

"Well, Burn, we've seen wild life," mused Tom sadly. "I'm glad I helped rout the Comanches. They've been robbed, I suppose, and I can't blame them. But they sure made a man's blood boil for a fight."

"What'll you do, Tom?" queried Burn.

Doan dropped his head. "It'd hurt too much to go back to Sprague's Post—just yet. You see, Burn, I can't forget Milly. Of course, she died long ago. But then sometime I see her in dreams, and she seems alive. I'd like to learn the truth of her fate. Some day I might. Pilchuck and I are going south of the Brazos. The last great hunt is on there."

"I'm goin' to settle on a ranch at Sprague's," said Burn. "Father always said that would be the centre of a fine cattle an' farmin' district some day."

"Yes, I remember. It used to be my dream, too. But I'm changed. This roving life, I guess. The open range for me yet a while! Some day I'll come back."

"Tom, you've money saved," returned Burn thoughtfully. "You could buy an' stock a ranch. Isn't it risky carryin' round all your money? There's worse than bad Comanches now in the huntin' field."

"I've thought of that," said Tom. "It does seem risky. So I'll ask you to take most of my money and bank it for me."

"It's a good idea. But see here, old man, suppose you don't come back? You know, we've seen things happen to strong an' capable men down here. Think how lucky we've been!"

"I've thought of that, too," said Tom with gravity. "If I don't show up inside of five years invest the money for your children. Money's not much to me any more ... But I'm likely to come back."

This conversation took place at Wheaton's camp, on the headwaters of the Red River, in April. A great exodus of freighters was taking place that day. It was interesting for Tom to note the development of the hide-hauling. The wagons were large and had racks and booms, so that when loaded they resembled haywagons, except in colour. Two hundred buffalo hides to a wagon, six yokes of oxen to a team, and twenty-five teams to a train! Swiftly indeed were the buffalo disappearing from the plains. Burn Hudnall rode north with one of these immense freighting outfits.

Tom and Pilchuck made preparations for an extended hunt in the Brazos River country, whence emanated rumours somewhat similar to the gold rumours of '49.

97

While choosing and arranging an outfit they were visited by a brawny little man with a most remarkable visage. It was scarred with records of both the sublime and the ridiculous.

"I'm after wantin' to throw in with you," he announced to Pilchuck.

The scout, used to judging men in a glance, evidently saw service and character in this fellow.

"Wal, we need a man, that's shore. But he must be experienced," returned the scout.

"Nary a tenderfoot, Scout, not no more," he grinned. "I've killed an' skinned over four thousand buffs. An' I'm a blacksmith an' a cook"

"Well, I reckon you're a whole outfit in yourself," rejoined Pilchuck with his rare broad smile. "How do you want to throw in?"

"Share expense of outfit, work, an' profit."

"Nothin' could be more fair. I reckon we'll be right glad to have you. What's your handle?"

"Wrong-Wheel Jones," replied the applicant as if he expected the name to be recognised.

"What the hell! I've met Buffalo Jones, and Dirty-Face Jones, an' Spike Jones, but I never heard of you...Wrong-Wheel Jones! Where'd you ever get that?"

"It was stuck on me my first hunt when I was sort a tenderfooty."

"Wal, tell me an' my pard here, Tom Doan," continued the scout good-humouredly. "Tom, shake with Wrong-Wheel Jones."

After quaintly acknowledging the introductions, Jones said, "Fust trip I busted a right hind wheel of my wagon. Along comes half a dozen outfits, but none had an extra wheel. Blake, the leader, told me he'd passed a wagon like mine, broke down on the Cimarron. "Peared it had some good wheels. So I harnessed my horses, rode one, an' led t'other. I found the wagon, but the *left hind wheel* was the only one not busted. So I rode back to camp. Blake asked my why I didn't fetch a wheel back, an' I says: 'What'd I want with *two* left hind wheels? I got one. It's the right one thet's busted. Thet left hind wheel back thar on thet wagon would do fust rate, but it's on the wrong side.' An' Blake an' this outfit roared till they near died. When he could talk ag'in he says: 'You darned fool. Thet left hind wheel turned round would make your right hind wheel.' An' after a while I seen he was right. They called me Wrong-Wheel Jones an' the name's stuck."

"By gosh! it ought to!" said Pilchuck, laughing.

In company with another outfit belonging to a newcomer named Hazelton, with a son of fifteen and two other boys not much older, Pilchuck headed for the Brazos River.

After an uneventful journey, somewhat off the beaten track, they reached one of the many tributaries of the Brazos, where they ran into some straggling small herds.

"We'll make two-day stops till we reach the main herd," said Pilchuck. "I've a hankerin' for my huntin' alone. Reckon hide-hunters are thick as bees down on the Brazos. Let's keep out of the stink an' musketers as long as we can."

They went into camp, the two outfits not far apart, within hailing distance.

It was perhaps the most beautiful location for a camp Tom had seen in all his travelling over western Texas. Pilchuck said the main herd, with its horde of hide-hunters, had passed miles east of this point. As a consequence the air was sweet, the water unpolluted, and grass and wood were abundant.

Brakes of the tributary consisted of groves of pecan trees and cottonwoods, where cold springs abounded, and the deep pools contained fish. As spring had just come in that latitude, there were colour of flowers, and fragrance in the air, and a myriad of birds lingering on their way north. Like the wooded sections of the Red River and the Pease River Divide had been, so was this Brazos district. Deer, antelope, and turkey, with their carnivorous attendants, panthers, wild cats, and wolves, had not yet been molested by white hunters.

Perhaps the Indian campaigns had hardened Tom Doan, for her returned to the slaughter of buffalo. He had been so long out of the hunting game that he had forgotten many of the details, and especially the sentiment that had once moved him. Then this wild life in the open had become a habit; it clung to a man. Moreover, Tom had an aching and ever-present discontent which only action could subdue.

He took a liking to Cherry Hazelton. The boy was a strapping youngster, freckle-faced and red-headed, and, like all healthy youths of the Middle West during the 'seventies, he was a worshipper of the frontiersman and Indian fighter. He and his young comrades, brothers Dan and Joe Newman, spent what little leisure time they had hanging round Pilchuck and Tom, hungry for stories as dogs for bones.

Two days at this camp did not suffice for Pilchuck. Buffalo were not excessively numerous, but they were scattered into small bands under leadership of old bulls; and for these reasons offered the conditions best suited to experienced hunters.

The third day Tom took Cherry Hazelton hunting with him, allowing him to carry canteen and extra cartridges while getting valuable experience.

Buffalo in small numbers were in sight everywhere, but as this country was rolling and cut up, unlike Pease Prairie, it was not possible to locate all the herds that might be within reaching distance.

In several hours of rising and stalking Tom had not found a position favourable to any extended success, though he had downed some buffalo, and young Hazelton, after missing a number, had finally killed his first, a fine bull. The boy was wild with excitement, and this brought back to Tom his early experience, now seemingly so long in the past.

They were now on a creek that ran through a wide stretch of plain, down to the tributary, and no more than two miles from camp. A large herd of buffalo tropped out of the west, coming fast under a cloud of dust. They poured down into the creek and literally blocked it, crazy to drink. Tom had here a marked instance of the thirst-driven madness now common to the buffalo. This herd, numbering many hundreds, slaked their thirst, and then trooped into a wide flat in the creek bottom, where trees stood here and there. Manifestly they had drunk too deeply, if they had not foundered, for most of them lay down.

"We'll cross the creek and sneak close on them," said Tom. "Bring all the cartridges. We might get a stand."

"What's that?" whispered Cherry excitedly.

"It's what a buffalo-hunter calls a place and time where a big number bunches and can be kept from running off. I never had a stand myself. But I've an idea what one's like."

They crept on behind trees and brush, down into the wide, shallow flat, until they were no farther than a hundred yards from the resting herd. From the way Cherry panted, Tom knew he was frightened.

"It is sort of skittish," whispered Tom, "but if they run our way, we can climb a tree."

"I'm not—scared. It's—just—great," rejoined the lad in a tone that hardly verified his words.

"Crawl slow now, and easy," said Tom. "A little farther— then we'll bombard them."

At last Tom led the youngster yards closer, to a wonderful position behind an uprooted cottonwood, from which they could not be seen. Thrilling, indeed, was it even for Tom, who had stalked Comanches in this way. Most of the buffalo were down, and those standing were stupid with drowsiness. The heat, and a long parching thirst, than an overcharged stomach, had rendered them loggy.

Tom turned his head to whisper instructions to the lad. Cherry's face was pale, and the feckless stood out prominently. He was trembling with wild eagerness, fear and delight combined. Tom thought it no wonder. Again he smelled the raw scent of the buffalo. They made a magnificent sight, an assorted herd of all kinds and ages, from the clean, glossy, newly-shedded old bulls down to the red calves.

"Take the bull on your right—farthest out," whispered Tom. "And I'll 'tend to this old stager on my left."

The big guns boomed. Tom's bull went to his knees and, grunting loud, fell over; Cherry's bull wagged his head as if a bee had stung him. Part of the buffalo lying down got up. The old bull, evidently a leader, started off.

"Knock him," whispered Tom quickly. "They'll follow him." Tom fired almost simultaneously with Cherry, and one or both of them scored a dead shot. The buffalo that had started to follow the bull turned back into the herd, and this seemed to dominate all of them. Most of those standing pressed closer in. Others began to walk stolidly off.

"Shoot the outsiders," said Tom quickly. And in three seconds he stopped as many buffalo. Cherry's gun boomed, but apparently without execution.

At this juncture Pilchuck rushed up behind them.

"By golly! you've got a stand!" he ejaculated in excited tones for him. "Never seen a better in my life. Now, here, you boys, let me do the shootin'." It's tought on you, but if this stand is handled right we'll make a killin'."

Pilchuck stuck his forked rest-stick in the ground and knelt behind it, just to the right of Tom and Cherry. This elevated him somewhat above the log, and certainly not hidden from the buffalo.

"Case like this a fellow wants to shoot straight," said the scout. "A crippled buff means a bolt."

Choosing the bull the farthest outside of the herd, Pilchuck aimed with deliberation and fired. The animal fell. Then he treated the next in the same manner. He was far from hurried, and that explained his deadly precision.

"You musn't let your gun get too hot," he said. "Overexpansion from heat makes a bullet go crooked."

Pilchuck picked out buffalo slowly walking away, and downed them. The herd kept massed, uneasy in some quarters, but for the most part not disturbed by the shooting. Few of those lying down rose to their feet.

When the scout had accounted for at least two dozen buffalo he handed his gun to Tom.

"Cool it off an' wipe it out," he directed and, taking Tom's gun, he returned to his deliberate work.

Tom threw down the breech-block and poured water through the barrel once, and then presently again. Taking up Pilchuck's ramrod, Tom ran a greasy patch of cloth through the barrel. It was cooling rapidly and would soon be safe to use.

Meanwhile, the imperturbable scout was knocking buffalo down as if they had been ninepins. On the side towards him there was soon a corral of dead buffalo. He never missed; only seldom was it necessary to take two shots at an animal. After shooting ten or twelve, he returned Tom's gun and took up his own.

"Best stand I ever saw," he said. "Queer how buffalo act sometimes. They're not stupid. They know somethin' is wrong. But, you see, I keep knockin' down the one that leads off."

At last, after more than an hour of this incredible stolidity to the boom of gun and the fall of their numbers, the resting buffalo got up, and they all moved round uneasily, uncertainly. Then Pilchuck missed dead centre of a quartering shot at a bull that led out. The bullet made the beast frantic, and with a kind of low bellow it bounded away. The mass broke, and a stream of shaggy brown poured off the flat and up the gentle slope. In a moment all the herd was in motion. The industrious Pilchuck dropped four more while they were crowding behind, following off the flat. A heavy trampling roar filled the air; dust, switching tufted tails, wooly bobbing backs, covered the slope. And in a few moments they were gone. Silence settled down. The blue smoke drifted away. A gasp of dying buffalo could be heard.

"Reckon I never beat this stand," said the scout, wiping his wet, black hands. "If I only hadn't crippled that bull."

"Gosh! It was murder, wusser'n butcherin' cows!" ejaculated the boy Cherry. Drops of sweat stood out on his pale face, as marked as the freckles. He looked sick. Long before that hour had ended his boyish sense of exciting adventure had been outraged.

"Lad, it ain't always that easy," remarked Pilchuck. "An' don't let this make you think huntin' buffalo isn't dangerous. Now we'll make a count."

One hundred and twenty-six buffalo lay dead in a space less than three acres; and most of them were bulls.

"Yep, it's my record," declared the scout, with satisfaction. "But I come back fresh to it, an' shore that was a grand stand. Boys, we've got skinin' for the rest of to-day an' all of tomorrow."

CHAPTER 7

The middle of July found Tom Doan and Pilchuck far down on the Brazos, in the thick of the slaughter. Thirty miles of buffalo hunters drove the last great herd day by day towards extermination.

The prairie was open, hot, dusty, and vast. Always the buffalo headed to the wind; they would drink and graze, and go on, noses to the breeze. If the wind changed overnight, in the morning they would be found turned round, traveling towards it. All day they grazed against it. They relied on their scent more than on sight or hearing; and in that open country the wind brought them warning of their foes. But for the great number of hide-hunters these buffalo might have escaped any extended slaughter.

The outfits were strung along the Brazos for many miles; and as the buffalo had to drink, they were never far from water. Thus a number of hunters would get to them every day, kill many on the chase, and drive them on to the next aggregation of slayers.

One morning when Tom drove out on the dust-hazed stinking prairie he found a little red buffalo-calf standing beside his mother, which Tom had shot and skinned the day before. This was no new sight to Tom. Nevertheless, in the present case there seemed a difference. These calves left motherless by the slaughter had always wandered over the prairie lost and bewildered; this one, however, had recognised its mother and would not leave her.

"Go along! Get back to the herd!" yelled Tom, shocked despite his callousness.

The calf scarcely noticed him. It smelled of its hide-stripped mother, and manifestly was hungry. Presently it left off trying to awaken this strange, horribly red and inert body, and stood with hanging head, dejected, resigned, a poor, miserable little beast. Tom could not drive it away; and after loading the hide on the wagon he returned twice to try to make it run off. Finally, he was compelled to kill it.

This incident bode ill for Tom. It fixed his mind on this thing he was doing and left him no peace. Thousands and thousands of beautiful little buffalo-calves were rendered motherless by the hide-hunters. That was to Tom the unforgivable brutality. Calves just born, just able to suck, and from that to yearlings, were left to starve, to die of thirst, to wander until they dropped or were torn to shreds by wolves. No wonder this little calf showed in its sad resignation the doom of the species!

August came. The great herd massed. The mating season had come, and both bulls and cows, slaves to the marvellous instinct that had evolved them, grew slower, less wary, heedless now to the scent of man on the wind.

Tom Doan and Pilchuck reined their horses on the crest of a league-sloping ridge and surveyed the buffalo range.

To their surprise the endless black line of buffalo was not in sight. They had moved north in the night. At this early hour the hunters were just riding out to begin their day's work. No guns were booming, and it appeared that Tom and the scout had that part of the range to themselves.

"Wal, we spent yesterday peggin' hides in camp, an' didn't think to ask Jones if the buffalo had moved," remarked Pilchuck refectively.

"The wind has changed. It's now from the north," said Tom.

"Shore is. An' the buffs will be grazin' back pronto. That is, if they *are* grazin'!"

"Any reason to doubt it?" asked Tom.

"Wal, the breedin' season's just about ended. An' that with this muggy, stormy, electric-charged mornin' might cause a move. Never in my huntin' days have I seen such a restless, queer herd of buffalo as this one."

"No wonder!" exclaimed Tom.

"Wal, it ain't, an' that's a fact. Do I see hosses yonder?"

Tom swept the prairie with his glass. "Yes. Hunters riding out. I see more beyond. They're all going downriver."

"Come to think of it, I didn't hear much shootin' yesterday. Did you?"

"Not a great deal. And that was early morning and far away," replied Tom.

"Buffs an' hunters have worked north. Let's see. The river makes a bend about ten miles from here, an' runs east. I'd be willin' to bet the herd hasn't turned that bend."

"Why?"

"Because they'll *never* go north again. For two months the trend has been south, day by day. Some days a wind like yesterday would switch them, but on the whole they're workin' south. This ain't natural for midsummer. They ought to be headed north. 'Course the mob of hunters are drivin' them south."

"But how about to-day?" inquired Tom.

"Wal, I'm shore figgerin'. Reckon I can't explain, but I feel all them outfits ridin' north will have done their work for nothin'."

"What will we do?"

"I'm not carin' a lot. Reckon I've sickened on this job, an' I shore know that when I stay a day in camp."

107

Tom had before noted this tendency in the scout. It was common to all those hunters who had been long in the field. He did not voice his own sentiment.

"I've been wantin' to ride west an' see what the next ford is goin' to be like," said the scout presently. "We'll be breakin' camp an' moving south soon. An' the other side of the river is where we want to be."

For the first time Tom experienced a reluctance to a continuation of the old mode of travelling south. Why not turn north once more? The thought was a surprise. There was no reason to start north, unless in answer to the revulsion of hide-hunting. This surely would be his last buffalo-hunt. But he did not think it just to his partners to quit while they wanted to keep on. His reflection then was that Pilchuck was wearing out, both in strength and in greed.

They rode west, aiming to reach the river some four or five miles farther on.

It was a cloudy, sultry summer morning, with storm in the air. The prairie was not here a beautiful prospect. Tom seemed to gaze over it rather than at it. Westward the undulating grey rise of ground stretched interminably to a horizon bare of landmarks. Far in the east rays of sunlight streamed down between sullen, angry, copper and purple-hued clouds. The north threatened. It was black all along the horizon. Still, oppressive, sultry, the air seemed charged.

From time to time Pilchuck turned in his saddle to gaze backward along the empty range, and then up to the cloud bank. It appeared to Tom as if the scout were looking and listening for something.

"What're you expecting?" queried Tom, yielding to curiosity. "A thunderstorm?"

"Wal, I'll be darned if I know," ejaculated Pilchuck. "Shore I wasn't thinkin' about a storm. Wasn't thinkin' at all! Must be just habit with me. But now you tax me, I reckon I'm uneasy about that herd."

Pilchuck led west farther than he had calculated, and struck the river at a wonderful place where the prairie took a sudden dip for miles, shearing steeply to the shallow water. Here was the buffalo-ford, used by the herds in their annual migrations. Trees were absent, and brush and grass had not the luxuriance common to most stretches of river bank. From prairie rim to margin of river sloped a long, steep bank, even and smooth; and at one point the wide approach to the ford was split and dominated by a rocky eminence, the only high point in sight along the river.

The place seemed dismal and lonely to Tom as he sat on his horse while Pilchuck forded the river. Contrary to most river scenes, this one was lifeless. Not a bird or animal or a fish or turtle in sight! Loneliness and solitude had their abode in this trodden road of the buffalo.

At length the scout returned and rode up to Tom.

"Wal, I wouldn't care to get a team stuck in that sand," he remarked. "It shore ain't packed none. Lend me your glass."

The scout swept a half-circle of the horizon, and finally came to a halt westward, at a point on the prairie some distance from the river.

"See some small bunches of buffalo," he said. "Let's ride up on them, make a kill, skin what we get, an' pick them up with the wagon on our way south to-morrow."

"You're the boss," replied Tom.

"Wal, I wish someone was bossin' me," returned Pilchuck, enigmatically.

They trotted off over the grey prairie, and after travelling a couple miles, could see the buffalo plainly. Meanwhile a slight breeze began to blow from the north.

"I'll be darned!" ejaculated Pilchuck with annoyance. "Wind's turned again. If it blows stronger, we'll not slip up on this bunch."

Another mile brought increase of wind, and the wary buffalo, catching the scent of the killers, loped away over the prairie. Pilchuck watched them in disgust. "Run, you old dunderhead! Run clear across the Rio Grande! Tom, I reckon we're all spoiled by the past easy huntin'. It'll never be easy again. An' somehow I'm glad. Let's work back."

They turned about to face the breeze, now quite strong, cooler, with a heavy scent of rotting buffalo carcasses.

"Faugh!" exclaimed the scout. "I'd rather have nose an' eyes full of cottonwood smoke."

Tom's quick ear caught a very low rumble of thunder. He turned his head. The sound had ceased. It had come on a stronger puff of wind.

"What d'you hear?" inquired the scout, whose eye never missed anything.

"Thunder."

"Wal, it does look stormy. But I never trust thunder in this country," replied the scout significantly.

He halted his horse; and Tom did likewise. They gazed at the north. Dull, leaden mushrooming clouds were moving towards them, not rapidly, but steadily, in heavy, changing forms. They merged into a purple-black mass down which streaked thin zigzag ropes of lightning.

"Storm all right," observed Pilchuck. "Listen."

After a moment in which nothing was heard save the heaving of horses, the rattle of bridle, and creak of leather, the scout dismounted.

"Get off, Tom, an' walk away from the horses. Listen now."

Presently Tom again heard the low dull rumble.

"There," he said.

"Shore. That's genuine thunder, an' it means rain for this stinkin' dusty hot range. Listen some more, Tom."

The two men stood apart, Pilchuck favouring his right ear, Tom his left; and they remained motionless. Several times the mutter of thunder, distinct now to Tom, caused the scout to nod his head.

"Reckon that's not what I'm expectin'," he said gloomily. "An' we've no time to stand here all day. Listen hard, Tom. You're younger than me."

Tom's sluggish blood quickened a little. He had been two years with this old plainsman, during which there had been numberless instances of his sagacity and vision, and remarkable evidences of experience.

Pilchuck was worrying about that herd of buffalo. Thereupon Tom bent lower, held his breath, and strained his ear with all intensity possible. Again he heard the muttering long rumble, then the beat of his heart, the stir of his hair over his temple, the sweep of wind. Thunder again! That was all; and he abandoned the strain.

"Nothin' but storm," he told Pilchuck.

"I reckon my ears are old, an' my imagination makes me think I hear things," returned the scout. "But a moment ago...Try again. I want to be *shore*."

Thus incited, Tom lent himself to as sensitive and profound listening as was possible for him. This time he seemed to hear the thunder as before, somewhat louder; and under it another, fainter sound, an infinitely low roar that did not die out, that went on and on, deadened by another mutter of thunder, and then, when this was gone, beginning again, low, strange, unceasing.

Then he straightened up and told Pilchuck what he had heard. How sharply and intelligently the scout's grey eyes flashed! He made no reply except to raise one of his brawny hands. Leaving it extended, he froze in the attitude of an Indian listening. Tom again let his ear to the strengthening breeze. Thunder—then a long, low menancing roar—thunder again—and roar! He made his own deductions and, lifting his head, waited for the scout to speak. Long did Pilchuck maintain that tense posture. He was a slow, deliberate man on occasions. Sometimes he would act with the most incredible speed. Here he must have been studying the volume, direction, and distance of this thrilling sound, and not its cause. Suddenly, his big brown hand clenched and shot down to crack into the palm of the other. He wheeled to Tom, with grey lightning in his eyes.

"Stampede! The whole herd!" he ejaculated. "I've been expectin' it for days."

Then he gazed across the northern horizon of the prairie round to the point due east.

"You notice we can see only four or five miles," he

111

said. "The prairie rises slow for about that distance, then dips. That'd deaden sound as well as hide any movin' thing. We can't be shore that herd is far away. Funny how we run into things. Reckon we'd better ride!"

They mounted, and were off at a gallop that gave place to a run. Tom had lost his fleet, faithful Dusty, and was now riding a horse, strong, sound, and fairly fast, but no match for Pilchuck's hunter. So Tom fell behind gradually. He did not goad the horse, though he appreciated Pilchuck's brief hint of danger.

The scout rode east, quartering towards the river, and passed a couple of miles out from where he and Tom had stopped at the ford. Tom gradually fell behind until he was full a quarter of a mile in the rear. As long as he could keep Pilchuck in sight he did not have any anxiety about the separation. The horse could run, and he was surefooted. Tom believed he would acquit himself well, even in a gruelling race with the buffalo. It seemed strange to be running away from an unseen danger. While riding he could not hear anything save the rhythmic beat of hoofs and rush of wind. He observed that the direction Pilchuck had chosen was just a point east of the center of the black storm cloud. Far to its right showed the dim fringe of river timber. There was a wide distance between the end of that cloud and the river, most of which was gently sloping prairie. He had a keen eagerness to know what could be seen beyond the long ridgetop.

Next time he gazed at Pilchuck he was amazed to see him pulling his horse to a halt. Tom rode on with eyes now intent. The scout reined in and leaped out of the saddle. He ran a few paces from the horse, and stopped to lie flat on the ground. Tom realised that Pilchuck was listening with an ear close to the earth. The action startled Tom. Not improbably the situation was growing serious. Pilchuck lay a moment, then got up and stood like a statue. Then he abruptly broke his rigid posture and leaped astride. But instead of riding off he waited there, face to the north. Tom rapidly overhauled him and pulled his mount to a stand.

112

"Jude, what's wrong? he called sharply.

"I ain't shore, but I'm damned scared," replied the scout.

"Why? I can't see or hear anything."

"See that yellow dust way to the right of the black sky. Look! It's movin'! I'm afraid if we go farther this way we'll get headed off an' run into the river. We could cross, but it'd take time, an' when we got over we might have to run south. That's never do. We've got to go east or west."

"Jude, I hear a roar," said Tom.

"Shore. So do I. But it was the movin' dust that stopped me. Keep still now an' let me figger. If I've any prairie cunnin' left, we're in a hell of a fix. We've got to do what's right—an' quick."

Therefore Tom attended to sight of the low, rounded yellow cloud of dust. It did move, apparently slowly, and spread to the right. Against the background of purple sky it held something ominous. Tom watched it rise gradually to the left, though in this direction it did not spread along the prairie so rapidly. The ground sloped that way, and the ridge-top stretched higher than the level of the east, where the dust now rolled plainly. The roar was a dull, distant rumble, steady and ear-filling, though not at all loud. It was a deceiving sound, and might be closer than it seemed or farther away.

Suddenly it became loud. It startled Tom. He turned to see what Pilchuck made of that. The scout sat his fidgety horse, with his head extended, his long neck craned forward. Suddenly he jerked back as if struck.

"Doan, *look*!" he shouted in a tone Tom had never before heard. His voice seemed to merge into a rolling tumble.

Tom wheeled. Along the whole of the prairie horizon had appeared a black, bobbing line of buffalo. Above them rose the yellow dust and beyond that spread the storm-cloud of purple. The ragged front of the herd appeared to creep over the ridge-top, like an horizon-wide tide, low, flat, and black. Towards the west the level grey horizon was being blotted out with

113

exceeding swiftness as the herd came in sight. It spread like a black smoke, flying low. To the east the whole space before noted by Tom had been clouded with black and yellow. The front line of the herd then did not appear to be straight across; it was curving from the right.

One moment Tom gazed, rapt, thrilling, then his blood gushed out. The great herd was at last on the stampede, not five miles distant, running downhill!

"By God! we're in a trap!" yelled Pilchuck hoarsely. "We've only one chance. Follow me an' ride!"

He spurred and wheeled his horse and, goading him into a run, headed for the river ford. Tom spurred after him, finding now that his horse, frightened by the roar, could keep up with Pilchuck's. They ran straight away from the eastern front of the herd, which was curving in and quartering away from the western front. Tom had ridden fast before, but Pilchuck's start bade fair to lead him into the swiftest race of his experience on the range. He was aware of drawing away somewhat from the roar in the rear; on his right, however, the sound augmented. Tom gazed around. His eyes, blurred from the rush of wind, showed a league-wide band of black, sliding down the prairie slope, widening, spreading. He did not look behind.

Pilchuck's fleet horse began to draw ahead. The old scout was riding as he had never ridden away from Comanches. Tom remembered what fear these old plainsmen had of the buffalo stampede. It was the terror of the plains, more appalling than the prairie fire. Comanches could be fought; fires could be outridden or back-fired, but the stampede of buffalo was a rolling sea of swift, insane beasts. With spur and fist and voice Tom urged his horse to its utmost, and kept the distance between him and Pilchuck from widening farther.

Both horses now were on a headlong run strained to the breaking point. The wind hissed by Tom's ears, swayed him back in his saddle. On both sides the grey prairie slid by indistinct, a blurred expanse over which he seemed to sail. He could not see the river depression,

114

but before long he made out the rocky eminence that marked the site of the ford. Pilchuck's intention now was plain. At first Tom had imagined the scout meant to try to cross the river ahead of the herd; now, however, he was making for the high point of rock. This realisation unclamped Tom's cold doubt. If the horses did not fall, they could make that place of safety. Pilchuck was fifty feet ahead, and not only was he driving the horse at breakneck speed, but he was guiding him over what appeared the smoother ground. Tom caught the slight variations in the course and the swerving aside; and he had only to follow.

The straining horse broke his stride, caught it again, stretched on, and plunged to the bare rise of rocky ground. Tom hauled with all his strength on the bridle. He checked the maddened animal, but could not stop him. Pilchuck stood ten feet above the bank. He had dismounted. Both hands were uplifted in a gesture of awe. Tom leaped off just as the horse slowed before the first rocky bench. Dragging him up, Tom climbed to Pilchuck, who seemed to yell at him. But Tom heard no voice. The rocky eminence was about half an acre in extent, and high enough above the bank to split the herd. Tom dropped the bridle and whirled in fear and wonder.

His first thought when he saw the ragged, sweeping tide of beasts still a third of a mile distant, was that he would have had time to spare. The herd had not been so close as his imagination had pictured.

Pilchuck dragged at Tom, pulling him higher on the rock. The scout put his mouth close to Tom's ear and manifestly yelled. But Tom heard no voice; felt only a soundless, hot breath. His ears were distending with a terrific thunder. His eyes were protruding at an awful spectacle.

Yet he saw that sweep of buffalo with a marvellous distinctness, with the swift leap of emotion which magnified all his senses. Across the level front of his vision spread a ragged, shaggy black wall of heads, humps, hoofs, coming at the speed of buffalo on the stampede. On a hard run! The sea of bobbing backs beyond disappeared in a yellow pall of dust curled aloft and hung low, and kept almost the speed of the front rank. Above the moving mantle of dust farther back showed the grey pall of storm. Lightning flashed in vivid white streaks. But there was no thunder from above. The thunder rolled low along the ground.

Suddenly, his ears ceased to function. He could no longer hear. The sense had been outdone. There was no sound. But he saw yet the mighty onsweep, majestic, irresistible, an army of maddened beasts on the stampede, shaking the earth. The rock under his feet began to tremble. It was no longer stable. He felt the queer vibration, and the sensation added to his terror.

Transfixed, Tom awaited the insupportable moment for the rolling front ranks to reach the rock, either to roll over it like a tidal wave, or split round it. The moment was an age. Pilchuck was holding to him. Tom was holding to Pilchuck. The solid earth seemed about to cave in under them. Shaggy black heads bobbing swiftly, gleam of horns, and flash of wild eyes, hoofs, hoofs sweeping out, out, out—and the awful moment was at hand.

The shaggy flood split round the rock and two streams of rounded wooly backs, close-pressed as water, swift as a millrace, poured over the bank towards the river.

Pilchuck dragged Tom away from the back position to the front of the rock. As if by supernatural magic the scene was changed. Below, far on each side, the mass of buffalo spilled over the embankment to plunge into the river. Up and down the water-line spread white splashes; and over and into them leaped the second ranks of buffalo, too close to miss the first. Then what had momentarily been ranks on the slope closed up into a solid mass of black. Bulge and heave—great sheets of muddy water—a terrible writhing massing forward along that irregular front! Then the tide of buffalo swept on, over, once more a flat, level multitude of heads and bumps, irrepressible as an avalanche. They

116

crossed the river on the run; the stampede had been only momentarily retarded. Downriver below the ford, as far as the eye could see, stretched lines of buffalo swimming swiftly, like an endless flock of enormous geese. Upriver stretched the same, as far as the eye could see. The slope of the prairie to the water was one solid mass of buffalo, moving as one beast, impelled by motive as wild as the action. Above swept the dust, blowing as a storm wind from the prairie. Curling like a yellow curtain of smoke, it followed the buffalo across the river, up the long slope and out upon the prairie. Tom and Pilchuck were on that level between the moving dust above and the moving buffalo below. All views back towards the prairie whence the herd rolled were soon obliterated. Likewise the front ranks of the great mass disappeared on the opposite side under this accompanying mantle. But the river, for a while, lay clear to their gaze, miles up and miles down, and all visible space of water and ground was covered with buffalo. Buffalo more numerous than a band of ants on the march!

Suddenly night seemed to intervene. A gale swooped the dust away across the river; and in place of a yellow curling curtain of dust there came a slanting, grey pall of rain. It blackened as the grey light grew less. Blazing streaks of lightning played through the grey gloom. But if there was thunder above, it could not be heard in the thunder below.

Pilchuck drew Tom under a narrow shelf of rock, where, half protected from the deluge, they crouched in the semi-darkness. What seemed hours passed. Yet there was no end to the passing of the great herd. The rain ceased, the sky lightened and cleared, and clearer grew the black mantling of prairie and river. All was buffalo, except the sky. Then the sun broke out of the clouds.

Tom's stunned senses rallied enough for him to appreciate the grandeur and beauty suddenly given the scene by a glorious sheen of gold and purple streaming down from the rifts between the clouds. The dust was gone. The thousands of shining black backs moved on and on, rapidly, ponderously, swallowed up by the haze of the disappearing storm. And still the buffalo came over the prairie, obscuring the ground.

But at last the time came when the mass showed breaks in the ranks and then, in the rear line, more ragged than had been the fore. Tom's hearing seemed gradually to be restored. That, he realised, was only the diminishing of the vast volume of sound to the point where it was no longer deafening. It was a blood-deadening thunder that gradually lessened as the end of the herd rolled on from prairie, down over the bank, and across the river.

The thundering herd swept on out of sight. And the thunder became a roar, the roar a rumble, and the rumble died away. Pilchuck rose to his lofty height and peered across the river, into grey haze and purple distance that had swallowed up the buffalo. He seemed to be a man who had lived through something terrible.

"The last herd!" he said with pathos. "They've crossed the Brazos an' they'll never come back. The storm of rain was like the storm of lead that'll follow them."

Tom also got dizzily to his feet and faced south. What he felt about the last herd could not be spoken.

"Jude, I'm—going—north!" exclaimed Tom.

"Shake!" replied the old scout, quick as a flash, as he extended his brawny hand.

CHAPTER 8

From the crest of the long prairie slope beginning to colour brown and gold in the September sun, Tom Doan gazed down at the place that had been Sprague's Post. It had grown almost unrecognisable. Ranches dotted the beautiful sweep of fertile land. Near at hand the river wound away, hidden in green foliage, and far out on the plain it glistened in the sunlight.

The long wagon-train of hides and camp outfits lumbered across the prairie to enter the outskirts of the Post and haul up on the green square between the town and the river. Huts and cabins had taken the place of tents. Still, there were new wagons and outfits belonging to hunters bound for the buffalo range. Tom wanted to cry out about the pains and blunders they were so cheerfully and ignorantly travelling to meet.

Big wagon-trains such as this were always encountered at the Post. News travelled ahead of such large caravans; and there was a crowd on the green. There were half a dozen wagons ahead of the one Tom drove, and the last of these was Pilchuck's. The lean old scout was at once surrounded by hunters eager to learn news of the buffalo range.

Tom saw Burn Hudnall and Dave Stronghurl before they saw him. How well they looked—fuller of face and not so bronzed as when they had ridden the open range! Eager and excited also, they appeared to Tom. They would be glad to see him. If only he could avoid meeting their womenfolk! Then Burn espied him and made at him. Tom dropped the knotted reins over the brake with a movement of finality, and stepped down out of the wagon.

"Howdy, boys? It's sure good to see you," he said heartily.

They grasped him with hands almost rough, so forceful were they; and both greeted him at once in a kind of suppressed joy, incoherent and noisy, all the more welcoming for that. Then they hung on to him, one at each side.

"Say, have you boys taken to drink?" retorted Tom, to conceal how their warmth affected him. "I haven't just come back to life."

"Tom, I—we—all of us was afraid you'd never come," burst out Burn. "You look fine. Thin, mebbe, an' hard...My Gawd! I'm glad!"

"Tom—I've got a baby—a boy!" beamed Dave, his strong, smug face alight.

"You don't say! Dave, shake on that...I'm sure glad. How time flies! It doesn't seem so long—"

"We've got other news, but the best of it'll keep till we get to the ranch," interrupted Burn. "Tom, I've got that five hundred acres father liked so well. Remember? You can buy next to me, along the river. Dave has thrown in with Sprague. The town's boomin'! We've a bank, a church, and a school. An' wait till you see the teacher! She's—"

He rambled on like a boy, to be silenced by Dave's look. Then Dave began and, being more practical, he soon got out Tom's bag and gun and roll of blankets.

"You're comin' with us this hyar very minnit," he concluded as Tom tried to make excuses. "Burn, grab some of his outfit. Reckon this team an' wagon belongs to Pilchuck?"

"Yes, it does," replied Tom.

"Come along," went on Dave. "We've orders to fetch you home before these hyar town girls set eyes on you."

They dragged Tom and his belongings out of the crowd, pushed him up into a spring-wagon, and while Burn piled his baggage in the back, Dave climbed up beside him and started a team of spirited horses out along the river road.

If the welcome accorded Tom by Burn and Dave had touched him, that given by their women-folk reached deeply to his heart. They were all at the front of Burn's fine ranch-house. Burn's wife was weeping, it seemed, for joy; and Sally Stronghurl gave Tom a resounding kiss, to his consternation. Mrs. Hudnall, whose motherly face showed the ravages of grief, greeted him in a way that made Tom ashamed of how he had forgotten these good people. She took possession of him and led him indoors ahead of the others. They had all seemed strange, hurried, suppressing something. They were not as Tom remembered. Alas! had he grown away from wholesome simplicity? They wanted to welcome him to their home.

Mrs. Hudnall shut the door. Tom had a sense that the room was large, lighted by windows at each end. Clearing his throat, he turned to speak. But Mrs. Hudnall's working face, her tear-wet eyes made him dumb. There was something wrong here.

"Tom, you're changed," she began hurriedly. "No boy any more! I can see how it hurts you to come back to us."

"Yes, because of—of Milly," he replied simply. "But you musn't think I'm not glad to see you all. I am. You're my good friends. I'm ashamed I never appreciated you as I should have. But that hard life out there—"

"Don't," she interrupted huskily. "You know how it hurt me. But, Tom, never mind the past. Think of the present."

"My heart's buried in the past. It seems so long ago. So short a time to remember! I—"

"Didn't you ever think Milly might not have been

lost?" she asked.

"Yes, I thought that—till hope died," replied Tom slowly.

"My boy—we heard she wasn't killed—or captured—or anything," said Mrs. Hudnall softly.

"Heard she wasn't? My God! That would only torture me," replied Tom poignantly. He felt himself shaking.

"Tom, we *know* she wasn't."

He staggered back suddenly, released from bewilderment. He realized now. That had been the secret of their excitement, their strangeness. His consciousness grasped the truth. Milly Fayre was not dead.

"Milly is here," said Mrs. Hudnall. "We tried again and again to send you word, but we always missed you. Milly has lived here—ever since she escaped from Jett—and the Indians. She's taught school. She is well—happy. She has waited for you.

Mrs. Hudnall pushed back the door and went out. Some one slipped in. A girl—a woman, white of face, with parted lips and great, radiant black eyes! Could this be Milly Fayre?

"*Oh—Tom!*" she burst out in a broken voice, deep and low. She took a forward step, with hands extended.

122

John Silver's Revenge

November had laid its drab hand over the rangeland. The dismal croak of raven broke the dull, soundless day. Clouds hung lowering over the dreary waste of plain and ridge, and the dim distant mountains. Purple gloom filled the valleys; sombre colors merged on the shaggy slopes; under the grey stone bluffs above the road the vines and sumach showed dull red, faded and seared.

The day, the journey, the desert of ridge and range seemed made for the hard errand that had driven Jane Silver to Hillands.

"Mother, let me down. I can walk some. You must be tired," said the child.

"I'm glad—we're up the hill," panted the mother as she put Lily down.

Low squat houses of mud and stone dotted the slop; gray weatherbeaten cottages clustered below them, looking down upon the flat roofs of Hillands. The town had once been prosperous, before the mines in the hill had failed, and the hordes of cattle roamed the ranges. Up in the notches of the hills were black ruins of mills, and along the winding road were old taverns with their high-walled bleached fronts. Down the deserted irrigation canal rose patches of weeds on bare dry beds of cracked mud. All these were doleful reminders to Jane Silver of the lapse of years.

Yet, after all, it was not so long, judged by actual time. Her memory in one flash transported her back to the ranch and the range of her girlhood. She saw her father, the prosperous old cattleman, loud-voiced, with slap of hand on knee; her mother, sweet of smile, ever busy at her tasks; brothers and sisters who had teased her, loved her in that swift-fading time of girlhood. School days, vacation days, the long rides with the cowboys! She walked again with lovers under the cottonwoods, not sure even now, in this bitter memory, of the one she had loved best. The smell of cedar smoke came back to her, of burning brush, of the horse corrals, and the cornshocks in the barn. There were faces that shone for her and flashed dark upon one another. She saw the rangeland white with snow, she heard the jingling music of sleigh bells, and she felt the smooth rush of the wagon-sled on the way to the dance. The laughter of girls and the banter of boys filled this haunting memory. Always she had slipped a sly hand to a lover on each side in the darkness, merry in her deceit, yet not unconscious of guile. That had been her undoing.

Gray and grim in contrast, returned the world of her womanhood. John Silver had been her father's choice, more than hers; yet John, older, graver than the cowboys, a splendid figure of a man, had appealed to the best in her, had seemed an anchor for her secret and wandering passion for conquest. And she had married him. Bond of marriage with its disillusion! She could not be tamed. Worst of all, she could not endure jealousy and suspicion. Then with these phantoms of her past, stood out the great shock, the dividing line, the error of her life. Jim Warner, rider of the ranges, debonair and romantic, a handsome devil, saw her and loved her. Something violent and desperate in the depths of her being had called to its like. After three months of marriage with John Silver, bitterly brought to task for the last time, she had let his jealous rage make of her the madwoman she had never been—and she had eloped with Jim Warner. Then came disgrace, slow desertion by friends and family, abandonment, cruel years of want, and now catastrophe.

"Mother, after all, you must carry me," said the child.

The appeal brought Jane Silver back to the saddest and most poignant and terrible errand ever undertaken by a mother. She lifted Lily again—how light a burden!—up the worn red stone steps of Judge Silver's house. The sun peeped out of a rift in the clouds and made a warm spot on the Judge's porch. Lily, clasping an apple, sat down to rest. She panted a little and drops of sweat stood upon her blue-veined forehead. Over Lily hovered something shadowy, mystical, spiritual, and it softened the mother's pain.

Jane knocked as one knocked on the door of doom. It opened wide and a man filled the narrow space. He was lean and dark, vastly changed, yet somehow there was a thrill in her recognition. John Silver had never divorced her, had never loved another woman. For a moment amazement appeared to hold him transfixed.

"Jane!" he ejaculated incredulously, and he took a quick step. Then he seemed to shrink. "So. It's the Judge you're heah to see," he added, bitterly. "Wal, come in."

A different kind of past came back to Jane. To see the man she had wronged, to realize the havoc she had wrought, hurt more than any memory. Yet if John Silver had suffered the rust of actionless years, if he had shown the corroding lichen of hate, Jane felt she might have borne this ordeal.

"John—Judge Silver, I've been driven to come," replied Jane, hoarsely. "The doctor says my girl, Lily, is failing. Oh, God, it's hard! I've nothing, no people, no friends who will help me. And those old women at Turners, where I live, they say if there's a call on the county to bury anyone, the application must be made to the county magistrate *before* ..."

"Wal, wal, so that's your errand," returned Judge Silver. "Where's your child?"

"She's outside, resting," said Jane, hurriedly. "You won't need to see her, will you?"

"I reckon so. An' why not?" he queried, with the lightning of his gray eyes on her.

"I've no reason, no sensible one," went on Jane, painfully. "But I hoped it wouldn't be necessary. Lily is such a strange child. Not like other little girls! I never understood her. I'm afraid. Oh! so terribly afraid she knows what my life has been."

"I reckon I'll have to send for Doctor Bartle an' let him see her," replied the Judge.

"Lily was low yesterday. She has queer spells. Today she'd bright. Oh, she's uncanny sometimes. It wrings my heart. But she's so sweet, so lovable, so like an angel. Then she was the smartest girl in her class. I had to take her out of school. I've never been sure it was the study that broke down her health."

"Ha! Outcast mother, outcast child!" returned Silver. "How old is she now?"

"Nine years. Nine this month."

"Only nine! Wal, wal, I reckoned it seemed longer than that, since . . ." rejoined the Judge. "It's too bad. Poor little girl! She wasn't to blame. The sins of the parents are visited upon the children."

"Judge Silver, I'm deathly afraid. If she learns why I'm here . . . Oh, she mustn't know. I beg of you."

"Wal, I reckon I've no call to be kind to Jim Warner's child, but I'd never let her know, that's shore. Jane, there's no law about this county buryin' the dead. In fact the magistrate is the law. If the doctor says your child is dyin', then I'll decide on the case."

Jane could not utter her thanks, nor make another appeal on behalf of the errand that had forced her to face him. She sat clasping and unclasping her hands, questioning this lean austere face with piercing eyes. The woman in her sensed the wrong never forgotten, never avenged; the mother in her feared the righteous wrath of one whose opportunity had come, who must indeed be noble to withstand the temptation fate had thrust upon him. Yet, she had it in her power to change his hate, to rob his revenge of its sweetness, thought she might not break his will. Locked deep in her heart hid this power, and no scorn, no humiliation, no flaying her could ever bring it to light.

"Heah, Jane," he said, "swear on this Bible to tell the truth an' nothin' but the truth."

She heard some one within her, who seemed other than herself, repeating after him the words of the oath. As one fascinated, she watched his slow deliberate movements, his turning the leaves of an old ledger.

How absurd, aside from the point, these queries were as to her people, her birth, her age, whether she was married or single, her occupation, and proofs of poverty! Methodically he wrote down answers that he well knew without asking. Then all at once a change came over him. He looked up to face her with eyes she found hard to meet, and began more deliberate questioning, beginning with relation to the present hour and working back toward the past.

He would have the detailed story of her journey from Turners to Hillands. He probed the reason of her errand. He would have knowledge of where she lived and how she lived, of the poverty and sickness of her household. When Jim Warner had deserted her! What that abandonment had meant! He wanted to know the actions and the gossip of her neighbors. Then the years she had followed Jim Warner from range to range; and so on, endlessly back to the staggering fact of her downfall.

Jane realized now that her appeal to Judge Silver as the dispenser of county charity had been laid aside, that she must face him woman to man, and drain this cup of gall to the dregs. Not to answer never occurred to her. She had to speak. She was on trial to bare her soul, to confess that the wrong she had done him had earned its retribution, to feed some abnormal passion of curiosity and agony in him. She saw him slowly transforming under the poignant influence of a love recalled from its grave. His lean face and figure took on the lines of his youth.

No longer did it seem the dry, worn judge who arraigned her, but the dishonored and discarded husband, leonine in his wrath, white-faced, strong, and terrible. He laid stark and naked the facts of her elopement with Warner. If she had any shame, his fury and his will beat it down, so that she confessed even the miserable kisses she had bestowed upon her lover. The smothered jealousy of the years demanded fuel for its insatiable fire. Jane told him all. Self-abasement and degradation were hers to the fullest.

Then he got no farther than the catastrophe of his

life. He repeated, "You jilted me, dishonored me, disgraced me, abandoned me? Yes! You never loved me?" he thundered.

"Ah, John! You cannot make me confess that," she replied sadly. "I did love you. But I was a wild thing, hateful of restraint. If you had understood me, I'd never have ruined both our lives. If you had not been jealous and had not unjustly suspected me of dishonor, I'd never have betrayed you."

That stabbed him. The quiver of his intense face told how the truth struck mortally home. Jane had never understood until then the boundlessness of what his love had been. She felt in the presence of an appalling revelation, something unquenchable as the fire of the sun, an emotion which made her long-past wayward infatuation so base and pitiful. If, as a young wife, she could only have gauged the depths of this man's love! What might have been! Across the years now, from her woman's travail, she saw John Silver clearly.

"Woman, wife still, do you come to me?" he thundered, beating his breast with clenched fist. "Do you come heah beggin' me to save your child from the paupers' field?"

"Yes, John, I've come, replied Jane. "What's done is done. God only knows how it happened or why! It can't be undone. But if I had my life to live over, I'd never wrong you."

He towered over her for a silent, endless moment, while the white passion of his face gave place to a more normal hue. He changed again, though not back to the Judge Silver he had been. There remained something of the old John Silver.

"Wal, Jane," he said at last, sighing heavily. "I'll do what you ask. Meanwhile, you an' Lily stay heah with my folks, until . . ."

It was another afternoon, and Jane Silver sat by Lily's bedside, haunted by the shadow in the child's eyes.

A fly buzzed behind the window-shade, telling of the

autumn sunshine warm upon the pane. Lily lay with wide questioning gaze that seemed to grow wise. The soft lips were locked. After a while she closed her eyelids, dreamy and heavy with mystic thought, and lay as one asleep. Did she really sleep?

Jane Silver was used to long vigils by the bedside. But this one seemed to inaugurate a subtle change. The afternoon faded into twilight and then the gloom of early evening, which was the time when Jane's mind began to awaken and quicken. Soft footfalls sounded through the house. John Silver's old mother and his sister were busy preparing the evening meal. Low voices and faint steps came from the Judge's office. Jane's cold heart warmed as she thought of their quiet sympathy and kindness; and amazement, too, sometimes filled the brief intervals in which she wandered from the stern grief of the moment.

From outside the house there penetrated sounds somehow full of inscrutable meaning for her. Compared with the hamlet of Turners, this old town of Hillands was bustling with people walking and riding by. Footsteps! Clip-clop! Sauntering and hurrying steps passed along the road, and the jingle of spurs lent her a thrill. Could she ever hear that musical clink without a strange stir deep in her heart? For years she had listened for that sound; and then for more years she had listened from sad habit, not with hope. Here she was sitting in the first darkness of the November night, by the bedside of her dying child. And from outside came haunting sounds, sounds typical of the rangeland, clinking steps, trotting hoofs, roll of buckboard and freighter, the young, fresh, drawling voices of cowboys. These passers-by were unknown to Jane, yet seemed to come out of her past life. They had a message, but its meaning was not clear.

Later, when the black lonely night settled down over the house, Jane felt that she would be undisturbed in her vigil. But the wind from the rangeland moaned under the eaves; dead cottonwood leaves rustled over the ground, softly brushed the house, whispered of the coming of winter and ice and death, were silent, and then stirred again to a sad rustle. Mice gnawed at the wood in the wall, squeaked, and ran with tiny thrumming footsteps. The silence of the night hummed noiselessly—the wheels of life whirling and whirring on toward the end.

Through the window Jane watched a pale circle of light grow brighter over the black mountains. At length a white cold moving radiance silvered the cedars. Moonlight streamed into the room. On a white patch of floor the shadow of a swinging bough moved regularly, silently, weirdly. It swayed beyond the window to leave clear the moon-blanched square; it returned as steadily. It was a long dark moving finger pointing to a fateful hour. Light! Shadow!

Along the floor crept the square of moonlight, as if the time had come for it to sever its relation with the weird shadow of bough. It crept to the bed, slowly up the coverlet, slowly turning to marble Lily's frail hands, at last to illumine her face. How pure and strange and sad! But had Lily's suffering been physical? Whence that look of age, of wisdom, unreal on the beautiful face?

Jane Silver could not bear it; she shut out the moonlight. Yet that helped so little. Always, when Lily slept, there seemed another presence in the room. In slumber she was different from what she was awake. In the change from moonlight to opaque gloom, a deathlike whiteness hovered on Lily's face. Jane bent suddenly down closer, straining at the fierce pang in her breast. No, the child still lived. But was that an altered look, a slow, anguished passing from doubt to certainty? What did Lily know? Jane Silver shrank pitifully from the question that now knocked at the gates of her soul. Should she not have told Lily the truth? Then came a whisper out of the night, out of the past, out of the life she had pierced in thought, whence Lily was soon to flee; and it was not a whisper of hope, nor of peace, but of endurance.

The blackness paled, the gray light brightened, and

Lily's birthday dawned. Jane felt that the gentle life of the child had completed its cycle. Birth to death! Nine years that should have been the fleeting dreamful happy time of childhood! But Jane had begun to be dimly conscious that for Lily these years, almost from babyhood, had been travail. Something had forced the child's mind far beyond her age.

This day, then, Jane divined, would bring the rending climax of her sufferings.

She sat between the bed and the window, and when Lily slept, Jane would gaze down over the quaint old town, out to the dark mountains and the purple rangeland. This day November had gone back to October. Gone were the gray clouds, the gray mists in the valleys, the gray mantle of the peaks, and the gray gloom that veiled the distant ranges.

The sky was blue as the sea; great white cumulus clouds rolled over the mountain horizon; the sun shone gloriously and a fall wind whirled up the golden dust-funnels, and swept them pirouetting and expanding, far out on the bleached range.

Time had been when Jane Silver's heart had throbbed with love for this rangeland, so free, so vast, so unbounded. Undulating plain and swelling ridge! How they enfolded with their deceiving distance the many leagues! They seemed the same as in her youth. Red and white cattle dotted the foreground. A long meandering line of cottonwoods, half bare and half with dead leaves, marked the course of the canal. A patch of trees, a little shack and windmill, scattered here and there, removed this swelling plain from the aspect of a desert. Beyond them it spread and rolled, growing purple in the distance. She felt herself a part of that rangeland, but she had failed it. The glory and freedom and simplicity of the open had been hers all her girlhood, but she had not taken them into her being.

The mountain kingdom Jane had found in her womanhood to be a better teacher, because it did not haunt her with regret and remorse. All her life the mountains had been distant, an unknown land, barrier from the wilderness beyond. All this day the purple peaks ministered to her. In the clear light she saw the seams and scars of age, the pale cliffs, and the dark canyons. She saw the shadows of the cloud-ships sailing along their slopes. These upflung domes of rock were mute monuments to the travail of the earth. They taught endurance. Lift up thine eyes to the mountains whence cometh thy help!

Had they been the secret of John Silver's strength? Jane trembled when she thought of this man. Lover and husband, yet a stranger to her in those wild years of her girlhood! She asked herself why. Only because she had been a shallow, vain, ignorant child whom no one could understand. If she could only have called back the past! Then John Silver had every reason to despise instead of love her. Jane remembered his patience, his long talks, his hopes and prayers, entailed in the futile longing to make her a woman.

And now he loomed a strange and vast figure in her anguished mind. His old mother had spared Jane any look or word of reproach. She expressed pity for Jane and love for the child. But with pride, perhaps with purpose, she had talked of her son, John. And all the fixed hateful impressions of Jane's memory were suddenly as if they had never been. She had never known John Silver. Now she saw him through the wide-open eyes of womanhood. They, swiftly, strangely, her abasement flooded out on the tide of passionate exultance. He had loved her greatly, he had never remarried, he had climbed above hate, scorn, revenge. Ah! he might love her still! But that sweet wild thought died at its tumultuous birth. It was the last gasp of the vanity that had been the bane of her life. Jane sighed. Poor incomprehensible creature she was!

There came a tap on the door. Jane rose noiselessly and, opening it, she encountered John Silver on the threshold. His fine dark face showed signs of recent agitation. He entered the room with a strange glance toward the quiet figure on the bed.

"Is she asleep?" he whispered.

132

"Yes. She's slept on and off all day," replied Jane.

"I've been to Turners," added the Judge, abruptly. Jane's lips formed a query she could not speak.

"Jane, I wanted to know about you," he said, answering her look. "So I went. Why didn't you tell me how, how poor you'd been? I reckoned I'd saved you that. I never knew. No one ever spoke of you to me. Jane, those damned gabby women at Turners! Shore they riled me. Why'd they hate you so? Because you were pretty, I reckon. Wal, wal, that's no great matter. But what they said about Lily hurt me deep."

"I'm sorry. Tell me what it was," faltered Jane, with a numbness creeping over her.

"They say the children taunted Lily," replied Silver, darkly. "They say she's known for years that she's nameless. Jim Warner's child! That that's what ailed her!"

"Oh, heaven, of late I feared, and now I know!" whispered Jane. Her life fell around her in utter ruin. How mocking and terrible the result of her blind pride to hide and spare! Some day, a little later, Lily would be old enough to understand, to pity her mother—that had been the shibboleth. Too late! The innocent child had suffered for the guilty mother.

"Jane—" whispered the Judge, leaning down with a strong and beautiful light on his face, "she shall be buried as Lily Silver."

"What do you mean?" gasped Jane.

"I've never divorced you, Jane. You're still my wife. Lily must have my name. You shall stay heah. My home is your home, as it would be Lily's if by the grace of God she could live."

"You'll take me back? Give my child your name before the world!"

"Jane, I reckon so. I love you still."

With bursting heart Jane sought to cry out her agony, to fall before him and clasp his feet, to find utterance for a mighty and mounting storm, to wrench from her depths what now seemed the hate and revenge of a wayward girl.

133

"John, come with me," she whispered. Though she led him, it seemed she needed his support. And he clung to her, as one in a dream.

"Is she asleep?" he asked, husky and low. Indeed he feared she was asleep forever.

The light fell upon a face as white as snow, framed with golden curls. Only the closed mystic eyelids suggested pain. The mouth was sweet, as if about to break into faint smile of relief.

"John, look at her. Lily is your child!"

He uttered a choked cry, gazed with intense fixity at the strangely changing face, turned to Jane with staring eyes of anguished rapture, and back to the child.

"My God! My God! I—never—dreamed. O Jane, I see, I believe!"

And he fell upon his knees beside the bed.

Suddenly Lily's eyes opened wide. They seemed like windows of a soul in transport.

"Mother, I wasn't asleep," she said with a smile that seemed not of earth. "I heard you both." And she burst into tears.

Jane bent in fear and trembling over the bed. Not for years had Lily cried. The little white face quivered as she turned to the Judge.

"You're my—honest father," she sobbed.

"Yes, dear. But I never knew till now," he replied, huskily.

"Everybody will know. I will tell them. My father! I am not going to die!"

On Location

The tracks of Wesley's strayed horse led up the cedar slope and over the windy ridge-top into the pines. A roar of motor trucks heavily loaded came from the road down beyond the green slope. Wesley emerged presently at the edge of Bonito Park, where the forest thinned out and ended in the grassy oval shining like a silver lake under the black-belted white covered peaks.

A dark thread of road bisected the valley. Along it cars were moving, headed Wesley's way toward the desert. Riders appeared to be rounding up a big drove of horses. Wesley halted to light a cigarette, his eyes studying this scene, so unusual for lonely Bonito Park. A truck without sides rolled along. Sight of it, loaded with gleaming airplane propeller and engine, recalled to Wesley that Meteor Pictures had been on location there filming a western.

Then Wesley espied his horse, Sarchedon, cantering around near the other horses, raising the dust like a colt.

"He would, the son-of-a-gun," soliloquized Wesley, as he rode on. "That darn hawse is shore ruined. Ever since I lent him to Lee for that last movie!"

Trucks loaded with camping equipment and supplies passed Wesley into the forest. Evidently the company was going down into the Painted Desert. By the time Wesley rode up to the cabins that marked the site where the company had camped, the two score and more of horses had been bunched. Some were tossing nosebags high and others were kicking and snorting for grain. This bunch of thoroughbreds belonged to a friend of Wesley's, Lee Hornell, and Arizonian who had made big money with the motion picture companies.

As Wesley approached the horses, he passed several

135

parked automobiles, all occupied by actors, still with their make-up and costumes on. In the last car a strikingly beautiful blonde fixed flashing blue eyes upon him. Wesley stared back at her.

Then slim, hawk-nosed, red-faced Lee Hornell left a group at the road-side and called: "Howdy, Wess. Took you plumb long to find us here. We're leavin' for Red Lake."

"Howdy, Lee. Didn't know anything about it. What's that airplane propellor for?"

"Say, you backwoods cow-puncher, that's to throw up a dust storm!"

"Dog-gone! These movie hombres are shore queer. I reckon you could use an elephant."

"You bet. Have you got one?"

"Shore have. A white elephant. That danged hawse of mine, Sarch."

"Sarch? Is he gone again? I should think you'd rather count his ribs than his tracks. We haven't seen him."

"You're a liar, Lee. I have. Right there." And Wesley stretched out a gloved hand.

"Aw, hell! Wess, lend Sarch to me, Won't you please, pard?"

"Not on your life. You darn near spoiled him last time. Why Sarch is nuts on sugar ever since that movie dame fed him a barrel."

A lanky cowboy approached Lee. "All grained, boss. Hadn't we better rustle after the trucks?"

Lee addressed a tall hatless individual who was nervously pacing to and fro with gaze on the road. "Mr. Hinckley, shall I shoot the horses along?"

"No. Wait till Brubaker gets here. If Pelham's double doesn't come, we're sunk. You shouldn't have let the trucks go on."

"But, Mr. Hinckley," protested Lee. "We're two days late on the Red Lake location. Rimmy Jim sent me word he had the Indians and a thousand mustangs waiting. Double or no double, Brubaker said we had to go."

The director threw up his hands and gave Lee a wild look. Then one of the group called that Brubaker was coming. A car like the head of a comet with a tail of yellow dust appeared speeding across the park.

Wesley casually glanced in the direction of the dazzling blonde. She met his eyes with a subtle smile that quickened his pulse.

"We've been held up two days waiting for Bryce Pelham's double," Lee was explaining. "Got a wild hoss stampede to film tomorrow. Workin' doubles for both stars. Hinckley is bug-house now."

"Wal, Lee, it's not skin off your nose," drawled Wesley. "Didn't you tell me once that these delays just lined your pockets?"

"Shore. But it's hell to work with these directors even when everything clicks."

In short order the dust-rolling car arrived with a roar and a clank. Out leaped a stout young man, his eyes popping, his collar open, waving a sheaf of telegrams.

"Where's Pelham's double?" yelled Hinckley.

"He's not coming."

Hinckley tore his hair and yelped, and let loose a string of profanity. "Hell of a business manager you are," he ejaculated bitterly.

Brubaker did not even trouble to reply. He thrust the telegrams under the director's nose. It took a moment to force them upon Hinckley. "Ha!" he exclaimed, and ripped open a telegram to scan it contemptuously. Then with purpling visage he lore open another and another, all of them, suddenly to pitch them high and roar like a mad bull. "Retake—retake! Ha! Ha! Find double for Pelham. Ha! Ha! On no account let him risk life or limb! Ha! Ha! As if the conceited, sap-headed ass would! Hurry wild horse sequences! Budget overdrawn! Ha! Ha! Ha! These squawking producers!"

Brubaker and several attendants surrounded Hinckley, and for a moment there was a discordant medley of voices. At length they quieted the distrait director, who emerged from the group, his face black as a thundercloud.

"Lee, line up your cowboys!" he ordered. "Bru, drag Pelham out here, so we can see if any of these ginks can match him."

Lee ran shouting to his men, while Brubaker hurried

137

up to the last car in which Wesley had observed the beautiful blonde girl star. In a moment Hinckley's assistant appeared dragging at a handsome young man. Booted and spurred, wearing blue jeans and a gun-belt, this tall actor roused considerable interest in Wesley.

"What is it all about?" the actor protested, shaking himself free.

"Sorry, Bryce," replied the director, meeting him. "They didn't sent Jerry or anyone. Not a double for you on the lot. I've got to pick one here."

"Here? Out of this lousy gang of gawks!"

"No help for it. I'm on the spot, too... Don't rave now. All the shots are long shots, except the fight between you and the heavy. We'll shoot that somehow—"

Wesley had first hand evidence of the blood pressure and high-strung tempermerment credited to actors. In fact, Mr. Pelham ranted like a tragedian, and Hinckley betrayed how rapturous murder would be for a director. He wheeled away from the gesticulating, emoting star to Lee's line of eager-faced cowboys.

"No! No! *No!* Hell no!" he wailed as he strode down the line. By actual count there were twenty-six riders of the range, all typical, lean, bronzed, rough. A number of them could, no doubt, have doubled very creditably for Mr. Pelham in the dangerous parts of the role he was supposed to portray. Not improbably in the eyes of the director, their bow legs alone elected them to a discard. The star and the camera had to be satisfied.

"Lee, round up more..." raved the director. Then his fierce gaze alighted upon Wesley. With three leaps and a lunge he reached Wesley to pull him out of the saddle, and with a shriek of relief and joy he attempted to line him up beside Pelham. But with a resounding thump on Hinckley's chest the surprised Arizonian frustrated that move.

"Look out!" shouted Lee, almost choking, as he sprang between the men. He put his hands back to get hold of Wesley. "Hinckley, you—he... this isn't Hollywood."

138

"Hell you say! I wish it was," retorted the director, hotly. "What's eating you, Lee? This cowboy is the best double I ever saw for Pelham."

"That might well be. But you're not approachin' it proper," panted Lee. "Mr. Hinckley, this is Wesley Reigh, young rancher hereabouts.... Wess, old pard, shake hands with Director Hinckley of Meteor Pictures."

"Lee, I reckon I ought to sock him," drawled Wesley, coolly. "Jerking me off Brutus that way! Why the hawse might have busted a laig for me."

"Wess, if you sock anyone, it'll be me," yelped Lee, ready to weep. "Have a heart, old pard. Hinckley was beside himself. Big company on location. No double for the star. Enormous expense.... Wess, you're the best sport in ..."

"Pardon me, Mr. Reigh. I am a bit upset," interposed Hinckley, whose brain had evidently begun to function. "Aren't you a—a range rider? You're togged out like a real cowboy."

"No offense, Mr. Hinckley," replied Wesley, easily. "I was just scared. Brutus might have piled me."

"I'm sorry. But you're a perfect double for Bryce Pelham. Same height. Only a little wider of shoulder. You're made for it.... Help me out, Mr. Reigh, and name your own wages."

"Aw, I wouldn't do atall," declared Wesley. His confusion might have been partly due to the blue flame of the blonde star's eyes, which he happened to see bent upon him. She was close enough to have heard the conversation.

"Can't you ride?" exploded Hinckley.

"Reckon I don't fork a hawse so well any more."

"Lee, what's the dope? Will he do?" implored Hinckley.

"Say, Wess is stringing you," burst out Lee. "He's the best range rider in Arizona. Right up to date. His father is John Reigh, our biggest cattleman, running eighty thousand head. And Wess is foreman of six outfits. Ride! Say, he can ride any hoss, anywhere, any time.

And that stunt you asked about, A cowboy ridin' full tilt—bendin' over to pick up a scarf or a dollar? Mr. Hinckley, the Navajos won't let Wess ride any more at their chicken-pulls."

"Chicken-pulls. What are they?" inquired the director, seemingly greatly impressed.

"They bury a chicken in the ground up to its neck. They shave and grease that. The idea is for a rider to ride hell-bent-for election and grab the chicken by the neck. Wess never fails."

Hinckley turned to Wesley with a relieved and appealing smile. "See here, Reigh. We've got you with the goods. It'd be easy for you to race your horse and pick up a running girl—who weighs only a hundred and five pounds. I'd like to introduce you to the actress whom you are to rescue. If you don't fall for a chance like that with Vera Van Dever, you'll be the first man."

Hinckley made for the last car, and engaged the blonde beauty in private conversation. Meanwhile Wesley, feeling himself trapped in the interest of his friend Lee, and inexplicably weak, ventured to win some corroboration from the disgruntled actor.

"Mr. Pelham, I'm shore you agree that I'd be a failure as your double?"

"You'd be a flop and a wash-out," returned the star, resentfully.

Lee interposed eagerly: "Aw, Mr. Pelham, you're daid wrong. If Wess looks the part, he'd fit it to a T. Why, he can act swell. He's so good that the Normal College girls in town had him in their play."

"A hick actor, eh? That's worse," sneered Pelham, manifestly further alienated by this information. "I'm sick of insulting my public with doubles that a blind audience could see didn't resemble me. Moreover, I want a double who is an actor."

"But Mr. Pelham," protested Lee, holding tightly to Wesley's arm when he started and reddened at these insulting remarks, "You movie stars won't risk gettin' crippled."

The star fumed under that and his obviously sharp retort must have been checked by Hinckley's return. This, however, in no wise inhibited Wesley's caustic remark: "Mr. Pelham, if you're afraid of busting a laig or marring your beauty, why don't you insist on playing parts that don't call for a real man?"

Hinckley broke up this little by-play by drawing Wesley toward the car. "Listen, Reigh," he whispered, tensely. "Lucky break for you! Miss Van Dever likes your looks immensely. She's a big drawing card. Lent to us by Paragon. She hates westerns. I hope to God you'll give her a kick in this one."

Next moment Wesley found himself tongue-tied before the loveliest girl he had ever seen. Her wonderful eyes and her soft hand drew him irrestibly while her liquid voice lingered musically over his name and the words of pleasure she used in greeting him. Hinckley shoved him into the car and, slamming the door, yelled for the driver to step on it. Pelham let out a yell, too, but its content was indistinguishable. The car started with a crack and a whirr. Wesley fell almost into the actress' arms, which certainly opened to receive him.

"Rustled! Lee, the son-of-a-gun," cried Wesley aghast, sinking back helplessly.

Vera Van Dever clasped clinging hands round Wesley's arm and leaned to him. "Shanghaiied, you splendid cowboy!" she cried gayly. "But don't blame me. Only I'm tickled pink. I saw and heard the whole show. I liked the way you took it all. It's refreshing to meet some one who isn't movie-struck!"

"Don't jolly me, please," rejoined Wesley, in an earned effort to get his equilibrium. "It'll be bad enough without that. I'd like to help Lee out. I'll do my best, if only you—don't..."

"I won't, but believe me, Wesley, this is a tough break for Bryce Pelham. He's always scared to death some young extra or double will get his job. If you can act as well as a cigar-sign Indian, you'll give him a run.... I'm fed up on Bryce. He's hard to work with. You'll inject some pep into these wild-horse sequences Hinckley puts such store in."

"I'm supposed to rescue you—pick you up—or something like?" ventured Wesley.

"You'll pick up my double, Betty Wyatt. Damn it, I'd do some of these stunts, if they'd let me."

"Can you ride a hawse?"

"Indeed, I can. To be sure I wasn't born on one, like Betty Wyatt, but I could pull these stunts well enough."

"Then why don't you?"

"Listen to you! Wesley, my bosses would faint at such a suggestion. I'm a dancer, you know. *That* is insured for one hundred thousand dollars."

And, lifting her skirt, she laid an exquisitely shaped silken-clad leg over his knee.

"I—I reckon it's worth it," stammered Wesley, his gaze attracted as by a magnet. She left her little foot hanging over his leather-covered knee, and that, added to the soft warmth of her lissome body and the fragrance of her lovely head, that had come imperceptibly on his shoulder, scattered his wits, as well as his reluctance to enter into this adventure.

The car sped on, up over the pine divide, down the grade into the cedars, and at last out upon the desert. Miss Van Dever murmured at the colorful vista in the distance, but her enthusiasm did not extend to disengaging herself from Wesley's encircling arm. Still she asked many questions about the descent to the Little Colorado and the climb into the Painted Desert. After that she wanted to know all about Wesley—his ranch—his horses—his cattle—and his women.

"You mean my mother—sisters?"

"I meant your sweethearts. You must have some."

"Wrong again, Miss Van Dever."

"Call me Vera. . . . But haven't you had sweethearts—been in love?"

"I reckon, after a fashion. But nothing ever came of it."

"Aren't you in love *now*?"

Wesley caught his breath at the subtle query, invested as it was with this alluring actress's beauty. He wanted to tell her that if he was not, he pretty soon would be.

"I mustn't know my stuff, Wesley," she said cryptically, and whatever that was, she proceeded to fill that lack, to his utter rout.

The car sped on. Wesley noted vaguely the bad lands below Moencopie Wash. Beyond, at Tuba, sight of silver-ornamented Navajos and bright blankets in front of the trading post intrigued Miss Van Dever to the point of stopping the car and dragging Wesley out. She clung to his arm and led him all over the post, evincing an interest in the Indians, especially the dusky little children, that enhanced, if possible, Wesley's already exalted opinion of her. They were still in the post when Lee's cars went roaring by.

At length Miss Van Dever seemed inclined to resume the journey and her desire for conquest. She had just settled comfortably against Wesley when another automobile passed, and in this one he saw both Hinckley and Pelham peering at them. Miss Van Dever's silver laughter rang out.

"Are all cowboys as slow as you?" she murmured, presently.

"I reckon not. Some of them are pretty swift," he returned, boyishly.

"Wesley, in the movies, when the hero and heroine meet on the screen, some kind in the audience will yell. 'Now for the clinch!'"

"Yeah. I've heard that yell myself."

"Life is terribly short in this age," she said with a sigh.

Wesley was conscious that he was slow and stupid, but what he felt for this gorgeous creature went beyond flirtation. Her proud blue eyes and the poise of her head, notwithstanding the fact that it lay upon his shoulder, made it impossible for Wesley to react as he would have done to a saucy little minx of the range.

The afternoon was far spent. As the car climbed the long grade to the mesa, a sand storm swooped down upon it. Penetrating dust and cold put an end to Miss Van Dever's sentiment, if that had been what it was. She drew on a veil, and complaining bitterly of the cold and the horrid dust and rotten picture business, she had Wesley wrap her in a blanket, and she collapsed upon him. The driver had to proceed very cautiously through this yellow pall, so that they made but slow progress. When the dust cloud whistled by Wesley could see a dull magenta ball low on the horizon. This was the setting sun.

They reached Red Lake at dusk. Miss Van Dever's maid, who had been in the front seat with the chauffeur, led her off into the darkness, directed by Brubaker. Lee met Wesley to grasp him as if he were a long lost brother.

"Wess, you bunk in my tent," said Lee. "Got a stove. It's colder'n hell. Snowed some. . . . . Say, these movie people are sure the real thing. Got any cowboy outfit I ever saw skinned to a frazzle. They work, I'll tell the world. My trucks got here at four o'clock. Tents all up. Baggage unpacked. Beds made. And the cooks will be yelling 'come an' get it' pronto. Wess, you got to hand it to these movie folks."

"Wal, I been handing it, all right," drawled Wesley. "How about your hawses, Lee. And more particulary, Sarch and Brutus."

"Trucked them over with my best stock. They're eatin' their heads off right now."

"Which is what I'm needing. I had a biscuit and a cup of coffee at daylight this mawning."

"All same like good old ridin' days! Wess, I told Jerry and the boys not to push my hawses. They'll take a while gettin' here."

"Are you going to use them in that wild hawse stampede?"

"Yes. An' a thousand mustangs as wild as any broomtails you ever chased. . . . Ha! there's the supper gong. Let's go rarin'."

Presently under a huge tent, well-lighted, Wesley found himself straddling a bench to sit down at a white-clothed table, steaming with savoury viands. And directly across from him sat a distractingly pretty girl with curly fair hair and stormy blue eyes that immediately appraised him thoroughly and impartially. There were several other girls, all good looking.

"Wal, Lee, I reckon you had it correct," he drawled. "I'm in for a swell time." Lee, however, was too gastronomically active to talk. Whereupon Wesley endeavored to conjure up the enormous appetite he had hinted of. The supper was bountiful and as good as a Harvey dinner, which was the standard of cowboy excellence. Presently Wesley appeased his hunger to the extent of being able to look up from his plate. There were fully fifty persons at the long table, four of whom were young women. Neither Miss Van Dever nor Pelham were present.

"Lee, who's the little peach across from me?" asked Wesley.

"That's Betty Wyatt. She doubles for the star. And you work with her. Tough break, huh, pard? She was shore lampin' you."

"Yeah. I'm sort of leary," grumbled Wesley, recalling in dubious dismay how easy he had been for Vera Van Dever.

"Hinckley gypped you, pard," returned Lee, speaking low. "He and Pelham had a row. You see these stars are married or engaged—or Gawd knows what. And Pelham was as sore as a wet hen because Hinckley threw you in with Van Dever. I've got a hunch they framed you. Anyway, don't class Betty Wyatt with that proud golden-haired dame. Betty is western, all over an' deep down. She's a Californian, hard boiled, sure, an' knows her stuff. The company calls her Nugget, an' it suits her, believe me."

"Yeah. So that crazy galoot framed me? Lee, wait till I go out and walk it off. Then you can introduce me to the little double."

Wesley stalked out into the night. The desert wind, seeping along the ground, restling the sage, stinging his face with tiny atoms of alkali dust, brought to mind the nature of this Red Lake. Striding away from the noise and glare of the camp, Wesley halted on the ridge below the great octagonal trading post, the one and only white man's habitation in the barren region. It looked like a black fort, dark and forbidding, silhouetted against the cold sky. Below spread the dand slopes, down to the wide valley where the pale gleam of water identified the small lake which gave the place its name.

He stood motionless a while, feeling as always the strange sense of kinship with this solitude and wasteland. Red Lake was a gateway to the sublime canyon country of the north. But for once Wesley did not wholly respond to this influence. He was still under the spell of Vera Van Dever, still smarting at Lee's hint that she had been set to use her charms in the interest of the director. Wesley repudiated this suspicion. Nevertheless, it galled him, and, finding that he could not shake it, he went back to camp in search of Lee.

Passing near a big white tent, Wesley heard his name spoken by some one inside. The silvery laughter of the actress star pealed out like low bells. Then Hinckley's deeper voice cut in: "For Pete's sake, have a heart, Bryce. *I* told Vera to play up to the fellow. We had to land him for this double sequence."

"Oh, hell! Did you have to make me ride in an open car, through that hideous sand storm?" demanded Pelham hotly. "Did Vera have to ride sixty miles lying in his arms?"

"A little play like that in a good cause..."

"Bunk! She kissed him—and God only knows what else!"

Here Vera's mocking, sweet laugh sent a chill over Wesley.

"Registering jealousy, Bryce? I didn't think it was in you. No one but God ever will know what else I did. I'm a capable, obedient star. I obey orders, which you never do. Hinck's order was to hold this big boy in the car if I had to sit on his lap and make love to him."

"Bah! I know you, Vera. You got a kick out of it!"

"I'll tell the world! There's one cowboy who is a sweet innocent kid. It was a dirty trick to vamp him."

"Well, I'll tell you both," ground out Pelham. "If you pull any stuff like that again, I'll slug your sweet innocent kid and walk off the set."

Wesley thought it high time for him to walk off himself. In fact, he ran, burning with shame, furious with himself, utterly amazed that so lovely a creature could be such a cheat, that she could be married or engaged to such a poor excuse for a man as the actor. The nameless and beautiful emotion she had roused in Wesley died a violent death.

On the far side of the tents a bright camp fire, surrounded by Indians and members of the company, brought Wesley to a walk. What a fool he was to run like that! Run from whom? He felt hurt, sick, and disillusioned. He decided he would tell Lee that these double-crossing motion-picture people could make their western without him.

As he approached the fire he espied the girl, Betty Wyatt, standing in the light, a vivid contrast to the dark cowboy figures and the lean picturesque Navajos. She wore a white coat and her uncovered head blazed like gold. All feeling within Wesley seemed to rush to her. Here was someone real, of his own world, not sham, like all these moving-picture people. This girl did the dangerous work, took the hard knocks that glorified the star.

In another moment Lee was introducing him to the heavy, to a girl who was to play the part of a Navajo maiden, to others of the company, and finally to Miss Wyatt. Out in the open, with the firelight playing upon her face and the wind blowing her hair, she might have been recompense for a dozen stars, except that Wesley still felt like a burnt child!

"Lee has been building you up," she said gayly. "It'd never do to believe him."

"Don't. He's an awful liar. Like all cowboys, he loses his haid at sight of a pretty girl."

"And you're the cowboy exception to that rule?"

"Me? I'm no cowboy atall. I have to boss half a hundred of the lazy, lousy, looney buckaroos. But I wouldn't be coralled daid being a real one."

"You talk just like one. You look like one. I wonder?"

"Lady, if I've got to act like Pelham and save you, who're doubling for Miss Dever, wal, we're starting wrong."

"I hope you can't act like Pelham, any more than I can act like Miss Vera Van Dever," replied Betty, subtly changing. Wesley caught a tinge of bitterness. The laughter and glow left her face. He had struck a wrong note. The intimation of antagonism, almost contempt, for the stars, struck Wesley deeply and melted away his armor.

"That makes me shore we ought to get acquainted, outside of being doubles," he said.

"What you mean . . . acquainted?" He encountered a look that made him feel he would like to stand honest and square before this girl. Instinctively, she had put up the bars. It did not seem much of a compliment to cowboys in general and to him in particular.

"Let's walk a bit. I cain't talk heah. I'll show you something worth seeing." And, taking her arm, he led her away, from the fire toward the ridge overlooking the valley.

"Okay. But I'll freeze to death. I'm a California rose."

"You're limping," he said surprised, and turned to look at her.

"Are you telling me? I got hurt the other day. My trick was to jump my horse off a rock, down at Oak Creek. We went clear under. The water was so cold it damn near turned my blood to ice. I pulled the stunt okay. But riding out, I fell off too soon and the horse hit me."

"Oak Creek! Why, it's high now, and icy, you bet. That was pretty risky, Miss Wyatt?"

"All in the day's work. That's my job," she replied, flippantly. "I'm only a double."

"But do you have to—to take all these chances?" he queried, earnestly.

"Of course I do."

"Couldn't go in for regular movie-work—being an actress, you know, like Miss Dever?"

"Couldn't I?—I tried to, for two long years, and almost starved to death. At that, I'd have made the grade if I'd—well, just skip it. One day I had a job riding with some extras. They found me out. I've been doubling ever since."

"And you hate it?"

"Oh, my God! But I stick on my horse somehow. Fifteen bucks a day! *She* pulls down two grand every week. . . . Maybe I'll get a break some day."

"Shore you will," rejoined Wesley, and fell silent.

They passed Navajos gliding by with moccasined tread, and came out of the shadow of the huge trading post, looming like a bluff, to the edge of the ridge. Wesley kept on to a jumble of big rocks, among which he threaded a careful way to a protected shelf.

"We'll be out of the wind heah," he explained. "Hell of a place for cold wind, blowing sand, and stinging alkali dust—this heah Red Lake. But it's great. See that white glow above the bluff across there? The moon will slide up over the rim soon. And then you'll see why Arizona has it all over California."

But she did not look across. Instead she looked up at him. "All right, Big Boy. You've set the stage. Get going."

"Get going?—I'm not going anywhere," he returned, puzzled.

"I've been led around like this by a hundred cowboys."

"Yeah?"

"And I'm always curious to see what kind of a line they hand out. They haven't much originality. Now you—what's yours?"

"Oh, I get you." Wesley laughed at her half-naive, half-scornful explanation. Then he faced her to grasp that; as a matter of course, she expected him to take her in his arms. He wanted to. There was an allurement about her as strong as Miss Van Dever's, but entirely

149

different. There was more—a hard simplicity and honesty far removed from the wiles of the actress.

"Lee said they called you Nugget. How come?"

"My hair, I guess. It's real color."

"And Miss Van Dever's?"

"Was red last picture."

"Nugget. I kind of like that. It means solid gold.... Wal, Betty, if you expect me to talk and—and pet like a cowboy, you're in for disillusion."

"Good Lord! Am I hitting the pipe? But you *are* a cowboy."

"Shore. That was bluff of mine. I'm an Arizona cowboy, dyed in the wool, like my Dad was, and my Grand Dad. It makes no difference that I'm the luckiest dog ever—that I'm the boss of six outfits and eighty thousand haid of cattle. Betty, I'm just a plain sap cowboy. That was shore proved today."

"Don't take it too hard. Vera's specialty is making saps out of men."

"Aw! How did you know? You saw us in the car?"

"Yes. And I wasn't the only one. Bryce Pelham tore his hair out by the roots. Did that tickle me? I'm telling you, Big Boy."

"Hinckley put up a job on me, Betty," explained Wesley shamefacedly. "He sicked that blonde on to me. To vamp me! Land me for this double job. I was easy. I feel for her."

"Oh, Wesley, you didn't fall in love with that ... not really?" cried Betty, heatedly.

"No. But just short of it. Only a little more of her would have ... Wal, never mind, Nugget. Meeting you is a balance. I'm daid lucky."

"Meeting *me*!" she exclaimed incredulously, with her luminous eyes upon him, as if they had just seen him clearly.

"Yes. I can be my real self."

"But, Big Boy, I might be like lots of the movie girls—like *her*."

"Yes, you might. But are you? Tell me straight."

"I'm every way but *that* way, I am."

"That is the only way I'm counting. Look, Betty! The moon! Heah's where you go back on California."

The environs of Red Lake, all in an instant, had been transformed as if by enchantment. A full moon had sailed up over the black rim to flood the valley with a transcendent glamour of silver light. Like a burnished shield the lake glistened and glimmered in the middle of the valley of sand. Except under the looming bluff opposite, all blackness, weird shadow, and stark desolation had vanished in the magic of the moon. An ethereal softness fell upon the desert. Far across, through the opaque veil of light, loomed up mesas and escarpments leading off to mystic obscurity.

There was life down below that had not been visible until the moon shone out. A bunch of cattle trooped round the lake, slaking the desert thirst of the day. A moving round spot, gray in the moonlight, proved to be a flock of sheep coming in to water, shepherded by barking dogs. Off to the north straggled a line of mustangs driven by Navajo riders. Their mournful chant floated up on the cold air.

"How about it, Betty?" queried Wesley, after what seemed a long while.

"Ah! I forgot where I was," she murmured. "Arizona might win if . . . Let's go, Wesley. I'm frozen."

On the way back to camp it was she who held to his arm, not lightly, and she who was silent. There was something pregnant for Wesley in that silence and that contact, something that made him decide to accept the role of double, if only because he might share the danger with this girl, and in some way possibly minimize it for her.and in some way possibly minimize it for her.

Five miles from Red Lake, on the vast slope of the upland desert, the motion-picture company, with the cowboys and horses, and the Navajos with their hundreds of mustangs, had assembled to film the great stampede.

Hinckley had selected a sage ridge for the scene

upon which he depended for the climax and punch of his picture. To Wesley's experienced eye no more magnificent setting could have been found in all Arizona. If it could be filmed! If the gusts of a cold wind, blowing yellow veils of sand and dust, would hold off for the shooting! On the south side of a gentle rise of sage ridge, fairly well down, waited the immense drove of mustangs, corralled in the mounted circle of cowboys and Indians. This band was to be driven by shooting cowboys and yelling savages up over the ridge top in a wild stampede. Four cameras had been set up to shoot the action, one on a high rock to the extreme left, two across the canyon upon which the ridge verged, and the last on the crest of the ridge, precariously close to where the mustang horses would run. The action faced the sage slope to the north and the ruined front of white bluffs, and then the red rise of the mesa to the grand crowning wall of purple rock that wound away into infinity.

All morning Hinckley labored with details, angles, and light possibilities. At high noon he was ready for action.

"Now Lee, trot out this buckaroo you wished on me," he shouted stridently. "Oh, man, he's got to be good!"

In that moment Wesley was trying to assure Betty that his horse, Sarchedon, would not run her down.

"He's grand. But oh! so wild!" she exclaimed as she ventured to caress the noble arch of neck. "See how he flinches. Wesley, I'll have to ride him or die."

"Betty, you won't have to *die* to own him," flashed Wesley.

"Cowboy! What will I have to do?"

Lee dashed up to disrupt that colloquy. His hawk eyes glinted. Dust sifted off his sombrero. In charge of the cowboys and Indians, with the great drive at hand, he looked cool and hard, equal to the responsibility invested in him.

"Come, pard. Do your stuff."

Wesley rode out upon the ridge with him, where they were met by Hinckley, Brubaker, Pelham, and the camera men. The director had eyes only for Sarchedon.

"What a horse! Does he know what's coming off?"

"I'll say he does."

"All right, Reigh. See that red scarf there. Ride back to your stand. When I wave my arms, put that roan devil in high, and pick up the scarf at top speed."

Wheeling Sarch back, Wesley trotted to the spot designated and turned to await the signal. When it came, he spurred Sarch into a run across the ridge. In a few jumps the roan was going like the wind. Then, with Sarch at the top of his stride, Wesley swung down in perfect timing, to snatch scarf and tuft of sage off the ground. He had not tried that trick for a long time, but it was easy. Not easy, however, was it to pull Sarch out of that gait. He wanted to run. Wesley slowed him presently and turned to ride back to the group, which Wesley observed had been joined by Betty. At a distance he noted her strong resemblance to Miss Van Dever in stature and coloring. Moreover, she was dressed in smallest detail as the star had been the day before.

"Good," said Hinckley, rubbing his hands. "You'll do, cowboy. But don't ride down so thundering hard. I know I told you to. Never mind."

"The faster the better," interrupted Pelham excitedly. "And let him cut in quicker, so his back will be to the cameras."

"Bryce, I'm directing this sequence," retorted Hinckley irritably. "Hell of a lot you'd care if he ran Nugget down. It's a tough spot for her."

"She's doubling for Vera, isn't she? This is our big scene. It's got to be fast, hard."

"Rehearse," snapped the director, turning from the tense actor. "Reigh, listen. Vera comes riding up the slope in front of the stampede. When the mustangs show over the ridge, we trip her horse. Vera is thrown over his head. See! It'll be some fall. If she's unhurt, she'll be on her feet when you ride down to snatch her from under the hoofs of death. See! She'll catch your hand and spring to help you. *But*, if she broke her leg or

153

got knocked senseless, which can happen to doubles, she'll be flat on the ground, and you'll have to pick her up to save her life. However, it's more than likely Vera will roll free and come up on her feet. See!"

"No. You say Vera?"

"Oh, you dumb cluck! Vera is Nugget."

"All right, I see now. As far as I'm concerned you needn't rehearse this part. I'll get her, up or down."

"She weighs one hundred and five," retorted Hinckley, in terse voice. "Show me how you can snatch her flat off the ground."

"Wait, Wesley," interposed Betty. "Under my blouse I'm wearing a bolt of strong cloth. It's laced, but it's loose. Be sure you grab that."

Wesley smiled assuringly at the girl. She was pale and fully aware of her danger, but gave no sign of flinching. As he rode back to his stand he cursed this business that risked the life and limb of an unknown and courageous girl to swell the fame of a public idol. When he turned to face the gradual descent of the ridge he saw Hinckley with hand uplifted and down on the sage Betty on her knees waving at him. Then she slid over face downward in her protecting arms. The director yelled at the same time that he swept up his arm.

Wesley did not allow the roan to get his head this time. Nevertheless, Sarch hit from a lope into a run. Wesley glued his eye upon the little patch of blue that was Betty lying on the sage. Never even in his rodeo days, had he felt this stern and set coordination between his faculties and his muscles. He forced himself to imagine he heard the thunder of thousands of hoofs close behind him. Then he ran down upon Betty, swooped like a desert hawk, and buried his clutch in her blouse. Braced for the expected drag he felt the jerk of her weight, but he swept her clean off the ground as if she were an empty sack. Up he swung her into his arms.

"Ouch! You got my skin!" shrieked Betty. Then as he released that rigid grip she gazed at him with telltale eyes. "Oh, Wess, you're one grand cowboy! I was scared to death. But now I'd double on the edge of hell if you and Sarch were on the job."

"Wal, I reckon I'd go to hell for you at that," replied Wesley grimly and, holding her at ease, he rode back to let her slide down to the ground before the director and his group. They appeared to be in an exceedingly hot argument. Wesley gathered presently that some of them, particularly Pelham, were keen for the shot to be taken exactly as the action had been rehearsed that time. Hinckley, backed by the heavy, balked at the risk to Betty.

"Hold on! Give me air! Let me talk!" roared the director, his hair hanging wet over his flaming eyes. "It was great stuff, Bryce. Great for you! But it'll be good enough with Vera on her feet, if she's able to get on them."

"Alive or dead, *that* is the way she'll do it—or I'm through," rang out the star.

Hinckley appeared on the verge of apoplexy. His face turned purple. His neck bulged. "All right! All right!" he ejaculated hoarsely. "Have it your way, Pelham. But this is my swan song with you. I'd starve to death before I'd go on location with you again."

"You'll starve, old dear, if I give you the works at the studio," returned the star viciously.

"All set. Let's go," rasped the director.

"Hinckley, wait," called Wesley. "Make this clear to me! You want this stunt repeated exactly as I did it?"

"Exactly. And you're a marvel if you pull it. Just you watch me. When Vera—"

"You mean Betty Wyatt," interrupted Wesley. "I'm not saving Miss Van Dever's life."

"Yes . . . When Betty comes in sight, you watch me for your cue. This red scarf."

"How far will she be in front of the stampede when you trip her hawse?"

"Damn close, believe me. Vera—I mean Nugget—shows first—her horse plunging—rearing. A silhouette, you know. Then she'll tear across here. The mustangs show pell-mell. Right there we'll trip her horse. At the same instant you'll get my signal. The rest depends on you, and it's a hell of a lot, cowboy."

"It'll be okay, Hinckley, only I cain't wait for your signal."

"You cain't what?" yelled the director, imitating Wesley's pronunciation in his excitement. His eyes popped wide.

"Mr. Hinckley, I see it this way," returned Wesley, forcibly. "You don't know Indian mustangs. I do. They're wild. Once the cowboys open up with guns that bunch of broom-tails will bust into high. I've got to use my own judgment about distance. You're subjecting Betty Wyatt to grave peril. It oughtn't be done. But if you let me ride in there, not too soon to crab your picture, nor too late to allow for unforeseen chances, I'll guarantee to pull the stunt."

"You wait for my signal," bellowed Hinckley.

"Mister, I won't even look at you. I'll watch Betty and the mustangs. Got that?" returned Wesley forcibly and, turning to Sarch, he rode off to his post. A clamor burst upon his ears, so trenchant, so raucous that Wesley nearly succumbed to the humor of it. For a moment it looked like a free-for-all fight. Bobbing heads, upflung arms, a waving megaphone, and a shrill hubbub attested to the agitation liberated by his curt ultimatum.

Presently Betty disengaged herself from the group and hurried toward Wesley. She was not acting then. Her face, her wide, intent eyes, black with excitement, and her lithe form were instinct with her own emotions. Not even the vicarious garb she wore could rob her of her individuality.

"Oh, Wesley, that was swell of you," she said poignantly. "I love you for it. No one ever thought of me. . . . Hinckley told Pelham to go to hell. He sees it your way. And am I glad? This stunt gave me the willies."

"Forget it," replied Wesley. "When they trip your hawse, go over his haid relaxed. You'll light soft. And I'll pounce on you like a hawk on a prairie-dawg. It's a cinch."

"Wesley, I don't believe that fake blond dame was acting yesterday when. . . ."

Here Hinckley interrupted them. "Reigh, I apologize. You were right. I'm heartily glad for your cool grasp of the things that escaped me."

"Fine! You're talking, Hinckley," returned Wesley warmly. "I'm on edge. So is Betty. Lee is raring to go."

"We'll go. It'll be a knockout," cried Hinckley, his enthusiasm again flaring. He rushed back, his hair waving in the strong breeze.

Wesley stood up in his stirrups so that he could see everything. His teeth were clenched. A cold ripple ran up his back. Camera men were making final adjustments. Lee Hornell leaned from his horse for a last word with the director; then erect with his inimitable seat in the saddle, he loped away toward the black uneasy blot of mustangs and their guards. His red scarf streamed over his shoulder. Betty Wyatt appeared on a spirited white horse, riding to her stand. One glance sufficed for the Arizonian—she could ride. Vera Van Dever sat upon a high rock. Her mocking laugh jarred Wesley's strung nerves. Other members of the company were grouped near by. Pelham appeared to be bullyragging the director, who swung his megaphone on high as if to brain him. The star retreated with sullen stride.

Then suddenly the director spread high his arms, as if to embrace the perfect location. It was the homage of the artist.

Wesley awoke to the reality of his surroundings. The desert scene had gathered an appalling beauty. A strong wind came rippling the bright sage. It was dry and bitter, with a hint of invisible alkali. The lone cedar behind Wesley began to swish its violet-tipped foliage and moan a presage of desert storm. The sun, banked all around by huge columnar clouds, like purple ships with sails of silver, poured a dazzling light down upon the location about to be photographed. It brought out the caves and caverns of the ragged canyon, black in contrast to the pitiless white of the terraced cliffs. Dark cloud-shadows sailed swiftly up the vast sage-slope. And the grand purple wall, catching the full effulgence of the sunlight, blazed in incredible glory.

In the west the sand storm had gathered, and it was swooping its advance puffs of yellow dust and sheets of gray alkali along the colored desert floor toward the ridge. Farther back a low dense pall approached with an irresistible sweep, like an unearthly army hidden behind its skyhigh banners.

Wesley suddenly understood. He had been late to grasp what had stricken the director motionless, his arms uplifted. The elements had combined to glorify his picture. This scene, counterfeit of drama and stampede, would be truer than any actual race of frightened wild horses the West had ever seen. The rescue of Betty Wyatt would typify the innumerable and unrecorded feats of heroism that the pioneers, the gold-seekers, the hunters and scouts, and the range-riders of the plains, had performed with never a thought of their greatness.

"Cam-e-ra!" Hinckley's megaphoned voice rolled stentoriously over the ridge, to bellow back in echo from the canyon. Lee's gun, held aloft, belched fire and smoke. It's sharp crack loosed a terrific din of shots and yells.

Like a tidal wave, ragged with bobbing crest, the horde of trapped mustangs rolled into thundering action. The roar of ten thousand hoof-beats drowned the boom of guns and bawl of throats. Wesley felt the solid earth shake under his horse. The splendid spectacle drew a piercing yell from him, which seemed soundless in his ears. Across the chosen gateway of the ridge raced a flood of lean, wild noses, twinkling hoofs and flying manes—a terrifying stampede, rolling on like a juggernaut, smoking and streaking dust, straight at the frightened white horse and its apparently bewildered rider. Betty's cue in the sequence was to appear trapped. Hinckley had not needed subterfuge or acting. Lee had seen the peril. So had Wesley. The girl was trapped. The speed of those wild mustangs, maddened by the guns and yells, had been the unknown quantity to the director. But the cowboys had foreseen it. Wesley was ready for it. In that crucial instant, Betty ceased to play double for Vera Van Dever. She wheeled the white horse to goad him for her life.

Savagely spurred, Sarchedon shot like an arrow from a bow. As Wesley cut in after Betty the storm of wild mustangs zoomed over the ridge top. Fury of roar enveloped him. Fifty strides ahead, Betty's racing horse hit the invisible tripping wire. He plunged to a terrific fall, hurtling Betty far over his head. Like a catapulted diver, she winged that graceful flight. But when she struck, the force was so great that she ploughed through the sage, twisted sideways, rolled over and over, to lie prone, crumpled on her face.

Wesley hauled mightily on his rope-strenthened bridle. Sarch, with that rumbling avalanche at his heels, was almost impossible to check. It took two iron arms. He bore down on the blue form inert in the sage. Deadly, grim, and sure, Wesley bent far over in the saddle, suddenly to stiffen his legs and sweep with lowered arm. His clutching hand caught Betty—closed with steel fingers on blouse, belt, flesh. He held while Sarchedon's momentum swung the girl off the ground. Wesley felt his bones and muscles wrench. But she seemed light as a feather. Up on the pommel—safe! He reeled. A haze of red blinded him. He felt the mighty stride, the smooth action of the great horse under him. He heard the devastating thunder of hell at his heels. Sarchedon, carrying double, could not outrun the mustangs.

With clearing sight and brain, Wesley swerved Sarch to the left. His plan had been to gain the cedars. A red demon-like head, smoking, with eyes of fire and man of flame, forged past Wesley. Lean wild ponies, spectres in the flying dust, came abreast of Sarch. The engulfing stampede rolled like a maelstrom upon him.

Wesley saw cedars close at hand, dim through the whipping streaks of dust. Sarch would gain this shelter. His shoulder collided with a racing mustang. It went down to roll with four hoofs beating the air. Sarch lunged up a rise of ground, behind the cedars.

The muddy cataract of mustangs poured down the slope. All sound ceased for Wesley. As the yellow pall raced on with the stampede, Wesley covered Betty's bloody face with his silken scarf and bent his head to endure.

Like Sarchedon, he was inured to the hardships of the desert. This was a dust-laden storm, not one of the sandstorms that buried horses and men, and changed landscapes. It would pass quickly. Again his deafened ears admitted the rumbling roar of hoofs. They were rolling on, receding, lessening in volume. And soon the whistling wind obliterated all sounds of the stampede. That, too, swooped by with a parting shriek. Wesley lifted his head to wipe his wet and stinging eyes.

Sunlight again, pale, steely! The air was cold and acrid. It clogged Wesley's nostrils. Indian yells whooped from the slope. Sarchedon stood champing his bit and snorting. For him the incident was closed.

Wesley removed the scarf from Betty's face. Her eyes were wide open, dark with retreating pain or terror, beautiful in the realization of deliverance. Her mouth was redder than lipstick had made it. Bits of sage adhered to the raw flesh where points of blood began to show. Dust failed to hide a cut over her temple. Gently Wesley wiped the stains away.

"Wess?" she whispered. "We—pulled it?"

"Right-o. And I reckon we're all heah. But let's make shore." He felt her arms, her collar bones, her ribs, and her legs, fearful that pressure would extract a groan from her. But all bones seemed intact. Not till he shifted her to his left arm, thus pressing her back, did she cry out.

"Oooh! Have a heart—Big Boy!"

"Where did I hurt you, Betty?"

"My back. Holy cats! You tore my skin off."

"I reckon. But you're okay. We pulled it, and I'll bet, by God, no movie ever before equalled that stunt. Oh, how the sun and storm acted for us! What a setting, Betty! The desert gave us all her glory."

"I'm awfully glad. . . . Oh, my—that mob of beasts! I almost fainted off my horse."

"You did a grand stunt."

"Yeah? All the same, till I saw Sarch.... Oh, but he's wonderful! Wess, will you let me ride him—take my picture on him?"

"I shore will. He's yours."

"Mine?"

"Yes, darling."

"*Darling!* Oh, you cowboy!"

"I mean it, Betty. I've lived a long time in two days. These last few minutes! The hellinest ride I ever made—to save the girl I love!"

"Don't—don't kid me," she said weakly.

"I'm terrible in love with you, Betty."

"Oh, Wess! I fell for you on sight. Was I jealous of that hateful, lovely movie star? I'm telling you ... But now—Oh, Wess, is it a break for little Betty?"

"If you want to put it that way. Only I reckon the break is mine.... Betty, would you give up your career as double, and sometime star yourself—to be the wife of a young rancher? I can give you all a western girl could desire.... But that glittering career..."

"Hush! Beside what you offer, darling, that career is a burst bubble." She put her arms around his neck and lifted trembling, stained lips to meet his kiss.

Yells disrupted that ecstatic moment for Wesley. "Honey, they're yelling," he said, lifting his head. "I reckon they figure us daid."

"But we're alive, Wesley, alive, alive!"

He rode out of the cedars with her, and across the trampled sage-slope to the ridge-top. Hinckley with his company awaited them in strained expectancy. Wesley's keen eye caught the camera man shooting his ride across the sage with Betty in his arms.

"Cowboy! Don't tell me she's badly hurt," cried Hinckley. "It'd spoil the greatest finale I ever shot."

"I reckon she's okay. But it shore was a bad spill," replied Wesley, and he swung out of the saddle to set Betty on her feet.

"Betty Wyatt, you're disfigured for life!" exclaimed Miss Van Dever, in a tone that betrayed more than compassion.

"Yeah? To make you more famous, Vera!" flashed Betty.

Hinckley embraced Wesley, then wrung his hand in exceeding gratefulness. "Oh, boy! You were great, Reigh! It was a wow—a knockout! The camera man shot it all, every single detail to where the stampede and storm swallowed you. I never saw your beat for a rider and an actor."

"Wal, I was in daid earnest," drawled Wesley.

"You'll be famous. I'll offer you a contract."

Before Wesley could reply, Pelham interposed with his handsome visage distorted by jealousy and passion.

"Not with Meteor, you won't, Mr. Hinckley! And you'll have to retake that sequence!"

"Re—take?" gasped the director. "For Pete's sake— *why*?"

"Because I won't stand for it. I warned you. This lousy conceited cowboy turned his face to the cameras."

"*Ah!* Can you beat that? I ask you!" shrieked Hinckley. "Ha! Ha! He's handsomer than you, Bryce. Sure, I get it.... But look here. That shot is in the little black boxes. And when the studio sees it, *your* contract will fade out for this real guy."

Wesley strode forward to confront the frenzied actor. "Mister Pelham, this heah doubling stunt is done," drawled Wesley, in cool contempt. "I reckon you'll take back your dirty crack."

"Aha! All swelled up, eh?" retorted the actor wickedly. "Spooning with the star one day and stealing my thunder the next—too much for the glorified cowboy, eh? Here's another crack!"

As swiftly as he ended he struck Wesley a resounding blow. But for Hinckley, who blocked his fall, Wesley would have gone down hard. In an instant he recovered to rush at the actor.

That move appeared to liberate something dynamic in Hinckley. "Back! *Back!* Give them room!" ye yelled, fiendishly inspired. "On your job, Jimmy. Don't miss this! *CAM-E-RA!*"

Wesley heard, but his enforced entrance to an unforeseen contretemps, only increased his wrath and his purpose to give this crazy actor the beating he deserved. If it came to a rough and tumble, gloves and chaps and spurs would enhance his advantage. Wesley made at Pelham vigorously, meaning to give and take until he got his opponent's measure. During this period of the fight Wesley had the worst of it. Pelham showed a smattering of science. He could box. But no other of his blows upset Wesley. They lacked what a Westerner called beef. Moreover they had not been at it for more than a few moments when the actor began to sweat and pant. Compared with the range-rider, he was soft.

This dawned on Wesley with an exceeding satisfaction, which mitigated in some degree his surrender to rage. Pelham, manifestly realizing that he would not last long, redoubled his efforts to beat Wesley down.

The fight then became fast and furious. For every blow Wesley dealt, he received two. But his were sodden. Those to Pelham's midriff had decided effect. Once, in the whirl of battle, Wesley caught a glimpse of Betty Wyatt's face. It was decidedly no longer pale nor distressed. If the fight had been going against Wesley, Betty would not have betrayed such sheer primitive joy. Wesley heard her shrieks high above the shouts of the other spectators. Hinckley yelled through his director's megaphone a booming proof that his ruling passion had gone into eclipse. *Kill the ham actor, cowboy! Kill him!*

To Pelham's credit, he took a gruelling punishment without a yelp. But he was obviously so possessed by fury that he would have to be knocked out. Wesley recognized that, and the moment the actor's blows no longer harried him, he kept him back. Regaining his breath, Wesley bored in. As the fight progressed, his feeling had augmented with expended physical force. Blood on his face, on his hands, his own blood mixed with his antagonist's, maddened him, and he felt the lust to kill.

Plunging on the actor, then, Wesley beat down his

guard, banged him with right and left. A sharp upper cut to the nose upset Pelham, who sat down absurdly. Scarlet poured from his mashed nose. Whipped, tragic, he bounded up gamely, only to meet the same rain of swift blows. Back he staggered. Then Wesley swung with all he had left— and turned abruptly away.

Betty came running to him as he untied his scarf. "Oh, Wess! Wess! Are you hurt?"

"Wipe me off—Betty—I cain't see," panted Wesley.

Lee joined them, his hawk-eyes matching the fight in his convulsed face. "Aw pard! Every time he hit you, he hit me!"

"Yeah? I'll bet you don't feel what I feel. How's the handsome star?"

"Senseless yet. Mebbe daid. But he shore took it. Wess, we gotta hand bouquets to these motion-picture folks. I heahed Van Dever say: 'Served him just right, the big stiff! Always throwing a monkey-wrench into the works! But this picture with me in that stampede— riding to that fall—oh, what a climax! And oh, you cowboy, you can have me!'"

"Wal, I'll be doggoned!" ejaculated Wesley.

"Lee, she can't have that cowboy!" interposed Betty, with flashing eyes.

Hinckley waved to the cowboys and Indians, driving the tired mustangs back up the slope. Then he bellowed through his megaphone:

"All in the little black box! Let's call it a day and a picture. *SCRAM!*"

California Red

Preface

For years Ben Ide had chased and tried to capture the great stallion, California Red, probably the noblest of all the fifteen thousand horses who roamed the northern California plains. But he had always been unsuccessful. Now his chance had come—and he had to make the devil's bargain with a band of cattle rustlers in order to realize his greatest ambition.

Bright daylight came while the cavalcade drew close to Ben's ranch. They passed between the empty pasture and the frozen river. All the doors of the barn and the gates of the corral were open. Ben was about to declare himself forcibly when he saw Modoc rise in his stirrups as if to peer across the lake, then duck down quickly. Ben, sensing something most unusual, rode quickly by the rustlers to face Modoc, who had turned. Nevada was peeping over the rise of ground to the lake.

"What do you see?" demanded Ben.

"Wild red stallion—way out on ice," replied the Indian impressively.

"California Red...ON THE ICE?" cried Ben poignantly.

"Shore's your born, pard," returned Nevada, lowering himself into his saddle. "Only six hosses with him. The lake's frozen 'cept for circle in centre. They're takin' a drink. Look."

"No" whispered Ben, but he had not the will to do what he divined he should. Raising himself in the stirrups, he peered over the edge of the bluff. Wild Goose Lake was white with ice, and everywhere tufts of bleached grass stood up. Far out, perhaps two miles, he espied horses. Wild. He knew the instant his eyes took in the graceful slim shapes, the flowing manes and tails, the wonderful posture of these horses.

California Red stood at the edge of the ice. He was not drinking. Even at that distance Ben saw the noble wild head high.

"Nevada, watch Hall," said Ben, and fumbled at the leather thongs which secured his field-glass to the saddle. He loosened it, got it out of the case, levelled it. But his hands shook so he could see only blurred shapes. Fiercely he controlled himself and brought the round magnifying circle of glass to bear upon horse after horse, until California Red stood clear and beautiful.

Red as flame. Wilder than a mountain sheep. Ben saw him clear and close, limned against the white ice, big and strong, yet clean-limbed as any thoroughbred racehorse. While his band drank he watched. To what extremity had he been brought by the drought?

Ben fell limp into his saddle. Any other time in his life but this. What irony of fate. But he knew in another flash that he could not pass by this opportunity, cost what it might.

"Well, pard, it's shore tougher than any deal we ever got," said Nevada, in distress. "California Red on the ice. We always dreamed we'd ketch him waterin' on a half-froze lake an' lay a trap for him, or get enough riders to run him down."

"We can catch him," shouted Ben hoarsely.

"Nope. We cain't," replied Nevada tragically.

Ben felt something burst within him—a knot of bound emotion—or riot of blood—or collapse of

166

will—he never knew what. But with the spring of a panther he was out of his saddle, confronting Nevada.

"If it's all the same to you, I will," replied this man, cheerfully. "I can't ride hard, but I can yell an' fill up a hole. I've chased wild horses."

Ben ran back to his mount and with nimble fingers lightened his saddle, tightened the cinch, and untied his rope. The rustlers got off to stretch their legs.

"Cinch up," he panted. "Nevada, take two men, and go around to the left. Keep out of sight. I'll take—Hall and another man—with me. We'll cross the river. Modoc, you stay here till we both show on the banks. Then ride in. . . . We'll close in on Red slow. . . . Soon as he gets to running he'll slip—on the ice. . . . He'll fall and slide. . . . That'll demoralize him. . . . Rest will be easy."

Nevada rode off with two of the men, while Ben, calling Hall and Jenks, wheeled back toward the barn and went down to the river. The ice cracked and swayed, but held the horses. Once across, Ben led the way at a swift gallop round to the West of the lake, keeping out of sight of the wild horses. When he reached a point far enough along the lake, he swerved to the height of ground. As he surmounted it he saw Nevada with his two riders come into sight across the lake, and another glance showed Modoc, with his followers, emerging by the mouth of the river.

"We've got four men here. With us it makes seven."

"Aw, my Gawd Ben, you wouldn't."

"I would," hissed Ben. "I'll have that red horse. Say you'll help me."

"I'm damned if I will" yelled Nevada shrilly. His dark face grew dusky red and his eyes dilated.

"I never minded you of your debt to me," went on Ben, in swift inexorable speech. "I remind you now."

"Hell, yes." roared Nevada, "if you put it that way. But you locoed idiot, I'll never forgive you."

"Lighten your horses. Untie your lassoes," ordered Ben, and then, drawing his clasp knife, he opened it and strode back to Hall. He knew that he was under the sway of passion of power of which he had never before been aware. It made him unstable as water. At the same time it strung him to unquenchable spirit and incalculable strength.

"Hall, there's a wild stallion out here on the ice. I've wanted him for years. If I promise to let you and your men go free, will you help me catch him?"

Hall bent his shaggy head to peer the closer into Ben's face, as if he needed scrutiny to corroborate hearing.

"Yes, I will," he boomed.

Without more ado Ben cut his bonds and passed onto the next rustler. Soon he had released them all.

"You needn't go," he said to the cripple.

California Red was a mile out on the ice, coming directly toward Ben. His stride was a stilted trot, and he lost it at every other step. His red mane curled up in the wind. The six horses were strung out behind him. Discovering Ben, the stallion let out a piercing whistle and wheeled. Then his feet flew out from under him and he fell. Frantically he tried to rise, but his smooth hoofs on the slippery ice did not catch hold.

"Ah, my beauty," yelled Ben wildly, with all his might. "It's no square chase, but you're mine, you're mine."

The other wild horses wheeled without losing their footing and soon drew from the slipping, sliding stallion. At last he got up on four feet and turned towards his band. It seemed that he knew he dared not run. At every step one of his hoofs slipped out from under him. Ben caught the yells of his helpers. They were running their horses down the sandy slope toward the ice. Another wild horse went down, and then another. It was almost impossible for them to rise. They slid around like tops.

Meanwhile, swift as the wind, Ben was running his fast horse down to the lake, distancing his followers, who came yelling behind. Hall's heavy voice pealed out full of the wild spirit of the chase. Ben reached the ice. The sharp iron shoes of his horse cut and broke through the first few rods but, reaching solid ice, they held. Ben reined in to wait for the men to spread and form a circle.

Nevada was far out on the ice now, and he had closed the one wide avenue to the west. Soon the eight riders had closed in to a half-mile arc, with the open lake as an aid.

California Red turned back from the narrowing gap between Nevada and the lake. When he wheeled to the west, Modoc's group left a gateway for the wild horses nearest. They plunged and ran and slid and fell, got up to plunge again, and at least earned their freedom. This left two besides the stallion on the ice. He appeared at terrible disadvantage. Wild and instinct with wonderful speed, he could not exercise it. The riders closed in. Nevada rode between Red and the open water. Another of the horses escaped through a gap.

"Close in, slow now," bawled Ben, swinging the noose of his lasso.

The moment was fraught with a madness of rapture. How sure the outcome. Presently the great stallion would stampede and try to run. That was all Ben wanted. For when Red tried to run on that glassy ice, his doom was sealed.

He was trotting here, there, back again, head erect, mane curled, tail sweeping a living flame of horse-flesh. Terror would soon master him. His snorts seemed more piercingly acute, as if he protested against the apparent desertion of his band.

"Farther around, Modoc," yelled Ben. "Same for you, Nevada—on other side. Keep him in triangle...Now, men, ride in—yell like hell. And block him when he runs."

Suddenly, the red horse gathered himself in a knot. How grandly he sprang. And he propelled his magnificent body into a convulsive run, with every hoof sliding from under him. Straight toward Ben he came, his nostrils streaming white, his hoofs cracking like pistol shots. It seemed that his wild spirit enabled him to overcome even this impossible obstacle of ice, for he kept erect until he was shooting with incomparable speed.

At the geight of it he slipped, plunged on his side with

169

a snort of terror, turned on his back, and as he slid with swift momentum over the ice, his hoofs in the air, Ben's lasso uncurled like a striking snake. The noose fell over the forelegs and tightened.

Lusty yells from leather lungs. California Red had run into a rope. Ben hauled in his skillful horse. The great stallion flopped back on his side. The rope came taut to straighten out his legs, and stop him short. He could not rise. When he raised his beautiful head the Indian's rope circled his neck. His race was run.

Nevada came trotting up, noose in hand, white of face and fierce of eye.

"Pard, he's ruined us, but he's worth it, or I'm a livin' sinner," he shouted.

Ben gazed almost in stupefaction down upon the heaving graceful animal. California Red lay helpless, beaten, robbed of his incomparable speed. Every red line of him spoke to Ben's thrilling soul.

"Wal, Ide," boomed Bill Hall, slapping Ben on the shoulder, "I'm glad you ketched this grand hoss.... You're a good sport. Put her thar.... If I had time I'd tell you somethin'. But I see riders comin' along the lake an' we must rustle."

The Kidnapping
of Collie Younger

CHAPTER 1

It was Collie Younger who dared the picnic gang to go in swimming. This girl from Texas had been the gayest and the wildest of last June's graduates of Hazelton Normal College; and as on many former occasions, her audacity had been infectious. But despite the warm September sun, the water of Canyon Creek would be icy. Frost had long since come to tinge the oaks and aspens of that high Arizona altitude. It was one thing to bask in the golden sunshine and gaze into the amber water, which reflected the red walls, the fringed ledges, the colored sycamore leaves floating down, and quite another to plunge into it.

"You're a lot of daid ones," taunted Collie, with a shake of her bright head. "This picnic is a flop. The boys are playing poker. It's hot down heah. Me for a swim!"

"But, Collie, we didn't bring any bathing suits," remonstrated Sara Brecken.

"We don't need any."

"You wouldn't—"

"Shore I would—if we went up the creek in the shade. But it's nice and sunny heah. We can keep something on and dry off pronto."

"I'm for it," cried Helen Bender mischievously. "Anything to shock these boys out of their poker game!"

That settled the argument. Sara reluctantly followed her six companions down off the green bench to the huge rocks that lined the shore. Collie was the first to emerge from behind them into the open.

Roddy Brecken, who never had any money to gamble with and no luck besides, sat watching the red-sided trout shining in the crystal water. Espying Collie in her scant attire and slim allurement he drew with a start and a sharp breath. He had never seen such an apparition. In town, the couple of times he had encountered her since his return to Hazelton, she had appeared merely a pretty girl in a crowd of prettier ones. But this was different. Half naked, she was not so small; her form had more roundness than any one would have guessed; her graceful arms and legs held a warm tint of fading tan; and as she gingerly stuck a small foot into the water she leaped up with a shriek and a toss of her shining curls. Then, at the bantering of the girls emerging from behind the rocks, Collie daringly dove into the pool. She bobbed up splashing and blowing, to call out in a half-strangled voice: "Come on in. Water's great."

Roddy had arisen to make tracks away from there, as soon as he could unrivet his feet. But his retreat was checked by the spectacle of the six girls hurrying over the rocks. It appeared to Roddy that his gaze took in a great deal of uncovered white flesh. The girls made haste to wade in and submerge their charms.

Their squealing laughing melee broke up the poker game. The other six boys came trooping down, headed by Roddy's brother John, upon whose handsome face the expression of amazement was displaced by one of disapproval and annoyance. The other young men did not take the scene amiss.

"I'm a-rarin' to go," yelled Bruce Jones.

"Let's pile in, fellers, as we are," suggested another.

"Don't be a lot of fools! Not for mine. The sun will soon drop behind the wall."

John Brecken's vigorous opposition to the idea did not deter two of the boys from joining the girls in the water. But the impromptu bathing was obviously destined to a very short duration. John might have spared his peremptory call for his sister Sara to come out. Presently all of them, except Collie, made for the shore, and if they had looked outrageous before they went in, Reddy wondered what words could be used to describe them now. The boys ran puffing up the rocks. "I'll say—it wa—was—c—cold," declared Bruce, making for an isolated place in the sun. The girls, huddling together, slopped out of sight into their retreat. Collie kept swimming and splashing about. Roddy conceived an idea she was doing it to annoy John.

"Collie Younger, you come right out of there," yelled John. "You'll catch your death."

"Cold water's good for me. Cools me off," replied the girl.

"Yes, and your hair will look fine tonight for the dance."

That clever sally had the desired effect. But Collie did not bother to wade around the back of the rocks, like the other girls. She boldly climbed up at the point where she had plunged off.

"You're a sight," declared John, whipping off his coat, and making toward her.

"What for? Sore eyes?"

John's vehement denial was at distinct variance with Roddy's rapt attention. The beauty and the daring of the girl were potent enough to counteract his resentment at her impertinence to John and an underlying disapproval of her lack of modesty.

"Yeah? Well, you don't have to look at me," rejoined Collie flippantly.

"Here. Put this on."

"I don't want your coat."

"Collie! You look—like—like hell!"

"Jealous, Big Boy? You would be. I'll bet if you and I were heah alone you wouldn't register such absurd objection."

"I won't have this," sputtered Brecken.

"*You* won't. Since when were you my boss? Jack, I'm fed up with you. We're not engaged, and even if we were, I'd do as I pleased."

"You bet you would," said John bitterly. "You get a kick out of such indecent display—"

"Who's indecent?" queried Collie hotly. "It's your mind, Jack Brecken. Shut up, or I'll drop what I've got on and go in again."

John flung his coat upon her and wheeled in high dudgeon to climb up on the bench, where the boys teased him good-humoredly. Roddy preferred to leave his perch on the rock and saunter up the creek under the trees.

It seemed good to get back to Arizona, to which he had returned only infrequently during the last few years. Canyon Creek had been one of Roddy's haunts as a boy, and the dry smell of pine, the stream rushing here in white wreaths about the mossy rocks, and eddying there in amber pools, where the big trout lay like shadows, brought back memories and dreams that hurt. What days he and John had spent together in these woods. Red squirrels chattered into the still solitude of the forested canyon. He encountered deer tracks in the dust of the trail. What a joy it would be to again take a fall hunt with John. The smoky haze in the glades, the brooding melancholy of the canyon, the plaintive murmur of insects, the intervals of unbroken solemn silence assured Roddy that the hunting season was not many weeks away.

He retraced his steps, sorry to leave the shade of the gray-barked sycamores, reluctant to join the crowd of young people again. The boys were all Arizonians, whom he had always known, but the girls, except Sara, were strangers from beyond Hazelton. Roddy had noted with an unwonted stir of feeling that his bad reputation had in no wise kept them aloof. In fact, it had seemed quite the opposite. The Texas girl, who had made such an exhibition of herself, had cast too many glances in Roddy's direction for him to believe them

174

casual. No doubt she was taking John down the line, and would do the same thing to him if she had the opportunity. He felt sorry for John, who was so obviously in love with her. And to feel sorry for John, to whom he had always looked up, was not a pleasant sensation.

But what eyes that girl had! He had thought they were hazel until he had seen them this day, as she stood bareheaded in the sunlight, and then he decided they were topaz. Their color could not have had anything to do with their tantalizing expression. And he admitted that the rest of her matched her eyes.

Roddy felt ill-at-ease. He had not wanted to attend this picnic with John, who, however, had insisted until he gave in. Absence and a gradual drifting had not changed his boyhood love for his brother. That, Roddy reflected, had been the only anchor he had known.

When he got back to the others the sun had gone down behind the fringe of the western rim. Deep shadows showed under the walls. The warm breath moving up the canyon had cooled. Roddy's last glance at the creek took in the green-gold sycamore leaves floating down stream.

The boys were packing baskets and coats to the cars parked some distance away. John, looking somber and with traces of his anger still on his face, stood apart, evidently waiting for Collie. It developed, however, that he was waiting for Roddy. "Collie's riding back with Bruce and Sara," he said. "I'm glad of that, for it'll give me a chance to talk to you. Let's rustle."

Nevertheless, John slowed up as soon as he drew Roddy away from the others. He had something on his mind and apparently found broaching it not so easy.

"Rod, my mind's been simmering ever since you came home," he began presently. "This break of Collie's today brought it to a boil. I told you I was simply nuts over her, didn't I?"

"Yes. But you needn't have told me. Anyone could see that."

"Is that so? Well, she has been playing fast and loose

with me. I'm sure Collie cares most for me, else she wouldn't . . . but she plays with the other boys, too, and it's got my goat. I'll simply have to throw a bridle on her. . . . Once my wife, she'd be all right."

"Brother, I reckon what you need on her is a hackamore," observed Roddy, with a laugh.

They reached the glade through which the road ran. The cars were leaving. Roddy saw Collie's face flash out of the last one, as she bent a curious glance back at them. On second thought Roddy decided Collie had looked back at him. John might not have been there at all.

"I'll tell the world," admitted John grimly, "I'm at the end of my rope. And if the plan I have fails, or if you refuse to do it, I'm sunk."

"Me! Refuse?" ejaculated Roddy, in amazement. "For Pete's sake, what could *I* do?"

"You can kidnap her, by thunder, and scare her half to death."

For a moment, Roddy stared at his brother, waiting for him to give an indication that he was joking. But John's face remained deadly serious. "Well," John finally remarked impatiently, "did you get what I said?"

"Jack, are you crazy?" Roddy finally ejaculated. "You must have it bad. Nothing doing!"

"Wait till you hear my proposition," went on John, white and tense. "Listen . . . Roddy, Dad left all his property to us, fifty-fifty. You hate the store and you'd never stick there long at a time. I've run the business, improved it, made money, I've given and sent you money every time you asked for it. I didn't begrudge it. I know how you feel about living in town. I've tried to understand you, sympathize with you. Some of your scrapes the last two years have been hard for me to swallow and have given you a bad reputation."

"Jack, I haven't been so hot," replied Roddy, dropping his head, ashamed, yet grateful to John for not being harsher.

"Well, I propose to buy you out. Will you sell? It would be better for the business."

"I'd jump at it, Jack."

"Fine. I'll give you five thousand, half down, and my half share in old Middleton's cattle and range. That property had run down. It's not worth much now. But it can be worked into a good paying business. The old fellow won't last long. That property would eventually be yours. A ranch in the Verdi, where there's forest left and game!"

"Right down my alley, Jack," returned Roddy, with feeling. "I know the range. Swell! But I'd forgotten you had thrown in with Middleton. What's the string to this proposition?"

"Do you like it?"

"So far it's great. And darn fair of you, Jack."

"All right. Here's the string. I've been thinking this over for sometime. I want you to kidnap Collie—drive her down under the Tonto Rim to that old cabin in Turkey Canyon. Treat her rough. I don't care a damn how mean you are to her, so long as you make yourself out to be plenty tough. Scare hell out of her. As it turns out we can easily keep the kidnapping a secret. We'll plan for me to trail you—find you on a certain date. Collie will be subdued, worn out with mistreatment and hard fare and fright, then I'll come along to rescue her."

For a moment Roddy felt an impulse to laugh. This could be nothing but a bad joke of John's. But in John's face was no suggestion of humor and his voice was anxious and urgent. Almost pityingly Roddy asked, "Jack Brecken, do you figure she'll fall for you then?"

"I hope she will. If that doesn't fetch her nothing will—the contrary little flirt!"

"But, man alive! She's from Texas. She's a live wire. She'd kill you if she found it out. And I reckon she'd kill me, anyhow."

"Yes, Collie will be game. It's a risk. But I've *got* to do it."

"How on earth could I get away with it? She's popular—has lots of friends. They'd raise hell."

"Ordinarily, yes. But this deal has been made for me. Listen. . . . Collie graduated last spring. But she stayed

177

on all summer, until now. She's leaving for Texas tomorrow. I've offered to drive her over to Colton to catch the main line express. All the girls will be busy or in school when I call for her. She'll say goodbye to them at the dance tonight. She intends to stop off at Albuquerque to visit an uncle for two weeks. And she'll not wire him till she got on the train. I'll send you in my old car, in which you'll pack grub, blankets, etc. You'll whisk her away—and at a time we'll set, I'll drive down to Turkey Canyon to get her."

"Just like that!" ejaculated Roddy, snapping his fingers.

"Will you do it?" demanded John tersely.

"I'm afraid I'll have to turn it down. I'd do almost anything for you, Jack. And if that kid has double-crossed you I could shake the gizzards out of her, but—but—"

"Why won't you?"

"Jack, it's so—so—hell! I don't know what. So ridiculous! And even if we could get away with it, it seems a dirty trick to pull on any girl—even if she has played you for a sucker. You can't really love her."

"I'm crazy about Collie. And I tell you again if you fail me, I'll be sunk. And don't forget my offer of the money and ranch." John's tone was verging on despair.

"Money doesn't cut much ice with me. But that Verdi ranch—I could go for that in a big way." cogitated Roddy.

"Well, here's your chance to get it, along with money to make it a fine thing for you. A place to settle down. You could quit this rolling-stone stuff. There'll always be good hunting and fishing in the Verdi. Why, that canyon runs down into the Tonto Basin."

"Sounds great, Jack," said Roddy, gripping the car with a strong brown hand. "Only—the girl part is the deal—that sticks in my craw."

"I don't see why. Listen, Rod! There's something coming to Collie Younger. She needs taming. I should think it'd appeal to you."

"Well, it doesn't," denied Roddy forcibly. But the

178

instant his words were spent he realized they were false. And that astonished him. The idea intrigued him—took hold of him. Suddenly, a picture of Collie flashed into mind—her rebellious face and challenging eyes, as she had walked unashamed and free, like a young goddess out of her bath. That picture proved devastating. Then he sensed a resentment towards this high-stepping Texas kid and an urge to avenge her trifling with his blundering brother, who had never had any luck with girls. All the same it looked like a crowning folly for him.

"Sorry, old man. I just can't see it your way," he said, and got into the car. John violently slammed the door shut and took the wheel. His state of mind might have been judged by his reckless driving up a steep and narrow road to the rim. Roddy gazed across the deep canyon, now full of blue shadows, to the long sweep of the cedared desert toward the west. Purple clouds burned with a ruddy fire, low down along the horizon. To the south, towards the Verdi, the canyon wound its snake-like trail of red and gold into the green wilderness. Facing northward, as John headed the car homeward, Roddy viewed the huge bulk of the mountains looming high, crowned with white. How hard to leave this Arizona range again!

John drove like a man possessed of devils and roared past the other cars half way to Hazelton. Dusk had fallen when he reached home in the outskirts of town. Then he broke the silence. "Rod," he said, "you may have changed. Once you were full of the Old Nick. But if sentiment and romance are dead in you, look at my offer as simply business."

"Jack, I'm no good. All the same I'd hate to pull a low-down stunt like that."

"You're not acquainted with Collie. She'd get a kick out of being kidnapped."

"Why don't you kidnap her yourself?"

"I would. But I figured it wouldn't work. It takes time, and besides I haven't an excuse to leave the business just now. The rescue act would be much better, and I'd be more of a hero in her eyes. Collie's a Southerner, brimming with romance. She's crazy over the movies. Goes to every picture. Once she told me she could fall for me much quicker if I did something heroic. That's what gave me this idea."

"That may be okay with you, Jack. But somehow it doesn't persuade me. She's spunky, and she won't be bossed. I'd say that was your great fault, Jack."

"I like my own way and I see that I get it. I've set my heart on Collie, the little fiend."

John's words smacked of arrogance, but Roddy could sense the panic behind them.

"But this deal of yours isn't on the level, rejoined Roddy curtly.

"Neither is Collie on the level."

"Oh, she isn't!" Roddy stared aghast.

"Not with men, that's a cinch. In the two years she has gone to college here, she had taken every fellow I know down the line. Cowboys are her special dish. She swears she adores them. But I noticed none of them lasted long."

"Well. It'd depend on how far she—"

"I don't know. But there have been times when I was so jealous and sick I wanted to murder her. Then she'd be sweeter to me than ever."

"Jack, I should think you'd be leary of such a girl—for a wife."

John waved that statement aside. "Come to the Normal dance tonight. See for yourself. She'll make a play for you. I got that today. You're husky and handsome. She's heard gossip about you. She's curious."

"But I haven't a decent suit to my back," protested Roddy.

"I'll lend you one. My clothes always fit you."

"If my reputation is so bad, I should think—"

"That will make you all the more interesting." There was a tinge of bitterness in John's voice. "Besides, Normal dances are always short of men. "Everybody in town will be invited. All the cowboys on the range. It'll be the first dance of the season and sure a swell affair."

John's importunity weighed powerfully on Roddy. Moreover, he grew conscious of a curious eagerness to see Collie Younger again. He gave in to it. And he had a stubborn conception of his own about that girl—a something born from the scornful flash of topaz eyes at his brother.

Roddy accepted John's brand-new dark suit and dressed himself with a growing amusement and interest. After dinner, he walked up to town. The cold night wind whipped down from the black peaks. Roddy wished for a fleece-lined coat, such as he used to wear while riding. For the first time since his arrival home he strolled into poolrooms and hotel lobbies, curious about whom he might meet. No lack of old acquaintances and some sundry drinks of hard liquor warmed Roddy into a heartening mood. He fell in with some cowboys and went to the dance with them.

The Normal College was an institution that had been established since Roddy's school days in Hazelton. He had never been inside the big building, which was situated a little way out of town in a grove of pine trees. The several hundred automobiles parked all around attested to a large attendance at the dance. Reluctant to go in, and thinking it best to walk to and fro a while in the cold air, Roddy gave his eager cowboy comrades the slip.

When he did enter the building, he experienced a pleasant surprise at sight of the many pretty girls in formal gowns, and clean-cut western boys with tanned faces, talking and laughing at the entrance to the colorfully decorated ballroom. A forgotten something stirred in his veins. It swelled with the sudden burst of tantalizing music which drowned the low murmur of voices. Roddy found himself carried along with the crowd into the big hall.

Roddy took to the side-lines, intending to find enjoyment watching the dancers. He quite forgot his reason for coming. But he had scarcely had a moment to himself when a gracious woman, evidently one of the hostesses, swooped down upon him and led him off. To Roddy's dismay he saw a whole contingent of girls in white and pink and blue, all apparently eager-eyed for a partner. Before he realized what it was all about, he found himself on the floor with a dark-haired girl. He was awkward and he stepped on her feet. Mortified by this, Roddy woke up to exert all his wit and memory to recall a once skillful lightness of foot and accommodations to rhythm. He had begun to dance creditably when the music stopped.

One after another, then, he was given four partners, the last of whom was a decidedly comely girl whose auburn-tinted head came up to his shoulder. With her, Roddy started out well. But any one save a cripple could have danced with this girl, Roddy assured himself.

"Don't you know me, Roddy?" she asked roguishly. Indeed, no. I'm sorry. Ought I?"

"Hardly. I've grown up and changed."

"Did I go to school with you?"

"Yes. But I was a kid in the first grade. I'm Jessie Evans."

"Jessie Evans? You couldn't be that long-legged, freckle faced, red-headed little imp who used to..."

"You've got my number, Roddy," she replied gayly.

"No? Well, of all things! You, little Jessie, grown into such—such a stunning girl?"

"Thanks. It's nice of you to say so."

Roddy got along delightfully with Jessie and graduated into something of his old ease at dancing. He did not realize at all what a fine time he was having until after that dance, when he encountered his brother and several of the picnic party. Then he remembered, and was at some pains to conceal his self-consciousness.

"Rod, I see you're stepping right out," remarked John amiably. Manifestly he was in good spirits, and looked very handsome with his strong dark face minus its brooding anger. Something had cheered Jack up. No doubt it was the bewitching little girl who clung to his arm.

182

"Howdy, Jack. Sure, I'm enjoying myself," replied Roddy. Then he bowed to Collie and the others.

"I'm glad, old man. It's good to see you here," said John, and his heartiness seemed free of any ulterior interest in Roddy's presence. "You must dance with Collie. Here, take her for the next."

"I'd be delighted, if she'll risk it."

"Is there any great risk?" drawled the Texas girl, looking up with her penetrating topaz eyes. She wore a gown that matched them and her hair. Her rounded arms and neck, almost as gold of hue as her gown, brought back strikingly to Roddy the picture of her that he could never forget.

"I'm a rotten dancer."

"You cain't be any worse than some of these hoofers heah," she rejoined, lifting her little hands to him as the music started. In a moment he felt as if he were holding a fairy. He responded to the stimulus by dancing better than he ever had before. When they got half way round the hall she said:

"Roddy, you're not a rotten dancer. But you'd do better to hold me closer. Not at arms' length!"

"I'm a tenderfoot—at dancing," he replied apologetically, but he tightened his clasp.

"Yeah? I hadn't noticed it. But I'd prefer that to these boys who dance so darn well they cain't do anything else."

Collie inspired as well as intoxicated Roddy. It was impossible not to take advantage of her suggestion. Then he felt her as substantial as she had looked that afternoon. Her curly fragrant head rested low upon his shoulder. She clung to him without in the least hampering his step.

Roddy, you didn't approve of me this afternoon down in the canyon creek?"

"I—how—what makes you think that?" he stammered.

"The way you looked at me. Maybe I did go too far before a stranger, anyhow. But Jack gives me a pain in the neck."

"You give him a worse pain than that," said Roddy, with a laugh. "There! I got out of step. Collie, I can't talk and dance."

"All right. But tell me what you thought—about me—this afternoon."

"Well, I didn't get beyond how pretty you looked."

"Oh! Not so poor, Roddy." She did not speak again until the dance ended.

"Come, let's beat it outdoors," she commanded, and dragged him from the ballroom. "Pinch somebody's coat or wrap. I'm a Southerner, you know. I love your Arizonie, but oh, it freezes me to death."

They went out under the giant pines. White gowns shone in the moonlight. Other couples passed them going in. It was wonderful out there despite the cold. Black and star-crowned, the peaks pierced the dark blue sky.

"You're not much of a talker, are you?" inquired Collie.

"Me? Gosh, no. I haven't any line," replied Roddy.

"Not much! You cain't fool this dame. I wish you had come back heah a year ago."

"Why?"

"Then I could have known you. I leave Hazelton tomorrow and I won't be back for a while. We might not meet again."

"I reckon you're not missing much."

Collie gave his arm a squeeze. "Don't be so modest, old dear," she replied.

They came to a huge fallen pine that stretched across the campus. "Lift me up," said the girl. Roddy put his hands under her arms and sailed her aloft to a perch on the log.

"How strong you are!" she murmured, as she smoothed down her gown. Her head was now on a level with his. The moonlight silvered her hair and worked magic in her eyes and enhanced the charm of her face.

"I've been cowboy, miner, lumber jack," he said lightly. "All professions that require strength."

"I've heard that you were a hard drinker, gambler, fighter—in fact a hard nut."

"I seem to have a good reputation."

"Is it true?"

"True? I reckon so."

"I wonder.... Roddy, you're the bestlooking fellow I've met heah. And you've a nicer manner than most. You remind me of a Southerner."

"My granddad was from Texas. My mother from Missouri. That's south, you know."

"Are you staying long heah?"

"I reckon not. I cain't stay any place long. Why do you ask?"

"Oh, I told you I was coming back," she returned, with a flash of her eyes.

"But what about John? I gathered you and he had been pretty friendly."

"Oh, John's sort of dotty about me, and I thought I was in love with him. But he's too slow for me and too bossy, so I'm going to give him the gate." There was an insolence in the girl's tone that antagonized Roddy.

"Does Jack suspect that?" he asked, wishing to lead her on.

"Not a chance. He couldn't believe it. Says I don't know my mind two days running."

"He appeared happy tonight."

"I made up with him—kissed him. If I hadn't done so, this last night heah would have flopped. I wanted to enjoy it.... I'm enjoying it very much—right now."

"Are you going to tell him?"

"Yes, in the mawning. Maybe I'll string him along till later. It'd be fun to do it at the train."

Her mocking, high-pitched laughter pealed out. Her eyes danced in the moonlight. That was the moment Roddy understood his brother and accepted his offer. To tame this imperious and ruthless young lady appealed to all that was wild and reckless in Roddy. Aligned with his loyalty to John, it set the balance.

"Jack asked me to drive you across to Colton," said Roddy, smoothly. "He's a Mason, you know, and has an important conference."

"He did? How jolly. I'm tickled pink," she cried ecstatically.

"When and where shall I call for you?"

"The cottage where I've been living with Helen and Mary is on Oak Street, right next to the Women's Dormitory. Do you know where that is?"

"Yes. What time?"

"Two o'clock sharp."

"Baggage?"

"Plenty. But no trunks. I'll have the bags taken out."

"Okay."

"It's a nice long ride over. I hated the idea of Jack driving me. He's so business-like about everything he does and he cain't enjoy the scenery. If we leave at two we'll have plenty of time. You don't want to hurry, do you?"

"Reckon I'll creep along, if you like."

"Then we can talk, too, and plan. . . . I'm not saying goodbye forever. . . . You'll write to me. . . . Roddy, if I was staying on heah, I'd fall for you something awful."

"Oh, yeah? Lucky you're not."

"For me—or you, darling?"

"You. I'm a bad hombre, Collie."

"So I've heahed. Wild guy—devil with the women. And you haven't even squeezed my hand. Pooh! That's a lot of baloney."

They walked back to the school building and sought out John who was standing alone. Roddy gave his brother a significant look.

"I told Collie that you wanted me to drive her over to the main line," he informed John, "and she decided she could trust me."

It was lucky that Collie was looking at Roddy, for such a flood of relief and gratification passed over John's features that Collie would have suspected something had she seen his expression.

Before John could answer, Roddy turned to Collie. "So long, Collie, see you at two tomorrow," he said, and walked off into the moonlight."

He had let himself in for it, he mused rather grimly. But the girl had it coming to her. She was an outrageous flirt, and had tried to do to him as she had done to John, and undoubtedly to numbers of other boys. She needed a lesson, a severe one, and it seemed that he, Roddy, was the one chosen to give it. There was a strange satisfaction in that thought.

Then his doubt set in again. After all, what business was it of his? Why shouldn't John carry out his own crazy plans. What had induced him, Roddy, to give in to the idea? He was a softy and she was taking him down the line just as she had taken John. It wasn't a sane thing to do, and he was damned if he'd carry it out. He'd go right straight to John and tell him it was impossible.

Roddy turned and started back under the trees. Just as he was about to mount the steps of the school building, a movement in the shrubbery at the side drew his attention. The moonlight flooded down on the tantalizing face of Collie and on the white arms that were creeping around the neck of a cowboy Roddy had never before seen.

Roddy's right-about-face was so swift that he almost lost his balance. "You win, John," he muttered to himself. "I'll go through with it!"

CHAPTER 2

Next day, the last of Roddy's many errands was to drive to the bank to cash the check for twenty-five hundred dollars that John had forced on him, along with the papers of a transfer of his share in Middleton's ranch. John had not been taking any chances of Roddy's flunking on his part of the bargain.

The teller did not have so large an amount of cash in the cage and had to send to the vault for it. "Can't use checks in the country I'm going to," John explained. "I'm not known, and anyway the backwoodsmen don't believe in checks."

"Well, be careful," the teller warned him. "There are always shady characters hanging around."

John laughed and pocketed his bills. "I'll be on the lookout," he assured the man.

It was after two o'clock when Roddy turned in the direction of the women's dormitory. He stepped on the gas to go tearing across the railroad track ahead of a freight train. And in less than two minutes he was passing the noisy sawmill, with its great cloud of creamy smoke rolling aloft, to sight the college building beyond. In another moment he spied Collie at the gate of a small cottage. His heart leaped. All day the adventure had been unreal till he saw her. As he slowed to a stop he observed there did not appear to be any one but Collie in sight. She looked very smart in a brown suit and carried a coat on her arm. A pile of suitcases and bags lay on the sidewalk.

"Howdy, Texas. Sorry to be late," said Roddy, as he leaped out. "Hop in the front seat."

"Oh, Roddy, I thought you'd never come," she cried, giving him a radiant smile. "I see stingy Jack gave you his old car. What's all the junk?"

"I reckon I'll need to be alone in the woods for a while—after this ride with you. So I'm going camping," replied Roddy, and he began to throw her bags into the back of the car. As he slipped in to the wheel he looked around to see if anyone was observing them. There were no pedestrians, but a car was raising dust at the railroad crossing. Roddy drove rapidly toward the open country. The deed was done.

Collie edged closer to him and hooked a little hand under his arm. Excited and thrilled, evidently, she had not noted they were travelling in the wrong direction.

"Oh, swell!" she ejaculated. "I'm tired. Had only three hours sleep," and with a sigh she sank against him. But she kept on talking, about the dance, about the girls, about Jack, and how she hated to leave Arizona.

Roddy was too excited to pay much attention to her chatter, but he could not help but be affected by the softness and warmth of her person. At his lack of response Collie presently remarked dryly that she hoped he was going to make the ride interesting.

"I'll tell the world," he assured her. In the little mirror he caught sight of a car gaining from behind. Roddy did not intend to allow any one to see Collie, let alone pass him, and accordingly he increased the speed.

"Collie, how'd you like to have me drive you clear to Albuquerque," he queried daringly.

"Wonderful!" she burst out, amazed and delighted. "But how long would you take—where would we—"

"A couple of days, loafing along. Chance for us to get acquainted."

"Say, Big Boy, you're doing pretty well. . . . Where'd we sleep?"

"I'd make a bed for you in the back seat. I have blankets and pillows. I'll sleep on the ground."

"Can we get away with it?"

"Cinch. We'd roll through the few towns there are. Camp in lonesome places. I brought grub, fruit, everything, and I can cook."

She leaned against him, silent for a long moment. Then she asked: "Can I trust you, Roddy?"

"I reckon it'll be risky," he replied with a laugh.

"Well, I'll take the chance! It'll be a lark—my last in Arizona.... Okay, Roddy."

Roddy was hindered from making a ready response to her immediate acceptance of his proposal. Her tone, when she had asked if she could trust him, scarcely savored of heedlessness; it had contained a note foreign to every other thing she had said to him. It gave him pause.

Roddy happened at the moment to glance into his rear-sight mirror, and found that the car behind was coming up fast. Then accelerating his speed, he turned a corner, only to be confronted by a bad stretch of road that would be hazardous for fast travel. He decided to let the car pass if it caught him before the narrow strip ended.

"Slide down, Collie, so that driver can't see you."

"Gee!" ejaculated the girl gleefully. "We're starting off well."

The approaching automobile was an old Ford with two occupants. They came on apace and were almost up with Roddy when he reached a wider spot where they might have passed him. They did not, however, make the attempt, until just at the end of the rough stretch, when they astounded Roddy with a honking rush.

It angered him. Instead of swerving he hit into high speed. And at that instant the front of the Ford shot into sight alongside.

"*Stop, that!*" came a hoarse bellow. "*An' stick 'em up!*"

Roddy went cold all over. The rattling car rocked almost abreast of him. A man leaned out from back of the windshield, automatic gun extended. His ham-shaped visage, with pointed chin covered by a reddish beard, seemed vaguely familiar. Somewhere, that very day, Roddy had seen it. In a flash Roddy stepped his car to its limit. As he forged ahead, there came a crash of splintered glass accompanied by a gunshot. His left sideshield had been hit by a bullet. A fierce indistinguishable command to stop filled Roddy's ears. He slid down in his seat as far as he dared, yelling to Collie to keep hidden, and drove on, the cold shock to his internals giving way to the heat of anger. A holdup! Where had he seen that man? Every second he stingingly expected another shot and bullet. But it did not come. This old touring car of John's simply swallowed up the road. Walls of green flashed by on each side. Presently Roddy dared to look back. Already he was further from the pursuing car than he had imagined. Almost out of range! Perhaps the holdup man had shot to halt him, without murderous intent. Roddy sat up and drove as never before in his life, and presently he had left his pursuers far behind and finally out of sight around a bend.

"Sit up, Collie. We showed them our heels."

She came up as if for air: "G—gangsters?"

"Search me. But that guy with the gun looked plenty tough. *Where* did I see him?"

"Step on it, Roddy."

"I was doing seventy back aways. Sixty now. This old bus can go some . . . Collie, that little play wasn't on the program."

"You ought to pack a gun," declared this young lady from Texas.

"I've got two in the car. But gosh! I never thought of them. . . . Where in hell—now. . . . By thunder! *The bank*. It was in the bank where I saw that lantern-jawed hombre. I went in to cash Jack's check. He saw me with the money. . . . Well, what do you know about that!"

"They'll trail us. And this country is getting wilder. Oh, I should have made you drive me to the train!"

"Too late now, Collie," he replied grimly, and he meant that in several senses.

Roddy slowed to a reasonable speed. He did not trust the car to hold together. The road was good and he had now no fear of being caught. The fences failed, and gradually the slashed area where the timber had been cut off. Patches of goldenrod blazed among the sagebrush under the pines. Presently he passed the forks of the road, where a signboard marked the branch that turned west down to Canyon Creek.

"Canyon Creek?" exclaimed Collie. Why, that's the road we took yesterday!"

"You're not liable to forget it, or this road, either."

"This road; I've been on it. We drove down to the Natural Bridge a year and more ago. . . . Roddy, it runs to the left of Canyon Creek, and that Canyon gets deeper all the way. It's a terribly cut-up country. How'll we ever cross that canyon?"

"We can't."

"But we've got to go east. We'll be farther and farther out of our way."

"Shall I turn back?"

"Oh, no. We cain't do that with those bums chasing us."

"There's a road which turns off to the west, down here at Long Valley. It goes to Wilcox. We can take that. But then we'll have to go back through Hazelton."

"No. We'll keep on and drive way around somehow. A day or so more won't make any great difference. . . . I'm scared yet, but I'll soon get a kick out of it."

Stretches of rocky, cedared desert alternated with straggling pine forest. Collie lapsed into thoughtful quiet and again leaned upon Roddy's shoulder. Once he felt her studying his face. Was she beginning to wonder? It was all one to Roddy, for she would soon learn of his nefarious design. They passed a ranch zone, poor range, sparsely grassed, and scarce in cattle. The depression had hit these ranchers as well as town folk. Beyond, they climbed into forest country again, passed through bare spots where in spring there were weedy ponds, and so on to the lake and cottages of Hazelton's summer resort. It appeared deserted now. Collie was asleep with heavy head slipping low on Roddy's shoulder when he drove by the lake.

Beyond this point Roddy seldom looked back. He had not thought, however, that the holdup men would abandon the pursuit. On that dusty road they could trail him as long as he stayed on it. There followed a twenty-five mile stretch that ate up an hour of hard driving. Circling Snow Lake he passed on through the woods to Crooked Valley.

This was where he had to turn to the left from the main highway into the forest. And he needed to do so without being seen by any of the people who lived there. Moreover, he did not want to leave any tracks into the forester's road that led down to Turkey Canyon. Selecting a grove well carpeted with pine needles, Roddy drove to the right, off under the pines, as far from the highway as level ground permitted.

Darkness was coming on apace. When he stopped, the jolt of the car awakened Collie. She sat up bewildered, her curls all awry. "Night! Where the heck am I. Gee, what a lonesome place!"

Roddy explained that he had thought best to hide here until their pursuers went by. He advised her to get out and stretch her legs while he unpacked something to eat and drink. After that he would make room for her to sleep on the back seat. Here in the woods it was much warmer than out driving on the road. He concluded to get along without a fire, but did not hesitate to use his flashlight.

When presently he was ready to walk back to the road to watch till the Ford went by Collie said: "Roddy, I'm not stuck on staying heah alone. Let me go with you."

"Stay in the car. This is no picnic," he replied, and his tone was gruff.

Collie's eyes flashed and she retorted spiritedly: "Well, you needn't be so huffy about it."

Before very long, Roddy heard the drone of a motor car far off in the woods. Reaching the road he chose a deeply shadowed covert under a pine from which to watch. Soon the drone of the car changed to a hum. Headlights gleamed intermittently through the trees. The car came on, passed by behind its bright yellow lights. And it was not a Ford. This afforded Roddy satisfaction, for that car surely obliterated his tracks. He settled down to wait patiently. How long since he had been in the forest at night! The wilderness song in the tree-tops awakened a dreamy memory of his hunting days in that country.

In half an hour or less he heard another automobile. At length the lights glimmered under the trees. This car slowed down before it reached him. When it passed, he recognized the Ford. The driver halted some few hundred feet from where Roddy sat. He or his companion got out with a flashlight and appeared to be scrutinizing the ground. Roddy grasped that they were looking for his tracks at the junction of the road to Wilcox. Muttering, impatient voices floated to Roddy. The waving light went out; a door clicked; the Ford moved on down the road out of sight.

Hurrying back through the woods, Roddy was at some pains to locate his car. He found it, and peered in the back to find Collie asleep. Then he got in, switched on the lights, and cautiously drove back to the highway. Reaching it, he crossed to the left side and followed that down to the Wilcox branch on which he turned. Half a mile farther in the woods, he turned off on the rim road.

This was a forest road, seldom travelled by cars. Grass and weeds grew as high as the running board; thick brush lined the sides, with an occasional black-trunked pine rising above. It led down into Jones' Canyon, at the bottom of which ran a creek difficult to ford in spring. But now there was only a dry wash. The slope up the ridge opposite, Roddy remembered, was steep and long. When he at last surmounted it to the ridge-top, he felt relieved. All was smooth sailing now.

Collie called out something that sounded like, "Where in the hell are you driving?" Manifestly the slow grinding climb and severe joits had roused her. Roddy told her to shut up and go to sleep. She exclaimed what a sweet boy he was turning out to joyride with, and then she was quiet.

The forest road took a gradual ascent for twenty miles. Giant pines and silver spruce lined it so high that Roddy could not see their tips. It wound along the crest of the ridge, now through level areas of dense forest, and then by heads of ravines that ran down into the canyons on each side. The woods smelled sweet with an odorous tang.

At length, some time late in the night, Roddy reached the Rim, where the road ran east and west. As the altitude was over eight thousand feet, the air was bitingly cold. Roddy turned east. At times he passed close to the edge of the Rim, where it broke abruptly into the great Tonto Basin. In the moonlight it showed its vast gulf, opaque and gray, reaching across to the black Matazels.

Driving became even more difficult owing to potholes, rocky places, sharp bends, hills and crosswashes. And often Roddy had to get out to drag aside rotten logs and branches that had recently toppled over. Therefore he had to advance slowly and carefully. The hours passed. He could keep account of his progress and whereabouts by the white signs along the road: Myrtle Creek, Barbershop Canyon, Quaking Asp, Leonard Canyon, Gentry Canyon, and at last, Turkey Canyon.

Here he turned away from the Rim, straight down into the forest. The road had the same characteristics as the one by which he had reached the Rim; only now he was descending the winding crest of a ridge between the canyons. Towards the end, this road became well-nigh impassable, and full of rocks and gutters and boggy places. When he reached the end of the ridge, where it broke sharply down, the east was lightening and dawn was at hand.

Bright daylight greeted Roddy as he drove off the ridge into the beautiful park that was his objective. The old brown log cabin, with its mossy shelving roof, appeared as it existed in his memory, though even more weathered and picturesque than before. Here and there in the lonely park stood lofty pines and spruces; silver grass, colorful with autumn asters and daisies, covered the slopes; a wandering line of willow bushes, half-bronze, half-green, showed the course of the murmuring brook that flowed by the cabin; a grove of aspens, white-trunked and gold-leafed, blazed at the far end of the park.

Roddy's second glance caught the tawny gray coats of great antlered elk disappearing under the trees. He heard the gobble and cluck of wild turkeys. Down the brook two deer stood with long ears erect.

And all at once a strange feeling assailed Roddy, something stronger than the joy of solitude and beauty in the wilderness, a wish that he might have come there to stay.

Shutting off the engine, he stepped out. The glistening frosted grass crackled under his feet. And at that moment Collie stuck her tousled bright head out of the car. She looked all around. When her eyes rested upon Roddy, they were wide open, the sleep had vanished, and the topaz hue had darkened wondrously.

"*Lovely!*" she cried rapturously. "Oh, what a paradise!" And she bounded out to hold up her red lips to him. "Mawning, Roddy. . . . You may—for bringing me heah."

Roddy did not kiss her—he did not want to—but he wondered at himself.

"You'll cuss me pronto," he replied grimly.

"Never, darling. I feel like Alice in Wonderland." And she began to run around like a child who could not see all the enchanting things quickly enough.

Roddy unloaded the car of his camp duffle and food supplies. He split dead aspen and kindled a fire. Very shortly he had biscuits browning in a Dutch oven, coffee pot steaming, and he was slicing ham when Collie returned with her arms full of purple asters, goldenrod, and scarlet maple leaves. Her piquant face, smiling upon him from above this mass of exquisite color, gave him a distinct shock.

"Chuck that stuff and help me rustle breakfast," he said surlily.

"Say, Mister, you won't go far with me on such talk as that," she retorted, her smile fading. She laid the flowers carefully aside and warmed her hands over the

196

fire. Evidently they were numb. Then she got a bag out of the car and opened it upon the running board. Presently she went by with a towel and other toilet articles, to approach the brook. Suddenly, a little shriek reached Roddy's ears. He laughed. She was a tenderfoot, even though she came from Texas. A few moments after that she came back, her face rosy and bright.

"Don't you supply your women with hot water?" she inquired scornfully. "Or didn't they ever wash?" Then she returned to the car to brush her hair and apply her makeup, about which tasks she took her time.

"Come and get it before I throw it out," called Roddy.

She had a ravenous appetite, which might have been responsible for her unusual silence. "I'll say you can cook," she said, presently, when she had finished. "I'll help you wash up."

Roddy did not reply. He was revolving in mind the need to tell her what he had done.

"You drove all night?"

"Yeah."

"You look tired—and cross. I'm afraid you're worried about those holdup men."

"Not any more. I gave them the slip."

"What place is this?"

"Turkey Canyon."

"That doesn't mean anything to me. But I saw turkeys. Oh, so tame and beautiful. Where are we?"

"Over a hundred miles from Hazelton. Half that from the road we drove down on."

"So far!" she exclaimed wonderingly, but perplexed. "Why did you bring me heah?"

"I've kidnapped you," he replied, with a dark gaze at her.

'You *what*?" Like a bent twig released she sprang up.

"I kidnapped you, Collie Younger."

"Honestly—you did?"

"Honest to God."

She sank to her knees in amazement. "Roddy!

... Have my sins found me out?"

"I reckon they have."

"Oh! I swear I didn't flirt with you. I was thrilled to death to meet a real Westerner, like some of the Texas riders my Dad used to tell me about. I—I liked you, Roddy Brecken. . . . And because—because . . . you took the chance to fool me, to get me heah in this lonesome place. You fell for me!" Incoherent though her amazement had made her, Collie's last words held a note of triumph which stung Roddy to immediate denial.

"Miss Younger, it may surprise you further to learn that I did not fall for you at all," he rejoined with sarcasm.

Flaming red burned out the rouge in her cheeks.

"Then you kidnapped me for money?"

"I reckon so, partly."

"Who told you I had money?" And as he did not vouchsafe any answer to that she went on, her voice gaining in intensity. "Jack *told* you. I once showed him a letter from my brother about our oil wells in Texas. Jack must have told you.

"No. He never mentioned it."

"Then how did you know?"

"I didn't. You just jumped at conclusions."

"What do you mean by partly?"

"Well, as an afterconsideration, some dough is okay."

"I don't get you," she returned, shaking her curly head. "Cain't you come right out with it? *Why* did you kidnap me?"

"You made a sucker out of my brother," flashed Roddy passionately.

"Oh!" she breathed softly, with a gasp of realization. "Yes, I did. I suppose the fact that the big conceited stiff deserved it will not get anywhere with you? Well, heah we are. What do you think you're going to do with me?"

He regarded her brazenly, hiding in that bravado the conflict he was undergoing. He had not ever seen such a pair of tawny-fired eyes.

"You'll never play fast and loose with another guy."

"Do you intend to—to murder me?"

198

"I reckon I'll shy short of that."

"Then what?"

"You're curious, aren't you?"

"Why wouldn't I be curious. It seems to concern me."

"It'll concern you plenty before I get through with you. You'll be taught a lesson you'll never forget, you damn cheap little flirt. You'll think twice before you drive men crazy just to safisfy some female love of conquest. I'd think more of you if you'd gone the limit with every fellow you ever knew. Have you done that?"

"Why you—you backwoods lout!"

"All right. Call me what you like. The more you cuss me the more kick I'll get out of handing you what *I* think you deserve."

"And what's that, Mr. Loyal Champion of Brother John?"

"Understand, Collie Younger," his voice rang out, "I don't care a damn for you. Last night you made one of your usual plays for me. It made me sore, instead of soft. All your prettiness, your white and gold skin, your curls, your come-hither eyes don't mean one damn thing to me."

"Roddy Brecken, you *are* in love with me," she cried triumphantly, and she held out her arms with a gesture which, if it was as deceitful and vile as he believed, merited giving her all that rushed passionately to his mind.

"Yeah, you'll think so. You would! When you slave for me, when I beat you, hog-tie you with a rope, and make a rag out of you, till I trade what's left of you for money you're not worth?" So convincing did Roddy's fury make his words that Collie actually took them for truth.

"Jack will kill you!" she whispered, ashen white under her rouge.

Roddy dropped his head. Too look at her then was insupportable.

"For God's sake, Roddy, do *I* deserve that? Oh, it's unthinkable. . . . Roddy, I swear I never did a dirty trick in my life, one that I *knew* was dirty."

"Well, begin now. Wash up these pans and pots. Use

199

hot water and sand. Then pack your bags inside the cabin and clean it out. I'll go cut some bundles of spruce for beds."

The cold brutality of Roddy's response to her impassioned speech took all the fire out of Collie.

"Beds—in there?" she echoed haltingly. "That buggy, smelly place! I'd rather sleep outdoors."

"Well, if you prefer to freeze—but I don't—we'll both sleep inside."

"Roddy Brecken, if I sleep with you anywhere, I'll be cold plenty. I'll be daid!"

"Wait and see. You're a bluff, Collie Younger, and I'm calling you. Once in your life you're going to get the kicks you girls brag you like and never try. You'll show yellow."

"Much *you* know about girls. I won't do one single damn thing you order!"

"You won't, won't you?" rasped Roddy and, fastening a powerful hand in her blouse, he jerked her off her feet and shook her until her curly head bobbed like a jumping-jack.

"You bum! You bully!" she choked out furiously. Then he let her go. And with all her might she slapped him. Roddy returned the blow in a heat that overcame him, and it was too violent for her slight weight and build. She went down limp as a sack. Rising on one hand, with the other at her red cheek, she glared up with eyes like molten bronze. A fierce animal pain possessed her. As it subsided she appeared prey to an incredulous awe. Roddy needed no more to see that not only had she never seriously felt pain, but she certainly had never received a blow until that moment.

"Rustle now, before I get mad," he ordered and, picking up his axe, he stalked off toward the hillside. In all the fights Roddy had ever had, and they had numbered legion, he had never felt the fury this girl had aroused in him. On that score, he tried to excuse himself for knocking her down. His threat to beat her had been merely a threat. She was as imperious as the savage daughter of a great barbarian chief. She was also the epitome of the female species when infuriated, a cat, a spitfire. Lastly she was intelligent, keen as a whip. Roddy grasped that the one single advantage he had over her, the only thing he could resort to, was physical strength. By being a brute he could cow her. Chafing under this, he chopped down a small spruce tree and trimmed off the boughs. He gathered them into a huge bundle. Taking this up in his arms, he staggered to the cabin and flung down the odorous mass under the projecting roof that had once covered a board porch.

He noted that Collie had packed all her baggage and the bedding as well to the cabin, and was now cleaning out the rubbish. He heard her sobbing before she came to the door with tears streaming down her cheeks. Roddy most decidedly did not undergo the satisfaction that such a sight should have given him. Instead, he felt like a cur. Whereupon he went back after another load of spruce, taking a long time about the task.

Upon returning he found that Collie had made a pretty good job of cleaning the cabin, had carried her bags in, and all of the spruce boughs and blankets. Peering in he saw her in the act of spreading the blankets over the branches. She had not ceased crying.

Roddy set to work packing his supplies in under the porch roof, where he intended to build a fireplace of stones and cook the meals. While he was thus busied, Collie came to the door several times. Her expression seemed subdued.

"Stop your sniveling or I'll give you something to snivel about," he said, trying to make his voice as harsh as possible.

She did not reply, but the spirit flared up again in her eyes.

"Take that bag and fetch it back full of pine cones," he ordered brusquely.

After that he kept her at odd jobs until she appeared ready to drop. She was dirty and dishevelled. Her brown travelling suit was ruined. A discoloration began to be noticeable on her cheek. But all this did not deceive or placate Roddy. He knew that at any moment

201

he must expect an earthquake or a volcanic eruption. All Collie needed was the spark. He advised her to go into the cabin and change to warmer clothes, outdoor garb, and boots if she had them. He chopped a pile of firewood, and prepared lunch. When he called her, there was no answer. He went into the cabin to find her lying on the blankets pale and staring into space with tragic eyes.

"Roddy, I've been pondering," she said without a trace of resentment in her voice, "you know women have a sixth sense—intuition, clairvoyance, mysticism, or what not. My faith in you has survived that brutal blow. I cain't explain it. There seems to be something wrong, unnatural, false in this situation. I don't get it. But despite what you've said and done—I don't believe you're rotten."

"Yeah? Well, come out and eat," he replied, in self-defense. He would be lost if he tried to bandy words with her or exchange intelligent thoughts or even argue. He feared she would see through him no matter how crude and hateful he could make himself. He was afraid of her in serious pondering mood. Collie followed him out without further words, but her look was enigmatic.

While Roddy ate, taciturn and silent, he brooded over how to follow up his advantage without sacrificing every vestige of self-respect. He hated her, he believed, yet . . . he did not finish the thought. He had to carry on. But an almost insuperable obstacle seemed to erect itself on the fact that, flirt though she might be, she was as game as she was pretty, and utterly in his power. This actuality made the pregnant difference.

CHAPTER 3

There was a moment that followed, how soon Roddy
had no idea, in which he seemed to waver between
what Collie had divined he really was and the character
he had assumed. For her the situation, all at once raw
and ominous, had brought out the graver, more
womanly side of her. For Roddy that was harder to
withstand than her provocative charms. He had to
shock her out of it, kill it quickly, or fail utterly of his
part in this impossible travesty. What of John's fatal
attachment for this capricious girl, of the deal made and
paid for?

With sombre eyes upon the appealing pale face, with
gaze the passion of which was not pretense, though its
reason was his own sick wrath at himself, Roddy
deliberately crushed her intuitive faith in him, killed it
with profane and coarse speech no man should ever
have spoken to a woman. The horror she evinced, he
knew, would soon merge into the loathing and fear he
wanted her to feel. Then he stalked out of the cabin
despising himself. There was little left, he thought
bitterly, but to prove his infamous character in deeds.

Roddy took his rifle and went up the glade to hunt
for turkeys. It was necessary to procure meat, although
the hunting season was not yet open. Once on the
wooded slope, however, he scarcely concentrated his
faculties upon the pursuit of game. He sat down on a log
to wipe his moist brow. The contending passions within
his breast were not harmonious with the serenity, the
beauty, the speaking solitude of this colorful forest. He
could not sit still for long. He had to move, to walk, to
climb. And he mounted the ridge that he had
descended to get down to the park. He leaned against a

huge fallen log, aware of the presence of a frisky red squirrel, the squall of a jay, and of the flash of scarlet and orange and silver all around him. His consciousness of these sights and sounds was mere sensorial habit that he could not help. His thoughts and emotions were engaged in a grievous contention against what he knew not, except that it was not concerned with what he had promised to do for his brother. It was deeper than that. For minutes, perhaps hours, he paced the glades, the aisles under the pines, trying to bring to order the havoc in his mind. Then, all at once, he heard a hum foreign to the sounds of the wilderness. Lifting his head, he seemed to suspend all his senses except hearing. The sound was not the drum of a grouse or the whirr of a turkey in flight. It was a motor, and the certainty again sharpened all his faculties. At first he thought the car was coming down the ridge from the Rim. But clearer perception proved it was ascending the hill. No car could have gone by, down into the park, without his hearing it.

"By heaven! Collie! he cried. "She would, the game little Texan! And I never thought of it."

Roddy ran to intercept her, and he ran swiftly, leaping logs, crashing through brush, dodging trees. How far the road! He might be too late. The labor of the engine in low gear filled his beating ears. He rushed harder—burst out into the road.

Not a hundred feet down the grade the car came lurching and roaring toward him. Roddy caught the gleam of Collie's face, the bright color of her hair.

"*Stop!*" he yelled, in stentorian voice, leaping to the middle of the road.

But she drove on, bumping to a short level, where the car gathered momentum. It bore down on Roddy. Collie leaned out to scream something indistinguishable. But her white face and piercing eyes needed no accompanying voice. She would run him down. Roddy had to leap to save his life.

Then in a swift dash he caught up with the car and bounded upon the running-board. "Stop, damn you!" he panted.

"Jump—or I'll sideswipe you off!" she cried resolutely.

Holding on, Roddy bent with groping hand for the ignition. He had a glimpse of her face, set and cold, her blazing gaze dead ahead.

"Jump! *Quick!*" she warned.

Roddy switched off the ignition. But the car kept rolling on a short down-grade.

"Brakes! *Look out!*" yelled Roddy, frantically grasping the wheel. Collie had swerved toward the bank. He pulled. But she was strong and had a grip of steel. *Crash!* Flying glass stung Roddy as he was thrown off backward. He hit the ground hard. For an instant car and woods vanished in a scintillating burst of stars. Recovering, he sprang up. The car hung precariously over the bank, the front left wheel cramped against a tree.

"Collie! Would—you—kill us?" he panted, his chest heaving.

"I'd kill you damn gladly," she cut out icily. Her eyes shone with an extraordinary sharpness.

"Come out of there," he yelled, seeing the car slip a little. Opening the door he seized her arm and jerked her out.

"You'll take it right now, Texas!" he panted grimly, dragging her back to the road. He was vague about all he meant to do, but it included such a spanking as no girl ever got.

"I won't be manhandled, you dirty bum," she panted, struggling to free herself. But failing, she assailed him furiously, beating and scratching at his face, biting the arm that held her.

Then she kicked him violently on the shin. Her heavy-soled outing boot struck squarely on the bone, that owing to an injury of long standing, had remained exquisitely sensitive. Roddy let out a yelp and, loosing her, sank down in agony. The forest reeled around him. Hard on that flamed up the fury of a savage. He saw the girl through red-filmed eyes. And utterly beside himself, as she kicked viciously at him again, he seized her leg and upset her. She screeched like a wild creature, and lying on her back kicked herself free. She sprang up but did not run. Roddy lurched erect to get his hands upon her. And when, after a moment of blind instinctive violence he let go his hold, she sank limply on the ground, her face ashen, eyes glazed, with blood running from her lip.

"You Texas—wildcat!" he panted gazing down with a sudden reversal to sanity. "Brought that—on yourself!"

He left her lying there in the middle of the pine-matted road. Out of breath, hot as fire, he limped over to the car. No serious damage had been done, but if it got started down the slope, and missed a couple of trees just wide enough to let it through, it would be a lost car. By rocking it he slipped the front left wheel off the tree. The right front wheel hung six inches above the grade. With stones blocking it up, Roddy thought he might back the car upon the road. He found one of Collie's suitcases on the seat, also a canteen of water and a coat wrapped around a parcel of food. These he removed to the ground, and cautiously getting in, he left the door open and started the engine. As he backed with full power on, the bank gave away and the car slid over. He lunged out just in the nick of time, and as luck would have it, fell on his bruised leg. Rising on one hand, mad with pain and the miserable circumstance, he watched the car go straight between the two trees and roll down into the brush out of sight, cracking and banging. Then there was a final heavy metallic crash on rocks.

"Ahuh!.... That's that," muttered Roddy and, laboring to his feet, he limped back up on the bank.

Collie lay where he had left her. As he approached he saw that her eyes were open, distended in dark horror.

"Oh—Roddy!.... I heard it.... I—I thought you'd—gone over ..." she gasped huskily. Fury in her, as in him, had evidently weakened at the imminence of death.

"You played hell—didn't you?" he queried heavily.

"The car—smashed?"

"It pitched over the cliff."

"Then—we're stuck heah."

"Get up. You're not hurt."

She did not deny that in words but, observing her closely as she dragged herself to her feet, he began to fear that he might have hurt her seriously. She could hardly stand erect, and her breathing seemed difficult.

"Can you walk?" he queried, conscious of shock.

"I'm alright. . . . After all, you're pretty big. . . . I'm only a girl."

Roddy went mute at that. She was not accusing him but excusing herself for having been badly whipped in the fight with him. Was that the Texas of it? She had tried to sideswipe him off the running board, she had tried to kill him, she had fought him tooth and nail; and having lost, she seemed to be as square as she was game. What a wonderful girl! Roddy saw her in an illuminating light.

"Come on," he said, proceeding to take up her bag and coat and the canteen. Down the road some little distance he found his rifle. Thus encumbered, he could not help Collie. Slowly she followed him, a forlorn little figure now. Measured by his feelings, that descent to the cabin was indeed a long and grievous one for Roddy. If the girl had tried her feminine wiles, instead of pulling as nervy a stunt as he had ever heard of, he would have had no compunctions over continuing his program. But a change had begun to work in him, a change of opinion and heart. Still he had to keep up the deception until John came for them.

Arriving at the cabin, Roddy deposited his burdens and waited for Collie. It appeared to him that she would just about make it before collapsing. He had to subdue an impulse to go back and carry her. He judged correctly, for upon reaching the cabin, Collie fell upon the tarpaulin spread under the porch roof, and leaned back against the wall, spent and white.

"I've got to kill some meat," he said. "We can't last here without meat. . . . I'll have to tie you up while I go hunting. If I'd done that . . ."

"I won't try to beat it again . . . I couldn't, Roddy.

Cain't you see when a girl is licked. Please don't tie me."

"I reckon I won't trust you."

"But you can. On my honor."

"On your what?"

Her spirit flared up faintly at that. "Of course *you* wouldn't."

Without more ado Roddy bound her ankles securely, cursing inwardly more because his hands shook so than at the heinous act he was performing. Then he slipped a pack-strap tight round her waist and arms, and buckled it through the chinks between two logs at her back. All the while he avoided meeting her gaze. But even so the magnificent blaze of her eyes seemed to shrivel him.

"Roddy, you're a lot of things, the least of which is a damn fool," she said as he picked up his rifle.

Stalking off, he pondered her taunt. But upon reaching the woods at the end of the park he forcibly dismissed everything from mind except the important issue at hand, which was to procure meat. To that end, he stole into the aspens, on up the narrowing apex of the park, peering all around, and pausing every few paces to listen. He had not proceeded far when he heard turkeys scratching. This was a difficult sound to locate. Apparently it was above him. The afternoon wind was strong from the north. He worked against that. He heard various other noises. Once he stopped short with abated breath at a distant burr that he took for a motor car. He waited long for a repetition. As it did not come, he concluded he had been mistaken. Nerves! He would always be hearing the hum of a car in the forest.

Roddy located the flock of turkeys busily and noisily engaged in scratching for pine nuts. The wind was right from them to him, and he kept out of sight while making the stalk. Creeping close, he shot two gobblers before the flock disintegrated in a flapping, thumping escape. Much gratified at his success, Roddy tied the legs of the turkeys together, threw them over his shoulder and picking up his rifle, made down the slope for camp. Straightway, then, his problem with Collie reasserted itself, perceptibly different again and more vexatious.

When he strode out from under the pines at the foot of the north slope, he saw Collie leaning against the cabin wall where he had tied her. As he approached, Roddy imagined her face even paler. Her eyes resembled black holes in a white blanket. She had watched for his return. Poor kid! Roddy's conscience flayed him. Right there he felt forming in him the nucleus of a revolt against John's preposterous plot.

He crossed the brook. He was within speaking distance and was about to hail Collie when something about her checked the words behind his lips. Her unnatural rigidity, her blanched face—No! It was a strained and lightning flash of eyes.

Roddy hurried on. What was wrong with Collie? Even as he interpreted that magic of her eyes as deliberate, a warning of impending peril, a harsh voice rasped out:

"Drop that rifle! Stick 'em up!"

Roddy obeyed. A man ran out of the cabin at Roddy. A thin red beard failed to hide his hard lips and narrow chin. He held an automatic gun levelled before him. A second fellow appeared, gun in one hand, rope in the other.

"Frisk him, Marty," ordered the foremost. In short order Roddy's big roll of bills, his knife and watch, and his wallet were tossed upon the grass. The cold gray eyes of the leader snapped as he saw them. Then, in short order Roddy was bound hand and foot and shoved like a sack of meal to the ground. His head bumped against one of his supply packs.

"Collie?" he burst out, as soon as he could speak.

"Okay. They had just got heah. Cain't you use your eyes? A Texas ranger would have been wise the instant he caught my look."

"Ah!—I saw—I thought....But I'm no Texas ranger," rejoined Roddy heavily.

The man called Marty was a Westerner, unmistakably, but a ragged lout whose sallow visage Roddy had seen on the corners or in the poolrooms of Hazelton. He picked up his gun, which he had laid aside to bind Roddy, and shoving it back into his hip pocket he

209

turned to his accomplice. Roddy recognized in this individual the man who had attempted to hold him up on the road the day before. He was under thirty. The singularly cold and fanatic expression of his pasty face proclaimed him an addict to drugs. He was counting the many bills in Roddy's roll.

"How much, Gyp?" queried Marty, his bleary eyes rolling eagerly.

"Over two grand. But that's not a patch of what we'll clean up. Marty, you steered me on to something good." Then he turned to Roddy, his scrutiny intense and penetrating.

"John Brecken's brother, eh?"

"Yes."

"Yeah, and John Brecken's best girl," leered the fellow Marty.

"And all tied up tight. That means that she didn't come willing," cogitated the red-bearded one, putting two and two together. "Kidnapped her, eh?" he asked, turning to Roddy.

Roddy made no reply.

"Oh, you won't answer. Well, you don't have to. It's as plain as the nose on your face. If you stole John Brecken's girl, he'll pay to get her back and he'll pay to get you back just so he can get even with you. Now, ain't that a sweet dish?"

"Yeah," chimed in Marty, "and John Brecken's rich. Owns a store, a garage, and an interest in the sawmill. He ought to come across plenty, Gyp."

"Who's the dame? Does she have any folks that would be happy to have their little tootsie-wootsie safe home again?" inquired Gyp.

"She doesn't live in Hazelton. College girl. Never heard her name.

Gyp approached Collie to get down on one knee before her.

"What's your name, sweetness?"

"I guess it's Dennis."

"Say! You're all bunged up besides being tied. Beat you up, did he!"

210

"No. I tried to escape. Ran the car over a bank."

"I see. That's why we couldn't find the car we tracked down here. Have your folks got any money?"

"My mother works to send me to college."

"Don't try to kid me, sweetheart. Could you get ten thousand dollars for ransom?"

"John Brecken ought to pay that much for me," replied Collie sarcastically.

The gangster arose with a light upon his pale visage.

"Plenty safe, Marty, I'll say. Lovely hideout to wait, good eats when we were damn near starved, a pretty little dame to sleep with—a swell layout! Lemme dope this out while you cook supper. My mouth's watering for turkey."

"I'm shore a no good cook," replied the lout, too heartily to doubt.

"Little one, you're on the spot," said Gyp to Collie.

"I'm afraid I cain't stand on my feet," she replied.

"Hey, girl snatcher, can you roast a turkey so it'll melt in my mouth?" called the fellow to Roddy.

"I reckon. But hardly while my hands and feet are tied."

"Untie him, Marty. And stand guard over him with a gun while he gets supper."

The instant Roddy was freed and on his feet he began to think of a way to turn the tables on their captors. There would still be several hours of daylight. He must work slowly, watching like a hawk, thinking with all the wit and cunning he could muster. Marty fetched the turkeys to him and Roddy began to pick off the feathers. Gyp went back to Collie. Roddy saw him sit down to lay a bold hand on her. Then, Roddy, with the blood turning to fire in his veins, dared not look again. But he could hear the man talking low, manifestly making love to Collie. While Roddy heard, he thought desperately. How much more than Collie's life had he to save now! That transformed his sombre spirit. He recalled then that his gun was in the side pocket of the car. But his rifle lay only a few paces away in the grass under some bushes. Apparently his captors had forgotten that. As a last resort, even with Marty sitting there with weapon in hand, Roddy decided he would leap for the rifle. But before being driven to that, he must wait and watch for a safer moment.

"You dirty skunk. Take your hands off me!" suddenly cried Collie, her voice rising to a shriek. It had such withering abhorrence that Roddy marveled how any man could face, let alone touch, any woman who spoke with such passion. The fellow on guard let out a lecherous guffaw. Roddy, acting on a powerful impulse, edged over to kindle a fire. On his knees he split wood to replenish it.

"Need hot fire—so it'll burn down—bed of coals," he explained huskily. But he put his big skillet on the blazing faggots and poured half a can of grease onto it, then added a quart of water. He had conceived a cunning though exceedingly dangerous plan.

When Collie broke into hysterical sobs, the gangster got up. "Say, baby," he said caustically, "if I wasn't hard up for a dame, I'd call you a wash-out. You cut that stuff, or I'll give you something to squawk about."

Then he took to walking to and fro, apparently in deep thought. Roddy was fearful that he might come across the rifle. But he paced a beat between the cabin and the camp fire. His concentration became so great that he forgot the others. No doubt he was working out details of the plot to extort ransom money from John Brecken. That plot no longer concerned Roddy. It would never even get started into action.

Roddy put on the Dutch oven to heat. The greasy water in the skillet had begun to boil. Roddy watched it, listened to it simmer. The last of the water in his bucket he poured into a pan with flour. It was not enough to mix biscuit dough. But he fussed with other utensils and supplies until the grease and water in the skillet threatened to boil over.

The moment had come. Strong and cool, with his passion well under control, Roddy had two arrows to his bow.

"Can I fetch a bucket of water?" he asked.

"No. Stay there," called Gyp, coming to the fire. "Marty, you get it."

Marty took the bucket and slouched toward the brook.

Gyp looked down upon the fire. "Say, it strikes me you're slow."

"Slow—but sure," replied Roddy, bending to grasp the skillet.

With an incredibly swift movement he came up with it to fling the scalding contents squarely into Gyp's face. The fellow let out a hideous scream of agony.

Roddy sprang to snatch up his rifle. Wheeling as he cocked it, he saw the blinded man fire from his pocket. Roddy shot him through the heart, and his awful curses ended in a gulp. He was swaying backward when Roddy whirled to look for the other fellow. At the instant he heard a bucket clang on rock and a yell. Marty emerged from the willows with his gun spouting red. Roddy felt something like wind, then a concussion that rocked him to his knees. A white flash burst into a thousand sparks before his sight. But as it cleared he got a bead on Marty and pulled the trigger.

The fellow bawled with the terror of a man shot through the middle. His arms spread out wide. The gun in his right hand smoked and banged. Roddy, quick as a flash, worked the lever and bored the man again.

Blank-visaged and slack, he swayed back to crash through the willows that lined the brook.

Then Roddy, blinded by his own blood, dropped the rifle and bent over, one hand supporting him, the other pulling out his handkerchief. Hot blood poured down his face. He heard it drip on the grass. As fast as he wiped it off it streamed down again.

Collie was calling: "Roddy!...*Roddy!*....Oh, my God—the blood!"

"I'm shot, Collie, but...where are you?"

"Heah! Heah! *Heah!*"

He crawled on hands and knees, guided by her voice.

"Wipe off the blood."

"I cain't. I cain't! Darling, I'm tied!"

"Can you see where I'm shot?"

"Yes. Your head—on top—all bloody . . . But Roddy it can't be bad. You've got your senses."

"I feel as if my brains were oozing out."

"Mercy! No! No! That cain't be, Roddy . . . Cut these ropes."

Roddy felt in his pockets. "They took my knife," he said, and then blindly he began to unbuckle the strap that held her elbows to her sides. It seemed to take long. He reeled dizzily. An icy sickening nausea assailed him.

"There! Let me get at that rope round my feet. . . . Damn, you would tie such a knot!"

He felt her bounce up and heard her swift feet thudding away and back to him. A towel went over his head and face. Ministering hands pressed it down.

"Oh, the blood pours so fast! I cain't see," she cried. "I'll feel." And with shaking fingers she felt for the wound. Then Roddy sank under a pain that might have been a red-hot poker searing his bared brain. Collie was crying into his fading consciousness. "Darling! Only a groove! No hole in your skull. Oh, thank God!" Then Roddy lost all sense.

When he came to, his blurred sight seemed to see trees and slopes through a red film. His first clear thought was of the blood that had trickled over his eyes. A splitting pain burned under his skull. But his weak hand felt a dry forehead and then a damp bandage bound round his scalp. The red hue, then, he grasped, was sunset flooding the park.

"Collie," he called faintly.

She came pattering out of the cabin to thump to her knees. Topaz eyes with glinting softness searched his face. "Roddy!"

"I'm okay, I guess."

"Oh, boy! You came to twice, out of your haid."

"Yeah? Well, I can get it now. My head hurts awful.

214

But I can remember and think. . . . Collie, I reckon I did for those two hombres."

"You sure did. That Gyp dog is lying right heah by the fire, daid as a door-nail, and the other is down by the creek. . . . I screamed like a Comanche when you threw that skillet of scalding water in his eyes. I watched him then. . . . I never batted an eyelash. . . . Saw you kill him! But when the other one shot you and you went down. Oh, God, that was terrible. I lost my nerve. And never got it back till you fainted."

"Collie, nerve is your middle name. You're one grand kid. Can you ever forgive me? Oh, you couldn't! I'm a sap to ask."

"Yes, I forgive you. Maybe I deserved it. If only I could get all this straight! But heah, let's talk of our predicament. . . . Your wound is not serious. I washed it out with mercurochrome. Lucky I had some in my bag. No fear of infection. I can keep your fever down with this brook water, which is ice-cold. But you've lost blood. Oh, so much! That frightened me. You cain't walk for a long time. Our car is smashed. Of course, those men hid theirs, but maybe we can find it. I wouldn't mind staying heah forever. It's so sweet and wild and lovely. I'm a Texas girl, Roddy, you'd find that I can cook and chop wood and shoot game, dress it, too. That'd be swell. But, oh, I'm so worried. You might need a doctor."

"Collie, everything will be—all right," replied Roddy with thought only to relieve her. "Jack will—come after us in ten days."

"*Heah?*"

"Aw! You see, I . . ." Roddy had betrayed himself and could not retrieve his blunder. He bit his lip. The girl's face flashed scarlet, then went as white as a sheet. And her eyes transfixed him.

"Roddy, you framed me."

He groaned in his abasement, and try as he might he could not stand those accusing eyes.

"Why in the world? *Why?*" she cried poignantly.

215

Then evidently she saw that his physical strength was not equal to his distress. "Never mind, Roddy. Forget it. That's not our immediate problem. There's plenty of work for little Collie, believe me. Now I'll make good my brag."

For moments Roddy lay with closed eyes on the verge of fading away again. But the acute pain held him to sensibility. He heard Collie bustling about the camp fire. She roused him presently to give him a hot drink. Dusk had fallen. The red light left the sky. He could not keep his eyes open. Collie covered him with blankets. He felt her making a bed beside him. Then all went black.

In the night he awoke, burning, throbbing, parched with thirst. Collie heard his restless movements. She rose to minister to him. She had placed a bucket of water at hand. She gave him a drink and bathed his face. The air was piercingly cold. Coyotes were howling off in the darkness. While Collie was tucking the blankets around him, Roddy fell asleep. Later he awoke again, but endured his pain and did not arouse her. The pangs, however, could not keep him awake long.

The daylight came, Roddy did not know when. There was ice on the water in the bucket, but he did not feel cold. All day he suffered. All day Collie stayed near to keep a wet towel on his face. He craved only water to drink. That night he slept better. Next morning the excruciating headache was gone. His wound throbbed, but less and less. He was on the mend.

That day Collie half-carried, half-dragged him into the cabin to the bough bed under the window. She made a bed for herself on the ground close by. She was in and out all day long.

When she had made Roddy comfortable, she brought him his package of money. "Took this out of Gyp's pocket," she explained briefly with an involuntary shudder.

Roddy thanked her in a weak voice. It was an effort to talk, but his mind grew active once more. He had no appetite, but forced down what food and drink she brought him. As he slowly recovered, it grew harder for him to face her. There must come a reckoning. He divined it; and her care, her kindness, her efficiency added to his shame. Night was a relief.

Next day he struggled to his feet and walked out, wavering, light-headed, weak as an infant. He noted that Collie had covered the bodies of the dead men with large piles of brush and tarpaulins. In another day or two, Roddy thought, he would be strong enough to bury them. Even now the buzzards were circling around high overhead.

While the warm sun was melting the hoar frost on grass and leaves, Roddy walked and rested and walked again, slowly regaining his strength. All about him were signs that Collie's vaunted efficiency at camp tasks was no vain boast. The camp fire had been moved under the end of the porch where Collie had built up a rude fireplace with stones. She had even strung up a clothes line on which several intimate garments were fluttering with an air of domesticity, and was busy now carrying buckets of water up from the creek. And this was the girl he thought would make such a poor wife for John!

That third day Collie had little to say to Roddy until late in the afternoon, when, as he lay on his bed in the cabin, with the gold sunlight flooding in at the window, she entered with an armful of purple asters.

"My favorite wild flowers, Roddy."

"Mine, too. . . . Isn't it funny that we have one thing in common?"

"I could tell you more."

"Yeah."

She knelt beside his bed and leaned close to him. "Roddy, you're doing fine. You'll be well soon. I'm so glad. We can have some walks—maybe a hunt—before . . . Tell me now, darling."

Roddy protested and denied and demurred, but in the end, from his procrastination, his lies, his evasions, she pieced together the whole cloth of this miserable travesty.

"You great big sap! Roddy, did you ever read the story of Miles Standish, who got John Alden to do his wooing for him? Don't you remember when Priscilla said: 'Why don't you speak for yourself, John?'"

"Never was much of a reader," replied Roddy evasively. His chest seemed to cave in.

She leaned over him with soft look and touch and tone. "That day at Canyon Creek, when I went in swimming in only my brassiere and panties to torment Jack—you fell in love with me, didn't you?"

"No! I—I thought you a little brazen hussy."

"Sure, I was. But that's not the point. You fell for me, didn't you?"

"I did not."

"Roddy! Then at the dance, when I asked you to hold me close?"

"Collie, you're a fiend. You're all—almost all, Jack. . . . No, I didn't fall for you then."

"When you kidnapped me?"

"Nor then, either."

"Big Boy, it took you long, didn't it?" she laughed, adorably. "Well, then, when you caught me running away in the car, and I kicked you, *heah*, on your shin?" And she laid a tender hand on his leg, to move it gently, caressingly, he imagined in his bewilderment, over the great bruise.

"Collie, don't you kid me," he implored.

"When you beat me half daid—was it *then*, darling?

"Collie, you win, callous little flirt that you are!" he burst out hoarsely. "It must have been at the creek, when you pulled your shameless stunt—and all those other times. But, honest to God, I never knew it till that dirty Gyp laid hands on you!"

"It doesn't make any difference *when*, so long as you *do*, Roddy," she said, more softly, leaning her face so close that he began to tremble. Could not the insatiate little creature be satisfied without flaying her victim? "Say you love me!"

"I reckon."

"More than Jack did?"

"Yes."

"More than any boy ever loved me?" she ended imperiously.

"God help me, Collie, I'm afraid I do," he replied, huskily. "Now I'm punished. I'll take my medicine. But don't rub it in. This has been a rotten deal for you. It's proved you to be one grand little thoroughbred. It'll help me, too, I hope, to make a man out of myself. And when you . . ."

She was bending to him, her heavy eyelids closed, her expression rapt and dreamy, her sweet lips curved and tremulous with the kiss she meant to bestow, when Roddy saw her start. Her eyes opened wide, dark, flashing, luminous with inquiry.

"Listen," she whispered. "A car!"

"By gosh! You're right. It's coming down the ridge. A forest ranger or hunter . . . Oh, Collie, it means deliverance for you."

"No, Roddy," she cried, a note of triumph in her voice, "I've got a hunch it's your brother Jack, showing yellow, jealous, scared, come to square himself with us."

"Jack?" questioned Roddy in astonishment.

From the window they watched the leafy gateway of the road at the foot of the ridge. Collie put a tense arm round Roddy. He felt that if Jack really confronted him there, the world would either come to an end or suddenly be glorious.

A bright car slid out of the foliage.

"Jack and his new car! Look at him, sneaking along so slowly!" cried Collie gleefully. Giving Roddy a squeeze, she rolled off the bed. To Roddy's amazement she disarranged her blouse, rumpled her curls, vehemently rubbed the make-up from her face, all in a flash. "Will I hand it to him? I'm telling you, darling . . . Lie down. Pretend to be dying. Let *me* do the talking." She moved to the wide opening of the cabin and assumed a tragic pose.

The front of the shining car showed beyond the corner of the wall. It stopped. The click of door and

219

thud of feet brought their visitor to the cabin.

"Collie! *Collie!*" It was Jack's voice, betraying a decided panic.

"So! You're heah ahaid of schedule? But too late, Jack Brecken!"

"Too late? What do you mean? Collie, what's happened?" he exclaimed fearfully.

"Happened! What usually happens when a man carries a girl off into the woods alone?" Collie's tone held all the drama of a wronged woman.

For a moment Jack was speechless. "Why—Collie—he stammered then, "you don't mean that, that Roddy—"

"He's only human, Jack."

"But hell! I didn't dream he'd—Roddy did that?" For a moment his tone was utterly incredulous. Then fury possessed him and he burst out, "The dirty dog! Where is he?"

Roddy listened spellbound, half in horror, half in admiration. What an actress she was.

"After all, you can't blame him," retorted Collie accusingly. "This was your scheme. I should think you wouldn't have dared. Roddy loved you, Jack, and that was why he fell for your crazy idea."

Her stinging words had the effect of quelling Jack's rage.

"Collie," he said, and his voice queried with anguish, "after you left, I realized what I had done. That's why I came to confess, to make amends. I—"

"Too late, Jack," cut in Collie, in solemn accents. "Your brother lies in heah, his head shot open!"

In the silence that ensued, Roddy heard John's gasping expulsion of breath.

"God, almighty! *You killed him!*" John's knees shook so that they were incapable of holding him. He sat down on the pile of canvas behind him.

Collie started. For a moment she could not find words, and the pause must have been a lifetime of hell to the stricken man. Then she stuck her head in the door to wink a glowing eye at Roddy.

"Jack Brecken, now that you've realized what could have happened, I'll tell you the truth," she pealed out, her slim form instinct with a liberation of passion. "Roddy is not daid. He's alive—and I love him—love him—love him.... Your plot miscarried, you big sap! Roddy kidnapped me all right, but we both were kidnapped by real kidnappers. They planned to make you pay ransom. Oh, that would have been great! But one of them got fresh with me and would have attacked me. Roddy outwitted him—killed him—and his partner. Jack, I was on the fence about you. I think I would have married you. Thank heaven, I found you out, and at last fell terribly in love with your wicked, kidnapping brother."

Relief struggled with anguish in John's pale face. "Roddy not dead?" he gasped, "and—and he killed two men—?" Then looking fearfully around, "Where are they?"

Collie's tone was extremely casual. "One of them is over by the creek," she drawled, "and you're sitting on the other."

THE ALDRICH REPORT
ON MEN
Peggy Aldrich

BT51158 $1.95
Nonfiction

In the tradition of Kinsey and Hite, The Aldrich Report on Men further examines the origins of sexuality this time from the male point of view. Here are the private thoughts of men about their sexuality and interaction with women—orgasm, masturbation, intercourse, foreplay, homosexuality, and more. A BT Original.

THE GHETTO FIGHTERS
**Translated and edited by
Meyer Barkai**

BT51159 $1.75
Nonfiction

First hand, authentic descriptions from diaries, memoirs, and other documents, recording the heroic battle of those who fought against the total destruction of Jews—freedom fighters in the ghettos of Warsaw, Vilna, Cracow, platoons of Jewish partisans roving the swamps and forests of Byelorussia, and fantastically brave breakouts from the concentration camps. Reissue.

DEADLIER THAN
THE MALE
J.C. Conaway

BT51160 $1.50
Mystery

Four men had been beheaded with no clues, no motive, no suspect remaining. Novice Private Investigator Jana Blake finds her first criminal case a bizarre chain of killings with no real lead. Join Jana as she stakes her sleuthing from the subways of Manhattan to its breathtaking conclusion in the sky over the East River! A BT Original.

**Soldier of Fortune
OPERATION HONG KONG**   BT51161 $1.50
Peter McCurtin   Adventure

When a Chinese agent is sent into the port city to
disrupt daily life and instigate riots and street fighting, Jim Rainey is called in. He hand picks a team
of mercenaries. And for a time he is in charge . . .
Hong Kong, exotic port of call was his. A BT Original.

THE FOUR FEATHERS   BT51162 $1.50
A.E.W. Mason   Adventure

Here is a reprint of this classic of storytelling com-
plete with suspense, honesty, loyalty, heroism, and
unswerving love . . . the story of Harry Faversham,
branded coward by three friends and the woman he
loves. Young Harry flees to the Sudan to devote himself to deeds of reckless daring and valor until he
can come home a hero. Originally published by Mac-
millan.

Lassiter/CATTLE BARON   BT51163 $1.25
Jack Slade   Western

Lassiter becomes a cattle baron when he inherits a
dead friend's ranch . . . and his wife! Against hus-
tlers, rustlers, a hanging judge, and a gunslinger,
he settles down to make it work. But when he is suddenly offered more than the ranch is worth he dis-
covers his real inheritance—one hundred thousand
dollars hidden somewhere on the spread! A BT
Original.

SEND TO: BELMONT TOWER BOOKS
   P.O. Box 270
   Norwalk, Connecticut 06852

   Please send me the following titles:

Quantity	Book Number	Price
————	————	————
————	————	————
————	————	————
————	————	————
————	————	————

**In the event we are out of stock on any of your
selections, please list alternate titles below.**

————	————	————
————	————	————
————	————	————
————	————	————

Postage/Handling ————

I enclose . . . . . . ————

FOR U.S. ORDERS, add 35¢ per book to cover cost of postage
and handling. Buy five or more copies and we will pay for
shipping. Sorry no C.O.D.'s.

FOR ORDERS SENT OUTSIDE THE U.S.A.
Add $1.00 for the first book and 25¢ for each additional
book. PAY BY foreign draft or money order drawn on a
U.S. bank, payable in U.S. ($) dollars.
☐ Please send me a free catalog.

NAME————————————————————
(Please print)

ADDRESS————————————————————

CITY ———— STATE ———— ZIP ————
Allow Four Weeks for Delivery